Quickies 3

Quickies 3

Short Short Fiction on Gay Male Desire

edited by James C. Johnstone

ARSENAL
PULP PRESS
Vancouver

QUICKIES 3: SHORT SHORT FICTION ON GAY MALE DESIRE

ARSENAL PULP PRESS
103 – 1014 Homer Street
Vancouver, B.C.
Canada V6B 2W9
arsenalpulp.com

The publisher gratefully acknowledges the support of the Canada Council for the Arts and the British Columbia Arts Council for its publishing program, and the Government of Canada through the Book Publishing Industry Development Program for its publishing activities.

Interior design by Solo
Cover design by Val Speidel
Cover photography by Paul Beard

Printed and bound in USA

This is a work of fiction. Any resemblance of characters to persons either living or deceased is purely coincidental.

National Library of Canada
Cataloguing in Publication Data

Main entry under title:
Quickies 3 : short short fiction on gay male desire / James C. Johnstone, editor.

ISBN 1-55152-144-X

1. Gay men's writings. 2. Gay men – Fiction. I. Johnstone, James C. (James Compton)

PN6120.92.G39Q54 2003 808.83'108353 C2003-911210-1

Contents

Acknowledgments

Getting to work on another *Quickies* anthology was a dream come true. So I would like to thank Brian Lam and his amazing, pioneering team at Arsenal Pulp Press: Blaine Kyllo, Kiran Gill Judge, and Robert Ballantyne, for this wonderful opportunity. I can't imagine working with a better, more dedicated group of people.

Putting together an anthology, while fun, and rewarding, takes time away from friends and family (not to mention chores, eh, Richard?). Therefore, for their often superhuman patience with me over the past years, as well as their love, friendship, and support, my special thanks and sincere appreciations go to my partner, Richard Rooney, my good friend and co-dad, Keith Stuart (hey, send me a story next time!), my daughter and the joy of my life, Jayka Mayne, and her Supermom, Laura Mayne.

For help in saving and maintaining my sanity during stressful times I would also like to thank Jeff Sefton, our friendly neighborhood computer wiz, and the best pal a guy could have, my cat Smokey. As well, for reasons best known to them, I would like to thank my boss and co-workers at the Gourmet Warehouse (Steve, Gerald, I'm expecting to see stories from you guys for *Quickies 4*); Alfredo Ferreira, Jeff Fisher, and Alex Verdecchia of the best gang a guy could belong to; Martin Laba and Danielle Marchand; Don Seaton, Jeff van Steenes, Howard Ehrlich, John Cameron, Cara Moody, from the AIDS Candlelight Memorial & Vigil organizing committee, and last but not least, all the wild (and wise) women (and men) who live in the 700-block of Hawks Avenue, my East End Vancouver home.

I would like to thank the following people for their support, generosity, and hospitality during past *Quickies* launches and book tours. In Vancouver: Janine Fuller and the staff at Little Sister's bookstore, Ron van Streun and the staff of The Odyssey. In Calgary: Rudy and the staff of the Arena Coffee Bar, David Crosson and the folks at *Outlooks*, and my pals, Doug Ferguson and Paul Orr. In Toronto: Dean Odorico and the staff at Woody's and Sailor (you guys are the best), the management and staff of This Ain't The Rosedale Library, and my T.O. friends Antony Audain, Patrick Duggan, Robert Thomson, Bob Tivey, Mohamed Khaki, and Paul Yee. In Montréal: the management and staff of the much-missed Librairie l'Androgyne, and writer, bon-vivant-man-about-town, my host, John Woolfrey. In New York: I would like to thank the good people at the New York Gay & Lesbian Center. In Boston: the organizers of the various OutWrite conferences that have allowed me to launch my books there. In San Francisco: I would like to thank Richard Labonté and the staff at A Different Light Bookstore, Kai M. Venice, who opened his home to the SF contributors and threw us all a party, and lastly, two sweet, fun-filled, and generous men, Alan Workman and Tony Speakman, who make San Francisco my American home away from home. Thank you all.

An editor hoping to create an anthology with significant international content is only as good as his network. The success I had in soliciting the over 200 stories I received from six countries around the world was made possible through the help and support of a number of key people, in particular: Daniel Collins, Shaun Levin, Andy Quan, Lawrence Schimel, Ron Suresha, Greg Wharton, and my good friend, Karen X. Tulchinsky. Thank you all.

Arsenal Pulp Press makes great books with fabulous covers. Thanks again to Val Speidel for her masterful rendering of Vancouver photographer and writer Paul Beard's boner-inducing photo. (As far as I know, the model lives in Vancouver, guys, so, na-na-na-na-nah.)

Lastly, I would like to express my deep gratitude to all the writing men and women from all over the globe who continue to share their gifts with me. I am honored.

For Bob Tivey:
my first love, still sexy at sixty.

Introduction

I'm out for a walk through my old haunt, Vancouver's West End, to think about how I want to write the introduction for this third collection of short short fiction on gay male desire. I thought a stroll around the gay village and perhaps a drink at one of the Davie Street bars would be just the thing to kick-start the process. I bussed it from my quiet, slowly gentrifying neighborhood of old wooden Victorian and Edwardian houses and got off at the noisy – by East End standards – traffic-congested corner of Robson and Burrard, planning to walk a rectangular route through the downtown peninsula.

It's been almost eight years since I left the wild West End for a quieter life outside of the city core. I rarely venture out to my old stomping grounds these days, and every time I do I am startled by just how much everything has changed.

When I first moved downtown in 1982, Robson Street was still a neighborhood shopping area, a happy jumble of cheese stores, green grocers, German delicatessens – people used to call it Robsonstrasse – restaurants, hotels, and even a decent seafood store. West Enders who worked downtown used to be able to shop for their dinner on their way home from work. If you were a single gay man, like me, you could shop for more than just your dinner on Robson back then. Now it's all upscale glass and granite restaurants and clothing shops, more tourists than locals. Now it's nowhere near as cruisy. *Ah, the good old days. . . .*

I weave through the milling crowd of shoppers and tourists wondering just how many more Starbucks can be squeezed in among the Japanese noodle stands and Korean bulgogi houses that seem to occupy every piece of non-retail space along the street. I walk by Jervis Street and sigh, recalling Neighbours, one of my favourite dance bars, which used to be across the road. My first lover, Bob, and I used to go there every Friday, then John Barley's in Gastown on Saturdays. The bars were so much more exciting back then – the Gandy Dancer, Faces, Neighbours, Buddy's, the Central,

John Barley's, Playpen South with its back room – all gone. Later, after Bob and I broke up, I continued to go to Neighbours, sometimes with friends, sometimes cruising alone. I met Edwin there – a tall, dark, blue-eyed, sweet HIV-positive DJ visiting Vancouver from Bern, Switzerland. We kissed and made out on the floor of the flat he was staying in while his host and his boyfriend made out on the bed a few meters away from us. Edwin was the first man to make me think the German could sound sweet and sexy. . . .

Lost in a blur of recalled sounds and images, I continue down Robson Street. Phallic hotel and apartment towers loom in the twilight sky on either side, reminding me of my quest. I turn south on Denman Street and walk towards the beach at English Bay. Denman Street is changed beyond recognition too, but it's still more gay than Robson. Gone are the decadent and fabulously kitschy Benjamin's Café and the quick and easy Hamburger Mary's where, if you hadn't scooped a date after a night of dancing and drinking at the bar, you could usually come up with a suitable prospect for a quickie over a chocolate shake and a hamburger. I remember late one night at Mary's seeing a man sitting on a stool with his dick sticking out of his uniform. What a cocky grin! Must have been an American. . . . Ha! Gone are those days, but the dark-haired security guard with tattoos and a flat-top holding the door open for Royal Bank ATM customers looks full of promise. Is that a work-mode nod he just gave me?

The closer I get to the beach, the more crowded Denman Street gets. I walk past my old gym at Denman and Comox remembering how, when I was single and living in the West End, I used to get up at five-thirty every other morning and walk down the hill for a workout. I would always follow the same route because, if I was *very* lucky, Bruce would be at his balcony with a coffee and a morning smile. A Bruce sighting before gym usually meant an extremely satisfying quickie afterwards. A good morning blow job sure helps to relieve accumulated office stress. Workouts on Bruce days were usually quick, but focused. Bruceless mornings, there was always the sauna. . . .

In a reverie I finally reach the foot of Davie Street, the main drag of Vancouver's gay village. Before I make my way up the hill I take a little stroll away from the crowds and smoke a joint. I then walk down to the beach, where I watch the last traces of firy orange disappear from the tips of the coastal mountains visible in the distance across the rippling mercury-steel-gray waters of English Bay.

On sunny summer days in the early eighties you would see entire rows of gay men clones suntanning in their brightly-colored Speedos along the seawall to Stanley Park. Certain parts of the beach were definitely gay turf and had names like "lavender logs" or "moustache point." In the evenings, you would see them alone or in gaggles, in their flannel shirts and 501s, making their *passaggiata* along the seawall to Stanley Park and the magic of the trails. Walks in the park go rarely unrewarded at any time of day or night. I remember many a bike tour and jog through those magic woods – the denizens were friendly and spandex biking shorts were so practical. . . .

I turn around and head back towards the hill, passing the concrete bathhouse, the scene of so many quickies – the place is legend. I wonder how much action goes on there these days, but I'm a married man, even if I'm on a mission. I pass Alexandra Park with its octagonal wooden Victorian bandstand and I remember another night back in 1990, the summer the Gay Games came to Vancouver. I was out for another late night walk and I saw two leather men going at it in the dark under the projecting eaves at the back. There were so many gay men visiting the city for the games, most with roommates, that public sex became a necessity. *If you go down to the woods today. . . .* The city and our community haven't been the same since.

I continue my journey up Burnaby Street past the apartment building known as Vaseline Towers, another phallic edifice at the corner of Bidwell. While I cannot remember having had sex here, its nickname attests to the fact that hundreds of gay men did. Stack-a-Fag, its larger and more notorious cousin, looms in the distance up the hill. Each building, every apartment, balcony and window in the West End seems to have its own erotic stories – some that even I had a part in. There's the Crystal Court where that hunk Patrick used to sunbathe nude on his roofdeck. Further down the block are the Santana Apartments across the street from the Princess (*okay, okay*) where I used to live. One sunny evening, my partner at the time, Keith, and I were treated to the surreal vision of two young men fucking in the window. The guy on top was young and enthusiastic. When he finally came his arms shot in the air and he jumped up and down in a kind of Rocky Balboa victory dance. It was hilarious.

Ah, the joys of West End apartment living! Everyone's got binoculars. If there wasn't something going on in the apartment across the street there was always something to look at on the streets below. Back then, sometimes it was me. I pause at the corner of Burnaby and Broughton. Ten years ago on a warm autumn night, a very hot, sweet-mouthed man gave me the most delicious blow job on this corner. The combination of the stone and the memory almost make me reel. Yes, I like quickies.

I gaze up at the lit windows of the apartments looming above me. Some are wide open and some are shuttered or draped closed. What's going on up there? There's my old apartment, the Princess. I glance up at the second-floor balcony where Doug used to live. It's bare and drab now, but when Doug lived there, that small balcony was a veritable jungle of many different white-flowered plants. The lush growth provided Doug with a discreet vantage point from which to observe the comings and goings on the street below. Doug and his balcony were rather well-known, shall we say. I have many fond memories of Doug's apartment, not the least of which was the one and only time I had sex there. It wasn't with Doug – he was out of town at the time – but with Richard, Doug's house-sitter, the man who three years later would become my partner. The night was pure fireworks. The sex was great, and we laughed a lot. By rights that evening should have led to something more sooner, but we were both in relationships at the time. I went back upstairs to the tenth floor and crawled into bed with Keith, who was already sleeping – posties get up early. I didn't see Richard again for almost a year.

I take one more toke from my joint and leave Burnaby Street for Davie Street, one block north. The street is busy – not as crowded as Robson was, but the buzz from the pot makes it somehow feel so. I do a quick tour of Little Sister's Book and Art Emporium walking by the shelves of erotica and see *Quickies* and *Quickies 2*, still face out on the shelf. Soon there will be a third volume: sixty-nine-plus stories, written by sixty-six writers – three of them women – from six countries around the world.

I'm stoned and still on a mission so I head out of the store and on to Davie Street, heading for Pumpjack. I'm in shorts and a linen shirt – not exactly the dress code for this Levi/leather bar – and there's already a line-up, so I hesitate outside the open window. I'm tempted, though. The music is great and everyone seems to be having a fun time inside. It's been so long since I've been to a bar. I'm about to go when I hear someone call out my name. There, at a table closest to the open window, is my good friend Jeff and his hunky partner Rob hanging out with some friends. I walk over to the window and end up spending almost half an hour chatting with them and taking sips from Jeff's beer. It's the best of both worlds. I'm enjoying the bar without really being in it.

Years ago, this was a French bakery/café called Au Petit Bout. It was a popular Davie Street hangout for years before it was sold and turned into a new and expanded Benjamin's. The décor and the food was the same as the old Benjamin's, but it never had the same appeal as the original. For whatever reasons the business failed. It's next incarnation was as Doll & Penny's Restaurant. Now it's a leather bar. *Plus ça change....*

I'm tired. I think I have had enough inspiration for one night, so I bid farewell to my friends and continue down Davie towards Granville Street. I pass the F212 bathhouse and wonder what sort of crowd is there by now. I remember the many nights I used to go there. It was fun, usually, especially the nights that Keith worked there. Richard and I used to go together sometimes, usually on Gay Pride Weekend. I think about the sauna, and the corridors with all those dark doorways. Behind each door waited a mystery; hidden beneath each white towel, an adventure.

The muffled pound of '80s retro coming from Numbers buoys me. I turn north on Burrard, amused by the fountains that line the road along the foot of the very phallic north tower of the Sheraton Wall Centre. They are set so that they spurt white ropes of water into the air, like so much ejaculate. It's too perfect. I giggle all the way to the bus.

It's a twenty-minute ride to my stop at Hawks and East Hastings. En route, the bus passes through what is now called the Downtown Eastside, Vancouver's derelict old downtown. All along Hastings Street are small hotels and rooming houses, many of them with bars or pubs on the ground floor. Years ago, these were the seasonal homes of loggers and miners, single men, most of them immigrants. Conveniently enough, the old red light district was a few blocks north on Alexandra Street. *More quickies.*

I get off the bus at Hawks Avenue and walk south toward my blue row house. I pass by an older man standing framed by the doorway of the four-storey brick rooming house at the corner of Hastings. He is solidly built and neatly dressed in khaki pants and a plaid cotton shirt open at the neck. He's puffing on a cigarette. I nod a greeting. He nods back. I wonder who he is, what sort of life he's had, and how he came to live here. Perhaps he is a retired Swedish logger, or a fisherman from Croatia. Were there always enough working women to go around in those camps? I wonder about the quickies he might be able to tell me about.

I walk the remaining blocks to my door. My tabby gay boy-cat,

Smokey, greets me with a happy stretch at the door. He's been waiting up for me. (Richard is away at a cabin at Mabel Lake.) Smokey follows me up the old creaky wooden stairs to my office. I turn on the computer. It's late but I have to write something. What is this book I've put together? What am I going to write, Smokey?

"This is an international collection of very short stories (about 1,000 words or less) that explore the complex world of gay male desire. Each story is a snapshot from the great male homosexual odyssey that, in spite of their brevity, speak volumes to the power that our desire and sexual imagination have on our lives. Buy it. Read It. I hope you like it."

Thanks, Smokey.

Quickies and *Quickies 2* have fans all over the world. I am deeply gratified by how the two previous books have been received and hope that this third book satisfies as well as the two prior volumes. I am deeply honored by the many talented writers, both men and women, who took time to send me their stories. It has been great fun putting this book together. I hope you enjoy the read.

James C. Johnstone
Vancouver, Canada
August 2003

Sam Sommer

Night Dance

It was the night of the milk-glass moon, of felted sky, when satyrs gambol on manicured lawns. It was the time of the wedding dance, the consummation jig of the dog-day cicada. It was ambergris and ozone, magic and mischief. It was a coming of age and coming undone. It was unlike anything I had ever experienced, and it visits me like an old friend, keeping alive the memory of my youth. It was a golden night, a time of miracles. It was the essence of The Wild Things, those Sendak behemoths that rule the night. It was my one moment of sanity, my embrace of life. It was the most precious, perfect, sensible thing I've ever done, and I'd like to remember it fondly, forever. It means entirely more to me at this moment than it did then, and perhaps because of that I can now paint its form, its design, its crimsons and golds as I've never been able to before.

In the way that music can move, the night was alive. It coerced me out of my sleep, summoning me from dreams in which I raced with antelope. It beseeched, appealed, called to me, perhaps not in words, but I heard it. Perhaps not in thought, but I understood it. Perhaps not in motion, but I felt it, nonetheless.

I woke in a sweat, the heat of the day still clinging to the walls of my room like moss, my pillow a lifeless lump beneath my head, beyond resurrection. I propped myself up on an elbow to look at the clock. I had slept only a few hours. The air outside was cool and fragrant, but I couldn't feel it – the veil of wire mesh stretched tightly across my window refused it access – too much of a barrier for the breeze to negotiate.

I sat at the edge of my bed, planting my feet flatly on the tile floor. Something danced within me, something wild and unfettered. It tangoed, whirled, leaped with pointed toes. It kazatskied, cartwheeled, backflipped. I felt slightly light-headed and off-center. I needed air. Like a caged animal, I needed to be free. I wanted something I wasn't sure of, something that escaped me, something I felt, but didn't yet understand. It was out there – outside the room. It was on the air, of the night, in the tall grass that waited to be cut, rich with dew.

The house and all within were fast asleep. I was the only thing that moved. I passed through the kitchen, careful not to disturb anything on my way to the back porch. I was not yet aware that the heat that had woken me, that kept me from falling back asleep was within me, and I would not be able to sleep again until it had been extinguished or consumed.

There was an unmistakable odor to the porch, a melding of scents, like perfume worn by movie-house matrons. The smells upholstered the walls and hung in the air. It was the odor of summer nights, iced tea and lemon, *The Sunday Times* and mystery novels, their pages brown with age. It masked the other odors of the night and sent me still further from my bed, out into the darkness, a colander of stars above my head.

I hadn't planned being out at this hour, breathing in the strangely drugged air. The deeper I breathed, the higher I became. It was euphoric and inextricably entwined with the night. Lost in its aura, I followed, dancing in step to the music that filled my head, the pulse in my ears, the rhythms and cadences of a million years.

I sat down on my front lawn and stared up at the sky: flawless, perfect, and impersonal. My fingers ran over the cool grass. I let the pointed tops of each blade send tiny shock waves through my palms, up into my chest and then down into my groin. They merged with the passion and the perfume that had already taken hold. I was aroused, unaccustomed, and confused by the strength of my desire – its willfulness. I only wanted to respond. I would join with the night, and we would dance together, if only for a few, brief, wonderful minutes.

Stripping off my shorts, I ran as fast as I could, bounding over lawns and driveways, my body lithe and free in a way I had never experienced, had never let myself experience. I felt purified, cleansed, anointed. Only then did I return to my own backyard where I prostrated myself beneath the heavy, low slung branches of an apple tree, my silhouette lost among its deep shadows. The moon saw my body shake, saw it heave and fall, ebb and flow as I spilled my young seed upon the ground, fertile and waiting. I had at last answered the call. There was nothing left now but to catch my breath, brush myself off, and return to my room. My first dance had ended, but the music that played for me that night had only just begun. I would hear it for a lifetime, although never quite in the same way ever again.

In an evening, I had untied the knot that held my childhood safely in place. The best part of me found its voice that night. It sang out loud and clear to the music that plays for each one of us, saying, I am alive, I live, I am.

Michael V. Smith

Beaver Foxes

At the campsite that summer, when Mom and her second husband Gary were in the middle of their outdoorsman phase, my brother and I began our slow but consistent growing apart. Mom and Gary set up on the beach, expecting only the fairest of weather, whereas Kevin and I pitched our tent under the shelter of trees.

Two years older, a couple inches taller, sprouts of facial hair where I had none, and full pubic hair compared to my still barren pits and groin, my brother was a mirror of what I was headed for. That's how I liked it. When Kevin grew his hair long, I refused to go to the barber as well. When he cut it, I cut mine, just above the ear, with a rat's tail to match.

There were a fair number of bathers that first afternoon, but as the day wore on people slowly packed their sunburned bodies into the coolness of air-conditioned cars and drove back to the luxuries of houses and plumbing. Only a few people were left on the beach by the time Kevin and I were told to go to bed.

Kevin raced ahead of me, grabbed his flannel pajamas from the tent, and hustled up the incline leading to the road.

"Where you going?" I asked.

"To the car." We'd parked just at the top of the small hill, in a nest of trees off the dirt roadway.

"Why?"

Kevin gave me a derisive look. "To change," he said, his voice implying I was criminally stupid.

I put on my PJS, slid inside the sleeping bag, and waited to fall asleep. Within a few minutes, Mom came in her housecoat and sandals. Shadows from her flashlight jumped on the sides of the tent. When I told her Kevin was at the car, she handed me the flashlight and told me to go get him.

* * *

As I approached the Monte Carlo, I notided a faint light inside. The large door was slightly ajar, though I couldn't see Kevin.

"Kevin?" I called. No answer. "Kev?"

"What?" His voice came from the bubble of light. He sounded breathy.

"Mom wants to see you."

"What do you mean?" From the back seat, he sat up wearing his pajama top. Not thinking, I shone the flashlight on him. He held a hand up to his face. "Hey, Curtis, careful!" he cried, squinting.

I turned the switch off. "Mom is waiting at the tent. She wants to say good night."

I stood there in the dark for a second before he turned his own light out and answered me. "Okay, I'll be right there." His face was invisible in the added darkness of the car, but there was some disappointment in his voice. He was up to something and I was miffed that he hadn't thought to include me.

* * *

The next morning, I woke up alone. I found Kevin way up the beach, talking with a girl. She was about fifteen, in a fluorescent green bathing suit with purple trim, holding a Frisbee. As I approached, the girl whispered something to Kevin and he looked over his shoulder.

"What do you want, Curtis?"

"Nothing," I said.

The girl looked at me and smiled wide. She was chewing gum, though it was only the morning. "Is that your brother?" she asked Kevin.

"Yeah."

"You wanna play with us?" she asked.

She tossed the Frisbee to me, which was the last time I got hold of it. They played for another ten minutes, never tossing it my way.

I stormed back down the beach, past our tent, and up the incline to the car. Remembering the night before, I wanted to get Kevin in trouble. He'd been hiding something or other. Under the bucket seats I dragged out a rolled-up paper bag with a magazine inside like I'd only heard tell about. The cover sported a curvy blonde woman in a too-small lace nightie. No word of lie, the masthead read *Beaver Foxes*, though I was hard-pressed to know what either animal had to do with the naked women inside.

I can't say it wasn't interesting, or educational, of a sort. But the material didn't make me gaga. Puzzled, I leafed through the pages, read a bizarre story or two (with parts blacked out or just plain missing), and browsed various indecipherable advertisements at the back.

Then things went click: So this is what he had, and that's what he was doing, I reasoned. Fair enough, but very odd. I couldn't understand it, like I couldn't understand what he saw in Missy. Thinking myself very rational, I decided I was too young yet to appreciate such adult matters.

With that, I slid the magazine into its brown bag and slipped it back under the seat.

* * *

That night, I woke, roasting in sweaty flannel pajamas, with the sweet smell of pine in my nostrils. I opened my eyes to see Kevin in front of me. I can't figure how the moon threw enough light through the trees and then the nylon for me to see, but I lay on my side, facing the dark outline of his back. At first I thought he'd woken up from the heat as well, because there was no outline for his top, just his neck bending smoothly into shoulder.

He was breathing quickly, with a rasp in his throat. I'd never tried it, but I knew what he was doing. Why would he grab himself when I was in the tent beside him? But, really, he was only thirteen. And I wasn't much better; I watched. Knowing how reckless it would be to say something, I lay still listening to the sound of him as the staccato of his breathing increased, then hiccupped, and finally subsided. In that moment, I understood what he'd been doing the night before. The magazine made sense. My brother was beautiful. He was my beaver fox.

After a quick clean-up, he flopped down on his pillow. Though it would never again be easy between us, together that night, we fell asleep.

Bob Vickery

Bill's Big Dick

It's Sunday morning, and Bill and I are still in bed. It's a Vermont Indian summer, and the day outside is bright and clear.

Bill stirs awake and kisses me. "So, when are we getting married?"

Here we go again, I think. "I told you, Bill," I say. "I'm not the marrying kind."

Bill sits up. "That's it," he says. "You're cut off."

"Come on, baby," I say. "Don't be like that."

Bill shrugs, but says nothing.

"Bill . . . ," I coax.

Bill turns away. I run my hand down his back. "Let me make you feel good," I say. "And we'll forget all about this marriage foolishness."

Bill shakes my hand off.

"Let me suck you off," I croon. "Let me feed on that big, throbbing, pulsating, red, veined manmeat." Bill ignores me. "Please, baby," I urge. "Sit on my chest. At least let me look at it."

Bill turns and gives me a level look. "All right," he says. "But no touching." He sits up and swings his leg over so that he's straddling my torso. His dick drapes over his fat ballsac, its knob resting on the little cleft between my pecs. Even soft, it's a monster, a red, thick spongy tube that coils out like some fleshy python. For all the time I've known Bill, I still can't look at his godzilla schlong with anything but awe.

I reach out to stroke it, but Bill slaps my hand away. "I said no touching," he growls.

My eyes trace the blue vein that snakes down the long pink shaft, ending in a knob that is as red and juicy and round as a ripe summer plum. "Please, baby," I plead. "Let me stroke it."

"I don't think so," Bill says.

I continue to stare. His balls are enormous: big, fat jizz factories that can pump out truly prodigious quantities of spunk whenever Bill shoots a load. They hang heavily in a fleshy, red pouch, cushioning his tremendous wanker. As I stare at them, I feel saliva pool in my mouth. "At least drop your balls in my mouth.," I beg piteously.

"Fuck you," Bill growls. He's leaning back, propped up on his elbows, and his dick and balls hang a tantalizing couple of inches from my face. I inhale deeply and get a whiff of musk and sweat and ripe sex. I could get drunk on that scent. Under the naked worship of my gaze, Bill's dick stirs, thickens, and slowly grows hard. I watch the fat red head deepen in color and swell to full ripeness. I grab for the meaty root like my hand has a mind of its own.

Bill seizes me by the wrist. "No!" he snarls. "You're cut off. Permanently."

"Just let me give it a squeeze," I plead.

Bill's eyes narrow. "You gonna marry me?"

I shake my head miserably. "Baby, I can't."

Bill glowers at me. "Then keep your hands to yourself."

Bill's dick is sticking straight up now, pointing to the ceiling, fully hard, twitching. . . . It's like some thick, gnarled tree root, veined, pulsing, engorged with blood. I've never seen a dick that came even close to this, this . . . feast of man flesh. And I know that I never will. "Okay," I groan. "I'll marry you!"

Bill stares hard into my eyes for a couple of beats. "You on the level?"

"Yeah, goddammit!" I snap, meeting his gaze.

Bill's mouth curls up into a sly smile, leaning back. "Okay," he says. "Then it's all yours."

"Slide forward," I urge. "Stuff it down my throat."

Bill's grin widens. "Sure, Curtis. Anything you say." He scoots forward and his dick head pokes against my lips. I lick the red fleshy knob tenderly, running my tongue around it, probing into the piss slit, tasting the little dribbles of precum that keep oozing out. I can only nibble down half of Bill's cock before the cockhead bangs against the back of my throat.

Bill cradles my head in his hand, and I look up into his eyes as he fucks my mouth. I slide my hand over his lean torso, tugging on the muscles, tweaking Bill's nipples, never breaking eye contact with him. He pulls his dick out and drops his balls in my face. I burrow my nose into the loose folds of scrotal flesh, and breath deeply, getting the full hit now of ripe ball stink. I suck one ball into my mouth and then the other, as Bill lightly slaps my face with his father-of-all-wankers. Bill starts whacking off in earnest, his hand sliding up and down the mammoth shaft. I wrap my hand around my dick and pump it, my strokes falling in sync with Bill's.

Our jack-fest continues on like this for the next few minutes. Bill's dick looms above my face like some huge, pink blimp, some phallic Macy's Thanksgiving Day balloon, some great queer shrine of the Western World. I focus my gaze on it worshipfully, feeling my pumping hand drawing my load from my balls. Bill's balls are pulled up tight now, and his dick twitches with the hardness of steel rebar.

"I could squirt any time now," Bill gasps. "How about you?"

"Yeah," I pant. "I'm just about there. Let's go for it."

Bill gives his wanker a few quick strokes. He groans loudly and blasts my face with a wad of hot jizz. Spurt after spurt follow, Bill's cock a veritable Vesuvius of erupting spooge. A few quick strokes takes me over the edge, and I arch my back as my own load spurts out and splatters against Bill's back. We thrash around in the bed, our dicks pumping jizz, crying out loud enough to bring the ceiling down on us.

Bill rolls over and collapses on the bed beside me. We lay there, side by side, staring up at the ceiling, panting. Bill turns towards me. "I want a big wedding," he says. "With all the trappings."

Fuck, I think.

Darrin Hagen

Tree House

We slept in separate sleeping bags, sweating from the neck down, our warm breath visible, collecting in cooling pools over our heads.

My eyes never left him . . . busying himself with rolling the next joint, telling some made-up tale of teen lust, this girl's tits, that girl's ass . . . hair falling into his stoned eyes, goofy grin on one side of his face, playing air guitar to something by Black Sabbath – everyone thought he was cool.

I thought he was hot.

The night before Halloween, as we were exploding homemade Molotov cocktails on a deserted gravel road, he caught my gaze and held it: devil smile lit up by the flames, eyes reflecting not just fire, but an icy heat, a stony challenge.

Be like me and I'll be like you.

Grabbing a gasoline-filled liquor bottle, I light the rag stuffing the neck and heave it up high, straight up into the black night, pierced with the arc of my firebomb, the arc too steep, the bottle heading back to a mark dangerously close to where we stand looking up, his shoulder against mine, his triumphant howl changing to something less sure of itself as we run, dodging our own weapon, laughing hysterically, holding onto each other, breathless.

The bomb hits the gravel and shatters, shards of fiery glass flying out, a pool of blue flame shoots across the road, then subsides.

We lean against the truck. I watch the fire, but all my senses are focused on him, how close he is to me, the smell of sweat and beer and smoke. He flicks his cigarette into the dirt, climbs into the truck, and guns the engine to life. I never know where we're heading next. He decides as he drives.

The headlights slice through fields and bridges. I see one hand in his lap, but I can't tell if the groping I sense is real or if I'm just watching so hard for it that I see it anyway.

There's a car we've been eyeing for weeks, sitting abandoned by the side of the road. We park next to it and step out of the truck. I expect him to find a rock and smash in a window or a headlight, but he just tries the doors.

One is unlocked.

There are no keys, the battery is dead. The glove compartment opens after a few good punches. There's a camera inside.

The headlights from the truck shine into the abandoned car. He's a wiry angry silhouette, edged in a bright halo. The steam from our lungs swirls above our heads. He takes the camera in one hand, looks at me with that evil grin and points it at me. I shoot him the finger and he gets it on film: a birthday party, a picnic, someone's grad, an obscene finger in the dark. . . .

Traces of the flash repeat on my retinas. I hear a zipper, suddenly the camera is handed to me, and I see his jeans down.

"Get a shot of this!" he says, mooning me, his lean muscular ass glowing, goosebumps on his skin. He arches his back for a good view for the camera, for me. The flash freezes the moment in time, but before the image fades he's on to the next indecency – his dick facing me, smiling for the camera, jeans around his knees, hard white stomach peeking out from under his black T-shirt.

"Make sure my face isn't in the picture." I move in closer. His cock, lying straight back on his stomach, is hardening, in reaction to the sudden cold or the sudden freedom.

He, points it straight up for a good picture. I reach past the camera to adjust his angle and, for a second, cold hands touch hot skin and an electric jolt flies between us.

Suddenly, the camera is wrenched from my hands and he says, "Undo your belt."

He's behind me. The flash from the camera as he moves in reaches past the car windows and lights up the long grass outside, letting the real world intrude for a second before it's vanquished again by the dark cold night that seals off this moment for just us. He's not laughing anymore. Then I feel a hand on my back.

"Spread."

The camera clicks furiously. It flashes as he enters me, as our bodies become one pounding machine, the breath escaping our lungs in icy gasping clouds, the sweat on our skin chilling immediately. The headlights from the truck still shine on us, and the shadow in front of me is mostly his head and shoulders, then an arm as he grabs my hair and pulls my head back and for the first and only time ever our mouths meet and his tongue searches for mine and as I release all over some stranger's front seat and as he pumps into me he says

"I. . . ."

The sentence hangs in the air unfinished, frozen, mingling with our steam and breath and sweat.

Maybe he can't finish the sentence.

Or won't.

Or doesn't even know how it ends.

We drove back to his parents' place, to the tree house where we spent every summer night until the mountain air got too cold. Everything was just as before, he was cool and I was trying to be as bad as him, and we climbed the rope ladder, drawing it up behind us, lighting a joint, leafing through magazines filled with shiny naked female skin, marveling at their power over our stiff young imaginations, and I knew that even though we had finally kissed in that car, that sentence would remain unfinished forever.

But that night, he zipped both sleeping bags together as one, and we climbed naked into it and he rested cradled in my arms with his head on my chest and our breath mingled over our heads like a cloud, hanging in the dark like an incomplete thought, an unspoken longing, escaping red hot, then turning cold.

Donn Short

Tommy Nights

Tommy's family lived in one of six row houses, next to ours, a line of two-story shacks, all alike, except that Tommy Gallagher lived in one of them. Tommy's bedroom faced onto the pitiful hardscrabble patch we all thought of as our common backyard. The landlord – also common – had long since given up repairing the rotting fence that marked our property from the empty lot next to it, but to me, it was that fence I remember most about those years.

When I was four, I relied on my father's strong arms to lift me high above the crowds to see the clowns in the Christmas parade that each year marched past our house. And in a similar way, I always think of that fence, as the boost I needed to get a better look at life as it unfolded – from Tommy's second-floor window.

At the end of each school day, we followed the same route home, went through the same routine once we got there. Tommy would look at me and smile and I would smile back. Tommy stood at his front door, I stood at mine, he a little tired and I – erect. Tommy would say, "*See you later*," and then we would each go inside, to the sameness to be confronted there, until the marvel of tomorrow would bring the two of us together again. "See you later." Such an optimistic way to say goodbye.

On one of those late afternoons when Tommy and I took our leave of each other, he spoke to me in a voice that seemed somehow different: "*See you later.*" The words were the same, but the tone had changed. Believing that Tommy and I shared the same desires, I judged the distance between this day's parting and all the others that had come before it, and I understood. I *knew*. "See you . . . *later*."

In the early dark that comes in autumn, I stood at Tommy's fence, *knowing* this was the place he meant for me to be. I saw the light come on in the second-floor window, watched Tommy moving to music, which I stood on tiptoe to hear. His hands moved, fingers first, through his long hair, and high above his head, his naked chest framed on either side by the curve of his arms, like two long-necked swans guarding the treasure which floated between them . . . that *face* . . . a wilful spectacle meant only for me.

After several evenings of such life-altering theater, there came a night when I saw hands reach out to claim the white-feathered heavenly bird that was my Tommy. He was no longer alone in the room, maybe never had been. On that night of the hands, he danced as he had danced every night. And so it was, night after night: Tommy dancing, arms above his head, and hands reaching out for him. There were many boys, different boys, who came to Tommy's *Swan Lake*, and boys who were too old to be called boys, on many nights: starry, starless, moon-lit and moonless nights. The only constants in the drama were the dancing boy in the window and the boy on the fence, the boy on shore. Barefoot and fearful of wading in, I watched, night after night, my face burning and my eyes wet, watching the flight of the erotic, which did not wait for me: half-faces and shadows, male shoulders and masculine backs and arms raised like sails in the kind of lovemaking that looks like battle at sea, and always ended with Tommy, his belly up against the wall, as cold and hot (I imagined) as the lovemaking itself. And then, they stopped, shipwrecked in each other's arms. And I waited for the tension in my own stiffness to subside and, head back, I relaxed: two last tears sealing defeat under sad, cypress lashes for me, the wretched earthbound.

One night, there was no light in the second-story room. I waited for it, but it never came – no light, no dance, no dice. There was nothing to do but go inside, fall asleep, and dream.

Early the next morning, I overheard my mother talking on the phone – too early to be anything but the local excitement over *bad* news. I crouched on the stairs, listening – something about Tommy Gallagher – but the universe had already begun to spin, pulling me from the room and away from the world in which I lived. Somehow, I managed to climb back onto the spinning planet, felt my feet again on the stairs, heard my mother cluck her tongue about Tommy Gallagher's accident in Little Lake. My mother was particularly bitter that year, her prized roses winning only second place at the Exhibition. Listening to her speak of Tommy, lying in a hospital bed fighting for his life, I could hear her taste the news, knowing what this must be doing to his mother, whose roses had won first prize. My mother was not as close to her son as she was to her dog. Strange to prefer a dog to your own flesh and blood, but I must admit: in that moment, given a choice between mother and the dog, I'd have taken Fluffy, too – if we're talking turkey.

A couple of mornings later, sitting across from her at the kitchen table eating breakfast, I watched her savor the saddest news of all. "The Gallagher boy died last night," she said, licking her lips. "Every year somebody drowns in that lake," she said. "Why not a Gallagher?" To hear her speak of Tommy so, to learn of history changing course in such tones, I realized it was possible to hate her even more.

Douglas Ferguson

Pretty in Punk

Our relationship was just like a John Hughes movie. Derrick was playing Andrew McCarthy's role, except that Derrick was a basketball jock with a cocky smirk, as opposed to a rich, cross-eyed preppy. And I was Molly Ringwald, except that, well, I was a guy. Nonetheless, it was high school, it was the '80s, and it was my first experience with "movie love."

Growing up in Saskatchewan, in a town where the kids line-danced to Def Leppard, and practically every activity evolved around hockey and beer, I was the novelty of my high school. I wore baggy black clothes from the Sally-Ann, wrapped shoelaces around my wrists, and decorated my cardigans with safety pins. I wore my hair in a hippie bob and listened to bands like Echo and the Bunnymen and Joy Division. I wanted life in dull Saskatchewan to reflect the teen movies of the time, and thought that my alternative style was a good place to start.

My friends and I were known as the school freaks. We'd loiter in the hallways and scoff at all the acid wash that would glide past us. We'd shout, "Hang the DJ," at school dances. We'd sneer disdainfully at the jocks and their preppy girlfriends.

But as far as jocks went, I knew that Derrick was different. Derrick was *cool.* He rode a skateboard. He used adjectives like "fly" and "dope." And he danced like Vanilla Ice. For over a year, I had fantasized that he'd come to need me in that dramatic way the heartthrobs in teen movies needed Molly.

On our first day of Grade Twelve, Derrick approached me in art class.

"Hey, man," he said. "Can I sit with you?"

"Uh, sure," I replied. My heart pounded in my ears, but I played it cool and nonchalantly flipped the hair from my face.

Less than a month later, we became inseparable. It wasn't long before my *Pretty in Pink* film fantasies had become a reality. While a couple of my friends criticized me for hanging out with a "dumb jock," Derrick took flack from his peers for hanging out with the "freak." But it was this drama that brought us closer together. And I felt smug whenever Derrick's peers would see us.

It wasn't until the spring, a couple of months before graduation, that Derrick told me the truth about his peers: that they weren't calling me a freak behind my back. They were calling me a fag.

Derrick had parked his four-by-four on one of our secret hangouts. It was on a low hill, just outside city limits, that overlooked the river valley. We sat on the hood of his car, stared at the stars, and talked about moving to Saskatoon together after grad. Derrick mentioned how he couldn't wait to leave this town so he would no longer be the subject of rumors.

I asked, "What rumors?"

Derrick said rumors that I was a gay, and had converted him to homosexuality.

"Well, maybe we shouldn't move in together," I said, "if you're so worried about what others are saying."

"I'm not worried," he said.

"'Cause, like, I do have my pride, you know. Don't do me any favors."

"I'm not," he said defensively. "I don't care if they think I'm gay. And I wouldn't care if you *were*."

I was quiet for a few moments. "Well, just so you know; I'm bisexual."

"And, like I said, I wouldn't care if you were full-on gay."

"Well, okay. I'm just gay."

"I still don't care," he replied. "You're my best friend."

Suddenly, Derrick wrapped his arm around me. I grew dizzy and placed a hand lightly on his neck. Before I knew it, the two of us were kissing. Overwhelmed, I remember only two things about that first kiss. Firstly, that "Reel Around the Fountain" by the Smiths was playing in the tape deck, which I had decided was the perfect song for the soundtrack of the movie that was our relationship. And, secondly, that his mouth tasted gloriously of Ritz crackers. A few minutes later, we heard a car approaching. We immediately stopped kissing and decided to call it a night.

His phone calls became less and less frequent after that. Like angst-ridden Molly, I would sit in my room and wait for the phone to ring. He acted like nothing had changed between us, but it was obvious that it had. A week later, he started dating this girl named Shayla. When he told me,

I insisted that we talk in private. It was a Wednesday, during lunch hour, and we sat in his blue Toyota, parked in a quiet residential area.

"Say it!" I shouted. "Just say it! You're ashamed to be seen with me!"

"That's not true!" he insisted.

I wept. I hollered. I smacked him in the chest for about fifteen minutes, then made my dramatic exit loudly slamming his car door. It wasn't until that night, weeping in my room, that I realized I'd ripped off my entire dialogue from *Pretty in Pink*. I had only made some substitutions: Instead of asking "What about prom?" I asked, "What about Saskatoon?" He said he wasn't sure if he wanted to move. I called him a "filthy, fucking, no good liar," though what he was lying about, I wasn't sure.

We stopped speaking to each other altogether. I was surprisingly fine by this. If John Hughes had taught me anything, it was that an upbeat ending would happen on graduation night. So I waited. And when graduation night came, I waited for Derrick to approach me, and tell me that he'd always believed in me. That he just didn't believe in himself. And that he loved me. *Always.*

Instead, I spent the night acting like I was having a better time than I really was. Derrick held Shayla tightly on the dance floor. And we never spoke again.

TK Chornyj

Skate Porn for Faggos

"What do you want for your birthday?" my best friend James asked me.

"Lots of fucking!" I smirked. I hadn't really thought about it, but it sounded like the right thing to say.

We were fifteen when we found each other. We'd spent that whole summer leering at boys downtown, egging each other on until we screwed up the courage to walk into the gay bookstore on Davie Street.

He'd held my hand once, but I'd pulled away. It was scary for me; I needed James and everything felt fragile. He took the rejection gracefully, and there hadn't been any weirdness afterwards.

James had dark curly hair, brown eyes, and lean limbs he wasn't used to. He nodded towards a guy jaywalking.

"Him?" James started our favorite game.

I made a puking face and pulled on my jacket. A silent version of our game continued on the subway as the train burrowed us back to our suburb.

As we turned the corner of my cul-de-sac, I noticed my parents' cars were gone and the house was dark, except for the porch light.

I stopped at our driveway and turned to James. "So tomorrow," I started to say, but something stopped me. James wasn't wearing his goodbye face. He was standing oddly close to me, and for some reason I kept walking.

He followed me to the front steps and as I reached for the screen door, he didn't take the usual step back.

Something stirred in me, maybe it was desire for James, I couldn't be sure. I was almost sixteen and a faggot so anything that stirred felt dangerous.

"What's going on, man?" I tried to make my voice seem gruff, but it came out husky.

James looked down and pressed closer. "I want to give you your birthday present," he said in a voice that reminded me of my little sister during a thunderstorm.

I swallowed. "It's not my birthday until Saturday," I said.

James shrugged.

My heart raced as we stepped into the house. I took my shoes off in the dark and walked tentatively into the living room I'd known my whole life. James stumbled in the dark and grabbed my waist to steady himself. He pressed against me and I felt the heat of his cock on my back. I pressed back and his arms slipped across my belly. We stood there for a long moment, the soothing embrace lulling my heart to a more normal rate.

"What do you want for your birthday?" James asked and his warm breath on my ear made the skin of my cock tighten.

"This," I said, and rolled my ass over his crotch.

"Like this?" He steered my hips with his hands so my asshole felt his burning cock, even through my cargo pants.

I pulled off my T-shirt as James unzipped my cargos. I heard my wallet chain hit the floor. James pulled my cock out of my boxers and gripped me until I was swollen like him. I heard his wallet chain fall. I imagined what his cock looked like because I was too nervous to turn and look. I imagined it was long and lean, like his arms.

He brought his fingers up to my mouth, and I sucked them inside. He explored my mouth briefly and his fingers easily slipped out. He added his own saliva to his fingers and rubbed our spit around my hole.

"Like this?" he asked again, and I groaned as his fingers went inside me. There was a mirror over the mantel on the other side of the room.

James followed my gaze, and we both kicked off our pants and I braced myself against the mantel. We made eye contact in the mirror, and without looking down, he plunged his fingers into my ass. My mouth began to water, and I used my own fingers to lubricate his throbbing cock. He closed his eyes for a second. His mouth gaped slightly and I thought that his lips looked very kissable.

He took his cock from me, and I held the mantel as he drove into me.

At first, I braced myself for his thrusts, but as I felt myself opening further, I used the mantel to thrust back, which gave him a look of surprise.

"Where do you want me to come?" he said.

I gave him a push. "On my back."

He gave me a few more hard thrusts and I closed my eyes, waiting for his load to land on my shoulders. He pulled out and I felt every ridge as he left me. Then everything went white.

I opened my eyes. The mirror was smeared with cum. I could barely make out the ecstatic face of my best friend, but to the left, her right, I saw the open door and the look of shock on my mother's face.

J.R.G. DeMarco

Model Behavior

Two more nights. Then I'd probably never see Nick again. We were both seventeen but I was a year ahead of him and would be graduating in June.

I'd had a crush on Nick since his freshman year; all dark hair, green eyes, and Greek features. He joined the frosh soccer squad and I got a chance to see him now and then in the locker room. What I saw made me crazy, but I could never make a move.

In my senior year, Nick joined the Model UN club and I followed right along. I was no fool; that group took week-long trips which meant we'd get to stay in motels together. I wanted in.

I made myself useful by taking the clerical work off Mr Walen's shoulders and convinced him to take me along on the next trip. Walen asked me to make rooming assignments and I was only too glad. I put myself in Nick's room. Duh.

When we arrived, our room had two beds and four guys.

"Who's taking the bed and who gets the floor?" Pete asked.

"The floor?"

"Yeah, I'm not sleeping with a guy."

"Me neither," Tom chimed in. "We can switch up, one night the bed, one night the floor."

"You guys are fucked up," Nick said. "I'm not taking the floor any night. I don't care who sleeps next to me."

My heart did a joyful little dance.

"That's how I feel." I shook with anticipation. "Nick and I will take that bed. You two fight over the other."

After the second night, I wondered why I was torturing myself. Each night, Nick took a shower before bed, then strolled out wrapped in a towel with his dick neatly outlined. In bed, I watched him saunter toward me, which made me giddy.

Nick made a point of dropping the towel in front of me and slowly pulling on a pair of loose boxers, showing everything in the process. He'd hop into bed innocently and then we'd talk. Soccer. The Model UN. Anything.

The heat of his body next to mine was unbearable. Sometimes as we talked, his leg would touch my hand. That was electric and my balls tingled.

Sleep was impossible. I lay awake waiting for him to roll over and touch me. He never did. Once I did feel his morning erection poking my leg and I nearly came in my shorts.

I decided to be more aggressive. Nick did the usual that third night except he couldn't find his boxers.

"Sleep naked," I laughed and pulled his towel off. Nick looked surprised but didn't move. Except for his cock, which began a slow bobbing arc up. Nick just looked at me and smirked.

"That's why I can't sleep naked. Boners all night long." He reached down and snapped it against his stomach.

"Oh." I gulped, unable to tear my eyes away. "Well . . . yeah . . . I guess." The air tightened around me.

Nick found his shorts and pulled them on, but his pink cock poked out and stared at me. Packing it back in, he hopped into bed a little closer than the night before.

My mouth was dry and my hands shook.

Nick rolled over to face me.

"My committee was no fun today."

"Mine . . . uh . . . mine, too." I stammered and looked into his sleepy green eyes. "Tired, though." With that I nested my head on the pillow and faced him. He breathed softly, smelling of mint and fresh air.

His breathing became regular. This was my chance and I was a coward. I drifted off cursing myself for wasting another night.

On the edge of sinking into unconscious sleep, I was jarred by Nick turning to throw his leg over me. Wrapped in his crotch the heat was incredible. His cock was hard and prodded my bare stomach insistently.

I froze, not wanting the moment to pass and wanting to be anywhere but here. Bristly leg hairs grazed my flesh and I shuddered. I slowly inched my hand toward his dick; I was nearly there when Nick turned, leaving my hand planted on his soft round ass.

I fell asleep like that and dreamt of drowning.

Next morning, Nick acted as if nothing had happened. It hadn't. I wanted to change that on this last night of the trip.

That night, Pete and Tom were out with other kids; I was alone with Nick. When Nick started his shower, I tensed up. Taking deep breaths, I listened to the water falling on his body and imagined being one of the drops rolling into his crotch.

Before I knew it, Nick was standing next to the bed. "Just one clean pair of shorts and I need those tomorrow. So I'm gonna sleep naked. You mind?" Even his voice aroused me. Dropping the towel, he hopped into bed, cock hard as ironwood.

"Up early tomorrow," he said around a yawn.

"Guess we should sleep." I flicked out the light plunging us into darkness. Cursing my cowardice, I felt Nick turn to face my back A few centimeters more and we'd be spooning, except his dick was so hard it would have to find a way into me.

"G'night," I murmured.

Silently, Nick moved closer.

Now or never, I thought, and rolled over, placing my face smack against his. My hand brushed his cock and it twitched. Still, he said nothing.

His breathing became ragged, then he moved and rested his cock in my hand. I wanted to scream and my heart tried breaking out of my chest. Slowly, carefully I closed my fingers around his cock and felt my own erection poking through my shorts.

Nick moved into me then.

"Yeah, Kev." His voice was throaty, his breath sweet. He moved to kiss me; grabbing my ass to pull me closer, he whispered, "What took you so long?"

John Briggs

Circulation

It was a Christmas vacation visit to my hometown library, the one where I had been scolded as a six-year-old for returning a rain-wet book, the same place where I had, at twelve, scoured the unabridged dictionary for dirty words, and where in high school I had pretended to flirt with Greta Johnston while secretly lusting after Tommy Barnes, who sat behind her. The lobby display cases were arranged with what I swear were the same artifacts and books from Christmases past that had greeted me as a child.

It was almost closing time, and the sun had been down for over an hour. My sister would be expecting me to join them for dinner soon, but I wanted to revisit the stacks, that quiet, overheated refuge of my adolescence, where hours had been spent exploring other worlds, assuring me that there was more to life than what I would encounter in my uptight little town.

In the nineteenth-century English literature aisle, I took in the sour smell of slowly cooking acid text: the books of my youth were decaying like old brittle friends. The overhead lights blinked. I assumed that a cough from the librarian making his closing rounds, the same man I had seen at the circulation desk, was calculated to hustle me out the door, but a second cough made me stop. "Wait for me here," he said, in his hushed but audible librarian whisper.

The nearly empty library engaged in a brief flurry of coat rustling and boot scuffing. Goodbyes were said, doors slammed, and darkness rose to fill each floor. I heard the sound of rubber soles on waxed linoleum. I am as guilty as most of not paying sufficient attention to those that serve the public. I had not looked at him closely enough . . . I knew only that he seemed a few years younger than me, was about my height, but with the build of a soccer player.

He moved toward me down the narrow aisle. I saw his silhouette against the red glow of an emergency exit sign. He said, "For years I've dreamed that some night, after closing, I'd be stalked up here." His fingers grazed my wrist. Our lips met, opened. We fell to the floor as we embraced, and he pulled shelves of mildewing volumes on top of us.

In minutes we were naked on the floor of the public library in the town where I had grown up. We were sweating on discarded clothes and leaves of books that had been in circulation for decades. What stains would someone find the next time that she borrowed *Middlemarch*? What aromas would be stamped beside the "Due Back" date?

Later, while he lay sweating on top of me and I traced the fine hairs clinging to his neck, he talked about his job. I hadn't realized that he was head librarian.

"I think I know you," he said. "I think you knew my brother, Tommy. Tommy Barnes? I'm his little brother Joey."

"You're kidding."

"You know, I always had a crush on you, but I don't think you knew I existed."

Joey Barnes. I remembered that he had indeed been on the soccer team, and that once he and the rest of the team had boarded the same late bus home with me. He had stood the whole way, next to where I was sitting, hanging from an overhead bar, his armpit hair unabashedly exposed to my view, blades of grass clinging to his thighs, only inches from my lips. I could smell the grass stains on his shoes, and the adolescent sweat rising from his sweat-stained shorts. I found myself getting hard again.

"Tommy's happily fat and suburban, by the way. Two wives, one divorce, six kids. How long are you in town?"

"Only for another few days," I said. "Maybe I'll stop by again before I go."

"I'll be looking for you," he said. While I tried to find all of my clothes, he stood there naked, reshelving the books that had fallen to the floor.

* * *

I returned a few days later, on the day before New Year's Eve. Joey was talking to someone at the circulation desk, but I was pretty sure he saw me. He was a handsome man in full light. I walked quietly up to level four of the stacks, and hid myself at the far end of nineteenth-century English literature again as the lights blinked, and the closing ritual was repeated. My heart raced and my underwear was wet with precum from my hardening cock as the lights below me were extinguished, one floor at a time.

I heard his rubber-soled shoes making their way up the narrow stairs. I waited for my eyes to adjust to the dark, then held my breath so he wouldn't hear me, but his footsteps stopped one floor below. I saw two inky shadows through the grated metal risers of the stairs. I heard the scratch of fingernails on denim, the drag of zippers, and Joey's breathless whisper explain, to someone else, "For years I've dreamed that some night after closing . . . ."

A nearby wall clock jumped audibly from notch to notch. I bolted to the nearest exit and burst out onto the fire escape, the tinny alarm swallowed by the falling snow.

Stephen Emery

Hook-Up Reunion

I'm trembling as I peer over the ledge. He's undulating across the dance floor below me, hands raised in prayer with the deafening drum and bass. His dance partner gyrates his backside just centimeters away from the crotch.

With the techno blast, my ears fill with blood. Bud's hair is shorter, his body a bit thicker in the shoulders, but he has the same half-sneering smile and perfect whites. The bastard is still cute after ten years.

I couldn't tell if Bud had something through the thin towel around his waist before he shoved me back against the wall, so many years before in high school. His post-football reek wafted into my nose as his three buddies jeered at my scrunched-up face. Bud's hand held the back of my head firmly against the locker room wall.

"You like to stare at guys in the shower, faggot?" he sneered with a crooked smile on his face.

I shook my head in frantic denial as his buddies laughed. No use, really, since moments before he had caught my glance at his crotch through the post-practice steam.

Grade ten was hell after that. I could handle being taunted by the freshman kids who were younger and bigger than me. I could handle being forced to kiss the wall, lunch trays flipped out of my hands, and buckets of water thrown over the stalls on me. What broke me was the yearbook photo with the caption taunting, "Sean Emery, Grade 10, Waterloo Tech: most likely to spend his life on his knees", which somehow got past the teacher on the yearbook committee before it went to print. The rest of the school knew I wasn't going for the priesthood. When my mom's divorce went through that summer, I was all too happy to make the name change with her and transfer out to another city.

My reverie shrivels in amazement as I watch Bud lean in to kiss the bottom boy. His next move grinding against the lad's ass on the dance floor shows that he has definitely been there before. And now he is out – here.

So I pluck up my righteous butt and glide down the stairs, I'm striding with all my years of die-in and kiss-in activist Queer as Fuck rage across the dance floor towards Bud Langdon and stare.

His radar is just as good as ever as he looks up at my eyes bearing down on him. I'm no longer the skinny faggot, though. My head is shaved and my body is buffed, forged after years of work-out rage at the Buds whom I would never let press my face into any walls ever again.

He blinks briefly without recognition, then spreads out a crooked smile of a stranger's invitation. After a couple of jarring tunes, he slides over in my direction. And I'm cool.

"I'm Brett," he croons. And then did he say "honey"? And did I hear a lilt in that once harsh voice? "Sean, sweet name for a nice looker," he said. Of course, I was just "the fucking faggot" to him back then. He never did care to know my name, did he?

Later, I'm walking him to my nearby place and into my bedroom. Stripping him, I ask what he does. Banking exec at a trading firm. It's famous. Pretty closeted, he tells me. So *he* has to be. I just smile.

I do him with my mouth and find all the tender spots soon enough, so that he's squirming, and rising to the edge before I let off and he's begging. He wants to fuck me. I deal. Not until I do him. He's not used to that, but I'm such a hunk. Doggie style, I tell him. Just go slow, he pleads. Then after I cum, I push his mouth on my dick and watch his head bob in the dark glass of my computer screen.

My cell goes off, phoning itself as I programmed it earlier. I fake a friend's emergency call. I watch Brett/Bud's face fall with disappointment. I tell him, sorry, he's gotta go. I sweetly ask for his card, then push him out the door.

Back in the bedroom, I flip on the screen and stop the cam, flipping its pics every few secs behind a mesh screen in the corner.

I select images of him on his knees getting it deep, his face on the pillow in full profile. Cut and crop facial close ups, just to be sure. I surf the corporate website on his card and copy some exec emails, then attach files and click the send key to his email, bcc to his company execs, and a few choice porn newsgroups to boot.

The message that I send with the pics reads: "Bud (AKA Brett) Langdon, formerly of Waterloo Tech, grade 10 class of '94: Most likely to spend his life on his knees, Thanks for the hot reunion – A close alumni."

Andy Quan

Shoes

Sex with Charles wasn't the first sex I'd had. But it was probably the first sex I'd had that wasn't romantic.

It wasn't hard to notice him. There were so few identifiable gay men at my small university that we all basically knew each other. The other men on campus were mostly sensitive straight boys, hippie kids, and lefty intellectuals mixed in with small-town rednecks and only a smattering of jocks, since the university's small sports program focused only on rowing and rugby.

Charles hung in the background of one of the gay cliques on campus. He had longish red-brown hair and a solid build, strong arms and chest. You could see that, even if you couldn't see the exact contours. None of us wore the form-fitting uniforms of gay men in the big cities, though occasionally, to be daring, our slightly more colorful (or slightly more fey) garments would have an extra shirt button undone, or the sleeves pushed up unusually high.

When Charles and I finally arranged to get together, neither of us were completely sure what it would lead to, and the planning of it was more with nervous energetic attraction than calm and cool lust. There was never a sly wink.

But by the time I had arrived at his apartment – his alone, unusual for a university student – I had some idea of what was to come. Still, I was in no rush, probably because I was still trying to figure out what I wanted. Was he boyfriend material? Was he sex material? How did those things combine and in what proportions?

I spotted a novel on his shelf. It happened to be my absolute favorite at the time. "You're reading this?" I pointed, obviously excited.

"Uh. Well, I was." He looked at me with a bit of confusion. "I couldn't quite get into it. Not much of a plot." He shrugged and it struck me that his voice was – not effeminate, what was it? – *nasal.* Slightly high-pitched, not girlish, but cloying.

"This is my bedroom."

Well, give it a go, I coaxed myself. I'm not here to talk literature.

We leaned in for a kiss, and managed, in that perfectly instinctual way, to tilt our heads in opposite directions, open our mouths slightly and to the same width and make contact, motors running, those thousands of muscles that make us smile and frown now concentrating on the pleasures of the mouth and tongue.

He wasn't a bad kisser.

We felt each other's chests and backs through our shirts. These days I'm like an expert at choosing fruit, squeezing and pressing at exactly the right places to find what I want at just the right ripeness. But then as an amateur, it was much more about patting and stroking, not even fondling; big hand motions, as if I were wearing thick mittens. He was the same.

He stopped abruptly. Leaned back, and lifted up his red rugby jersey over his head in one motion. I was disappointed that I didn't get to do this for him so I started to work on his jeans. He complied easily which made me feel awkward since I was still mostly clothed. I paused long enough without doing anything for him to catch on and undress me. Finally, we faced each other, mostly naked.

His body was softer than I expected. Puffier. I didn't know then how different men's bodies were from those in the gay magazines and newspapers I read. Nor did I know how to eroticize nearly any body: to focus on the personality of a bicep, respond to the alertness of a nipple, to find hidden strengths below different surfaces, to discover something sweet and dirty.

I looked at him and his shy, shrugging smile, suddenly noticed a shock of red pubic hair, and decided that touch was more pleasant than sight. I leaned in to kiss him. We ended up doing a horizontal, swooning sort of dance. We rolled over each other and messed up the sheets.

I went down on him: my mouth a homing pigeon; his cock, a home. He suddenly stopped all motion, breath more shallow, body stiff, his arms flat out beside him. His cock was quite nice really, a bit rubbery tasting, but of solid girth, though the rest of his body seemed lifeless. Had I killed him? Death by blow job?

He pushed my head away, whimpered, and came onto his stomach. He paused no more than a few seconds before leaning up, pushing me back, and sucking on my cock with a mechanical enthusiasm. It felt good but wasn't enough. Frottage was one of my first and favourite motions, so I reached down and pulled him up to me by his armpits. I rolled him over, rubbed away like a dog in heat, and came into the space between us which was still wet from his orgasm.

That was it, really. I don't think I even stayed for a shower, preferring to do it at home. I made feeble excuses when he telephoned, and then felt so embarrassed that I could barely talk or look at him when we came into social contact.

What was so wrong with not having good sex? Of him not turning out to be Romeo or Romy-root?

What comes around, goes around. What you do comes back to you. It's not a bad set of ideas. I want to believe them and sometimes I really do. But in the end, I think it's a crock. You do good because it's a good thing to do, not because you expect some reward. And people who do bad things probably have bad things happen to them not as a direct cause-and-effect but because they hang around in circumstances where they're more likely to occur.

So I don't believe that moments that I'm ashamed of like this need come back to me in a reversed form.

But when I'm snubbed, or my calls aren't returned, or I feel a bit used or confused, as I often do, moving about in big urban gay cities in search of friends, frolicking, and fucks, I try not to be angry. I can put myself in their shoes.

Shane Keleher

It's in the Shoes

The first time Peter noticed the tall stranger with brown hair was on a wintry Friday morning during midterms. Peter sat at his study carrel, surrounded by a sea of textbooks and study sheets, when he saw him stroll down the aisles of books. Peter didn't know his name and never would. This stranger looked to be a graduate student, in his mid to late twenties, tall, thin, and assured; he had thick, brown hair, and wore a dark grey sweater and blue jeans. His eyes were mischievous and he looked to be "at play." Peter watched as he gravitated towards an empty carrel beside one being used by a young male student.

This stranger waited for a moment and then slipped off his shoes, revealing white athletic socks. Peter thought that was odd until he noticed that the young man beside him also had his shoes off. Peter, looking for a distraction from his studying, eyed the two shoeless young men. The stranger then slipped his young neighbor a note and they both got up, first the younger one and then the taller stranger, and walked towards the bathroom. Peter's cock sprang to attention at the prospect of what was going on.

He didn't know what to do. Should he follow them in? Peter knew, in his shyness, that he would never dare go in, as much as he desperately wanted to. But he did switch to another carrel that offered a better view of the bathroom door. Minutes passed, then the tall stranger slipped out with a satisfied look on his face as he tugged his zipper securely into place. The younger one followed a half-minute later.

Peter's curiosity got the better of him from then on. For the next few weeks, whenever he was in the library, he spent more time looking for the tall stranger than actually studying. He kept wondering: How did those guys meet? Was the shoeless thing a way of identifying one another?

Then, one day in the library, he spotted a young guy in a study carrel, maybe a first-year student, medium height with a beautiful build and innocent eyes, with no shoes on. Peter grew excited and sat five seats away, stealthily watching him. The boy had his books open but was clearly not interested in them, as he continually scanned his surroundings. Peter didn't have long to wait before the tall stranger appeared from around the corner of some book stacks. The same routine unfolded before him: the stranger sat down, passed the young student a note, and with almost no time passing, they were off. Just watching the scenario got Peter so horny that he wanted to follow them into the bathroom, if for no other reason than to jerk off by himself. Sure enough, the tall stranger left first.

Peter made a decision there and then, He began to sit at the bank of study carrels, shoeless, on a daily basis. But to no avail – there was no sign of the tall stranger, nor did he see any other shoeless guys sitting at the carrels. As days became weeks, he began to believe that his chance was gone – that what he had seen was more rare and random that it was regular. As the semester headed into finals, Peter began to accept that his turn wasn't about to come up. He even started wearing his shoes again in the library. It had been over a week of wearing shoes when he finally spotted him again on a different floor in the library. And true to form, there was another young man in a carrel in his socks. Without thinking, Peter kicked off his shoes. The stranger looked around. When their eyes locked, the stranger headed over. Peter's heart pounded. He regretted it instantly. He was too nervous. He couldn't do it.

The stranger sat down beside him. Peter wanted to put his shoes back on. Suddenly, a note appeared under Peter's arm: "You're a lot hotter than your pic."

With a sudden burst of self-esteem, Peter crossed out the sentence and wrote "Washroom?" then returned it to the stranger. He was now one of them – the shoeless.

Jameson Currier

Chinatown

His name was Bob Kinnaman and he lived in Chinatown. I went to his apartment on a rainy autumn evening, calling him first from the pay phone on the street corner so he could come downstairs to the ground level and open the front door of his building for me. Upstairs, on the fourth floor, his apartment was large and spacious, the walls painted a deep shade of maroon and the rooms full of fluffy couches, oversized pillows, and vases full of long reeds and ferns. Everything seemed to happen rapidly once I was inside. He locked the door behind us and we stood facing each other, breathing hard. He pulled me against him and I tilted my face upward to accept his kiss. It was both strange and elating to taste him, to feel the hard scratch of his stubble against my own, to seek out the shape of his body beneath his dry clothes as his hands pressed harder against the wet chill of my skin. When we broke apart, he led me into his bedroom, where we continued kissing and he unbuttoned my shirt.

I was trembling while my clothes were removed; my nervousness getting the better of me. But as we landed on the mattress and he wriggled awkwardly out of his clothes, I lost my inhibitions and gave in to my feelings of lust.

His body wasn't flawless but to me it was beautifully necessary: a muscular frame maturing into middle-age, broad fleshy shoulders, a chest covered with dark swirls of hair. He positioned my arms around his shoulders and my legs around his waist so that we sat before one another like volumeless bookends and could grope each other's bodies as we continued kissing. Slowly, his mouth branched away from my lips to moisten my forehead, eyes, earlobes, neck, then the curve of my shoulder. In the grey light of the rainy city drifting into the room, the warm touch of his mouth against my cool skin was the most arousing sensation I thought I could experience.

He continued down the hairline of my chest, reaching my navel, pecking lower and lower until his lips reached my hardened cock. He nudged it with his nose, then slowly ran the tip of his tongue along the shaft. When he took me into his mouth, I let out a moan; I had never felt so alive, so deep and stiff and sexual that the adventure of it made me ache. Only after he had retrieved a towel to wipe the sticky fluids which had landed upon our bodies did I return to the complexity at work within myself and make an effort to leave.

"I hate it when guys just up and leave so fast," he said. His arms had found my waist and he drew us together, kissing my neck again. "It takes all the intimacy out of it."

I stayed there for a moment in his embrace, quiet but not calm. Inside, I was waging a fierce battle. Even though I felt a relief that this had finally happened, a layer of shame was working its way through me – I had come to terms with my sexuality, but had not yet conquered the enemy troops of morality, religion, and society. I fidgeted out of Bob's grip and began picking up my clothes. I had narrowed the million questions crashing around in my brain into a single one and, as I found and slipped on my underwear, I blurted it out. "When did you know you were gay?"

He lay on the bed on his stomach watching me get dressed in the dim light of the room, his upper body lifted off the mattress by his elbows. "I always knew," he answered. "I never doubted it. I was having sex with guys when I was twelve. And you?"

In the darkened room, his smile was wide and luminous, and I wanted nothing else to understand the direction he had accepted for himself and make it a part of my own now. "It doesn't seem so black or white to me," I answered.

"I didn't notice it was a crisis a moment ago," he said, the tone of his voice almost snide with insult.

I could not find it in myself to confess to him that he was the first man I had ever had sex with and I was still at war with what I had left behind – in another town and city and state. Then it occurred to me that something that was not so obvious about myself had been very obvious to him when we had first met in the library a few days before.

"Do you want to go for some Chinese food?" he asked me, when I was dressed. "We did make plans for dinner, too. There's a place downstairs Peter and I love to go to."

"Peter?" I asked. "Who's Peter?"

"My partner," he answered. "He's away for a month."

"You have a boyfriend?" I asked, with the same exasperated tone that Annette, my high school girlfriend back in my hometown, would often direct toward me.

"He's cool with this," Bob answered. His smile now appeared both charming and secretive, as mine must have seemed all those times when I didn't want to let Annette completely understand who I was. "We could do this again, you know," he added. "I thought it was sweet the way you found me."

Christopher DiRaddo

When I See Him, Maybe I'll Know

So I call. Pick up the courage to take the elevator down to the food court with a quarter on my break to call him.

I know the number already by heart but still look at the paper he scribbled it on as I dial. It rings three times before he picks it up. And there it is – his voice on the other end of the phone. I stammer my Hello, my Good morning, my How is it going? I wonder if maybe I should've practiced.

I can't tell if he is happy or surprised to hear from me, or maybe he just woke up. I don't remember what we talk about. My mind is all over his body, our bodies.

I never thought my body could do that.

I had been thinking about him all morning at work, still tired and slightly hung-over from the night before. My body all dehydrated and sore, craving water and oxygen. Under my shirt I can feel my nipples trying to burst out from under the cotton. I've had an erection most of the morning. I was playing with my dick too much in my cubicle, shifting it around, trying to hide it. I finally had to jerk off in the bathroom around eleven.

I can feel my chest pound as he talks to me. It feels like I can almost *smell* his voice through the receiver, and it reminds me of the taste of his breath and the other sounds he is capable of making. I'm getting hard all over again just thinking about it. A woman passes by with a kid in tow. The young security guard eyes me suspiciously. I turn away and try to inconspicuously shift my boner under my belt so they don't see.

We make plans. He wants to see me again. I hang up and the phone swallows the coin. I take the elevator back up to my office. This time on the way up, unlike all the other times, my thoughts aren't filled with the dread that normally characterizes my workday. Instead I think of him, and last night, and what this all means.

I get off the elevator and straighten my tie in the reflection of the company door. I go back to the bathroom and whip it out again. Thinking of his warm and groggy morning voice, I come all over the toilet seat.

The rest of the day passes by quickly and I get no work done. I think of possibilities as I doodle on scrap paper. What we did is there in front of me and I think about it any way that I can. I add things, actions, settings, words. I take it all further. And at the end of the day I come home, put on some music, cook myself dinner, watch some TV, and get ready for the next workday. Same old routine. But not. Not anymore. This time it's all different.

I'm going to discover things. Things about me and other people. And he'll help me. Indirectly. I won't ask him questions or expect him to teach me. When I see him, maybe I'll know.

Matt Stedmann

At the Bank

Well, I didn't think it could happen, but my creep-ass dead-end night job at the bank just got worse. It's not bad enough already that I have to spend night after night in a roomful of a hundred other drones, hunched over a keyboard punching in account numbers for check after check after check until I'm sure my head will explode from boredom.

Last night some new guy showed up. The little bastard just strolled in like he owned the place already and began to prowl the room as if he were personally in charge. Black hair in a really short buzz cut, piercing dark eyes, and a tight, muscular bod in jeans and a T-shirt (nobody cares what we wear on the night shift). He's got a nice dark tan and a stubble of beard, and his nose looks like it might have been broken once. The boy looks like some kind of fucking rough trade wet dream.

Talk about distraction. Keypunching isn't something you can just do without paying attention. If he's not gay and available, I'm in big trouble.

❧ ❧ ❧

I'm in big trouble.

I found out from listening to the breakroom gossip last night that the new guy's name is Eric, and he's straight, girlfriend and all. He's a supervisor for one of the other keypunch teams.

The trouble is, I can't stop watching him. Every time he goes past me, he drags my attention like a magnet. I want his roguish smile as he flirts with the college girls. I want his swaggering walk and that nasty scar under his right eye. I want to run my hands over the tight muscles of his chest and feel the hair I can see escaping from his collar. I want to shove my tongue down his throat and my hand between his legs and feel him from the inside.

I want him to be my rough-edged straight boy and I want him to be my bitch.

❧ ❧ ❧

This is weird: Eric touched my machine last night.

He slowed down ever so slowly as he went past, and lightly ran his fingers across the hard plastic of my machine where nobody else could see them. I was so surprised that I didn't know what to do. I looked up but he was already past me, acting as if nothing had happened. I kept watching him for a moment but he didn't do it to anyone else.

An hour later he did it again, this time tapping two fingers firmly on the casing as he went by. Nobody else ever touches my machine, not even the supervisors. We're not supposed to touch anybody else's machine. Why the hell is he touching my machine? I asked my friend Amy, "Does anyone else ever touch your machine?" when we were putting on our coats at the end of our shift, and she looked at me like I'd grown another head.

❧ ❧ ❧

This has got to stop.

He does it at least once a night now, but I never know when it's going to happen so I spend my entire shift restlessly waiting for his touch. Some times it's a quick tap of acknowledgment, other times it's a lazy caress or a long playful stroke. Of course he's never spoken to me, not once. He never says what he wants in words. I'm not sure that he even really knows.

His sister works in the next row and he keeps stopping to chat with her on his rounds. He'll lean there facing me and flex his long legs to emphasize his bulge or stretch his muscular arms over his head. He keeps glancing over to see if I'm looking. He never meets my eyes, but I know he wants me to watch him. He must stop by her machine two or three times a night. Nobody likes their sister that much.

Every time he walks past me I mis-key, nervously anticipating his touch. And he knows it too, the bastard. Every time I make a mistake my machine beeps loudly and I'm sure everyone in the room is watching me. Of course, that's probably all in my head. Our secret little dialogue is known only to the two of us, even though I'm trapped under the eyes of a hundred co-workers and the bank's damn security cameras, which watch our every move. He won't admit what he wants openly, but his fingers won't leave me alone.

If I manage to ignore him for a night, the next night he's back, his fingers more insistent. "Remember me?" they say. "I know you're watching me. I know you want me. You can't get away."

* * *

Last night was the worst.

Last night Eric touched my machine again, and this time it wasn't a quick, secretive stroke. He stood over me and slowly and deliberately dragged his entire hand across the top of the casing until I looked up to finally meet his eyes. He was standing two feet away from me, and yet I could feel the insistent pressure of his fingers as if they were sliding over my own skin.

Of course, he didn't look at me for the rest of the night. He didn't need to. All I could think of, over and over for the rest of my entire shift, was imagining his hand on my flesh, running it everywhere over my body.

I can't take this anymore. If he does it again tonight I just won't be able to hold back. I desperately need this crummy job, but I'll do it anyway. I've had enough. I'll trail him when he goes outside for a smoke or follow him into the men's room, away from the fucking security cams, and just do it. I'll slam him up against the wall, taste the pouting fullness of his mouth and the shocking stubble of his hair, rough under my fingers like his five o'clock shadow. I'll strip off that T-shirt and shove my hands into his jeans to grip that tight little ass of his.

And we'll just see what it is he thinks he wants.

Christopher DiRaddo

Closet

He closed the utility closet door behind us, drowning our faces in total darkness. I could hardly see him, save for a rough outline of his frame and features highlighted by the crack of light cutting through from under the door.

The room was a small office that doubled as a closet. No windows. Four tight walls. I could feel a small desk behind me piled with boxes and books. There was a shelf to my left. Patrick was in front of me.

Patrick was new to the firm. Another law student like me, shuffling through briefs and reviewing testimonies. I picked him out as a closet case on his first day on the job. Clean-shaven, trim suit, a sharp and boyish smile.

He had intercepted me coming back from the washroom. Asked me to help him get something out of storage. I could see the desire in his smile, a devious mixture of mischief and hunger; by far the most attractive thing I can ever find in a man. I used to foolishly chase after straight boys, but have now come to realize that it is truly the gay gaze that arouses my passion: bent boys whose faces become windows to the deep pull of their queer soul, whose breath expels exhaust from all the pent-up urges we, at some point, learn to succumb to.

Leaning in, he pressed his lips and body against mine while his left hand cupped the right side of my chest, the slurping sounds of our kisses lightly audible over the low rumble of the ventilation system. The room was dark, and as his tongue probed my mouth I could hear the chimes from the landing elevator down the hall, bringing people back up from the lunch break.

Inside this closed room I caught myself thinking about Seven Minutes in Heaven, a game we used to play as kids in high school, where one boy and one girl have to spend seven minutes together, alone in a darkened closet. But this time, instead of spending the seven minutes in the closet talking to Rosemary Adams about math, I gave in to my adolescence and knocked the boxes and books off the desk and onto the floor. This time, I pressed back, slid my hand into his shirt, and touched the warm smooth flesh of his skin.

I buried my nose in the shallow ditch where his heart lay, flat, hard, rising with his breath. I could feel his heart beat. Or perhaps it was mine. I ran my tongue across his broad chest, the nub of his nipple sandwiched between the grooves of my tongue as I licked him hard. Once more I inhaled his center, sweat and soap locked into a block of chest hair, before coming up again to meet his face. In that moment I wondered if Patrick and I would have been friends as kids, in school, on the playground, in closets at parties.

We stopped before it was too late, not wanting others to begin to wonder where we were. Adjusting himself, he opened the door and we both squinted as our eyes met the bright light. Our ears filled with the harshness of the outside noise and the hum of the halogen lights that hung over the corridors that led us back to our office. Like guilty boys who have sneaked ice cream, we wiped the wetness from around our lips and silently made our way back to our desks, leaving the closet door open.

Raymond Luczak

The Room of My Eyes

When he entered the room of my eyes that day, something changed. It felt at first vague, but became infinitely cool, real, concrete. I felt him rustling the sheets of my bed, and I felt his fingers pressing my body softly against his. I whispered his name as he did this, and all this before he revealed to me his name. I did not have to strain my ears to hear his voice or my eyes to read his lips. . . . When he entered the room of my eyes, I knew all that needed to be known, and yet I ached for much more. Whatever doors had been closed inside me were all flung open to his silent gaze, the flint-blue irises that made whatever words he chose to impart seem meaningless, trivial. I held my breath whenever he spoke, and my eyes swung madly on his every word. No, I knew he wasn't a god of any sort, but the power he did not know he had over me was far too gripping. I let myself drown in that clean-shaven face before me: his strong jaw, tiny pricks of freckles under his eyes, firm lips, his short blond curls, and those cobalt eyes. When I first saw him that day, I found myself exploring his eyes. It was a strange and unfamiliar room, but one in which I felt at once home. I wanted to turn boldly to him and to kiss him fully on the lips, right in front of all those strangers stranded in the elevator. I wanted to pull his body close to mine, grope through his suit the flesh he did not know he was blessed to have, and slide each of his fingertips into my mouth to let him know – *yes*. I would lick the dust from a day's work at the office accumulated on his black wingtip shoes. I wanted to trace his nipples through his freshly ironed shirt, then scorch each one with my furnace mouth. I wanted to feel my hands tremble as they traveled from his sweaty heels to his calves and to his thighs. I wanted to trace the mounds of his ass as he lay on his stomach, peacefully sleeping on my bed. I wanted to lick the sun off his shoulders. I wanted to pull open his armpits and let the nervous odor fill my senses. I wanted to kiss every sign he would try to convey on his hands: I would teach him the imprecise language of precise desire. I wanted to commit his entire body to memory so that should I ever be blinded in an accident, I would never forget his sensuous and violent ways beneath my sheets. When he entered the room of my eyes, I did not know yet how much I wanted him. I lay there the morning after, alone as always, and suddenly found myself so hard from remembering his face, whose name I did not know until I fingerspelled the name I'd call him if I would be allowed to do so. But where was I after all in the room of *his* eyes? His name had flashed only once in my mind, and yet I couldn't be sure. He was just a man who stood next to me, saying not even a word, but having given me only that slight smile. As he waited, I saw in his eyes a restless soul, and I wanted him in my arms, to soothe him, and to give voice to his yearnings. I wanted to listen more carefully than ever to his voice, to that something which had changed irrevocably inside me, in that emptiness of my hands held open: Oh, if I could, I would no longer feel the need to say *something* but simply rest my head on his shoulder as we stroll down the street, our arms around each other, the two rooms of our eyes having somehow conjoined into a room larger than our beds, ourselves.

Shaun Levin

How It All Began

We're about to cum in each other's mouths when his boyfriend Daniel walks in. Noah had warned me he might come home early, but I'm still surprised, and I still feel awkward. Noah waves to him, like you'd wave to the delivery boy from your office chair when he knocks on the door with a parcel, as he holds the back of my head, fucks my face, and shoots his thick warm cum down the back of my throat.

Rule NO 1: Don't let him come in your mouth when you're not paying attention. I'm coughing so much I don't even notice Daniel undressing and getting into bed. By the time I recover he's licking the last bits of cum off his boyfriend's cock.

"Wait," Noah says, pushing him away. "We need your help here."

I've never seen skin so pale, every vein visible, so hairless, and hair so red. It's down past his shoulders, and curly; he brushes it away from his eyes to look at me.

"You must be Shaun," he says.

"Enough chatting," Noah says. "Come and chew on his tits."

His mouth is warm as it lands on my nipple to suckle it. Noah eases me onto my back, so that Daniel's head is resting on my chest as he nibbles on my tit and fiddles with the hair on my chest. Noah's on his knees, holding up my cock, inspecting it, then leans forward to lap at the skin of my ball sac. And I think: Fuck.

"I'm there," I say.

"Already?" Daniel says.

"I know," I say. "But I have to."

And their mouths meet at the head of my cock as I jerk off onto their faces.

And that's how our threesomes began. I'd take the bus from Tel Aviv to Jerusalem three or four times a month, to the little house Noah and Daniel rented in the German Colony. We'd cook dinner sometimes, especially if it was a Friday and Daniel wasn't preparing for a lecture at the

Hebrew University, or Noah wasn't off in Gaza with some young Palestinian boy, selling dope to his friends after school.

"None of the symposiads," Daniel says, some weeks later, over dinner, his lecture on Plato's text imminent. "Not one of them has anything to say about threesomes."

"What *do* they have to say?" Noah asks.

"Which one?" Daniel says.

"How many are there?"

"Seven," says Daniel.

"Seven?"

"If you count Alcibiades," says Daniel. "Who wasn't there to start off with."

"Who?"

"Alcibiades," Daniel says

"Say it again," Noah says.

"Alcibiades," Daniel says.

"Oh, professor," Noah says, his eyes on Daniel's.

Daniel smiles at me: "Could you pass the salad, please."

Noah's love for Daniel was a kind of adoration, a playful submission mixed with genuine envy. Noah loved Daniel's intelligence and his background, he loved him for being what *he* wanted to be: A nice Ashkenazi boy from a well-educated, well-behaved, musical family; not some farmboy with a drug-dealer father from Syria and an Egyptian mother who cooked and washed up in silence while her husband was god knows where with his mistresses. That was where the shape of Noah's love was forged. His love for Daniel was so huge he couldn't bare to test it for reciprocity, so he diluted it with casual sex, especially with younger boys, like the yeshiva *bochers* he tells us about over dessert, when the conversation turns to fucking, in preparation for what is to come.

"Once," Noah says. "Daniel had to persuade this young boy I wasn't worth leaving the yeshiva for."

"You're not," Daniel says.

"Yeah," says Noah. "Especially after having your *goyishe* cock shoved up my arse and down my throat."

"How?" I say. "Show me."

Because somehow it's always up to me to make the first move. Like I'm the odd one out, the minority to be respected. The move from dinner table to futon has yet to be mastered. There is always a cue; in this case, a request for a demonstration.

"Come closer," Noah says, as he kneels before his boyfriend who takes out his big fat pink *goyishe* dick and shoves it down Noah's throat.

The thing is, Daniel's actually Jewish. A Lithuanian philosophy professor with a Jewish mother and a famous Russian painter for a father. He grew up under communism, hadn't been circumcised, and when he immigrated to Israel in the late eighties and started sleeping with Jewish boys, realized he was a bit of a novelty. He didn't like being singled out amongst the Jews, the way he'd been singled out amongst the *goyim*. So we're not that surprised when, six months into our threesomes, and a year after meeting Noah, Daniel pulls his cock out of Noah's mouth, lies down between us, and announces: "I'm going to New York to have it chopped off."

"Why?" I ask, reaching down to stroke his cock.

"They've got the best circumcision doctors there," he says.

"You know what I mean," I say, pulling his foreskin up over the head of his cock and running my finger around inside where it's moist with spit and sweat and precum, then licking it. "This is how Pooh Bear felt with his paw in the pot of honey," I say.

"Stop it," Daniel says.

"Yes," Noah says. "It's not kosher."

Which only makes me nuzzle in between Daniel's legs and swallow more of his cock. To be with the man who is loved by my friend; that is the wonder of all this. To be invited into a loving family: to be so content that every exaggeration is credible. Noah's at Daniel's side, kissing him, both of them peering across his flat hairless stomach at me. The *shabbes* candles are our only light. That is what our cocoon looked like. Those were the moments that sustained me when I was back in Tel Aviv cooking at Skizza Bar till three in the morning, drinking vodka gimlets to stay awake, then trying to write stories during the day.

Two weeks after Daniel left for New York, Noah called to tell me he'd received a letter from him: Daniel had been offered a job at Hunter College and he wasn't coming home.

"He asked me to join him," Noah said.

"So, why don't you?" I said.

"What about you?" he said. "I'd miss you."

But we both knew that that wasn't the reason. Though whatever I thought then, I think differently now. It *did* have something to do with me, but more with me as a witness, a companion, someone to help contain Noah's overwhelming love for a man who'd never be his. And the knowledge had been there from the beginning; I was being groomed for this moment of abandonment.

And then there were others.

George K. Ilsley

Clamp and Groove

When Tom and Sebastian met, in the shade of the oak tree at the edge of the reception, confusion helped bring them together.

"The future," Sebastian had said, "is insects."

But what Tom heard was – *The future is sex*, and he was provoked.

Tom glowed at the news. The future is sex.

And Sebastian felt *so good* for once, having but stated the obvious, and receiving a positive response.

Sebastian had put off talking about entomology as long as he could. But then Tom somehow managed to mention being a dyslexic bisexual.

Sebastian felt twisted out of position by this information, and by Tom's warm brown eyes fringed with lashes so black, so lush, they looked air-brushed. Momentarily stunned, Sebastian just blurted out, you know, in so many ways, the future is insects. There it was out in the open, and he saw the gleam in Tom's eyes, and Tom's bigger goofy grin. Sebastian felt welcome.

And so, having fallen silent on the topic, Sebastian lured Tom home and before the kettle had boiled they were looking at large glossy pictures.

"These aren't true bugs," Sebastian was quick to point out. "True bugs are another family. I'll show you those later."

Tom noted the books, the photos, the fascination, the large poster of a praying mantis captioned THE TRUTH IS OUT THERE.

"What did you say under the tree?" Tom asked. "About the future?"

"The future? The future is insects."

"Oh."

"What did you think?"

"I thought you said sex."

"Oh, I have pictures like that. I didn't want to just whip them out. Should I?"

"Sure," said Tom.

Sebastian pulled out another folder. "Look – these azure snout weevils are really going at it. Look at their feet, aren't they cute? So Dr Seuss. And the eyestalks on her, see how they're cocked forward, you know she's thinking, oh yeah baby."

Tom had to laugh.

"Wanna see more? Insects making out like mad?"

Tom watched Sebastian's face as he talked, listening not to the impenetrable flow of words as dense as a dictionary, but to the sound of excitement. These elaborate creatures lived in a complex chemical environment, Sebastian explained, where love and war are dictated by smell.

In the biochemical universe, formula is the message. And programming is attributed to an elusive, pernicious instinct. And as Sebastian says, everything he needed to know, he learned from insects.

He handed Tom a photo. "Look at this. One male mounting another male who is mating with a female. The one on top is called a superfluous male."

"A super-what?"

"A superfluous male. As far as I'm concerned," Sebastian stated, "there's no such thing."

Tom smiled. "Why not just say, threesome?"

"Yes," says Sebastian. "A tiny, marvelous threesome."

I've been there, Tom thought.

"Now where are those dragonflies?" Sebastian rummaged while he talked. "They mate in a wheel. Of course dragonflies are somewhat of a sexual overachiever. Males have two sexual sites. Sperm produced in one location is moved to another. And the dragonfly penis has a little scoop on the end so he can scrape out any other dragonfly sperm which happens to be there before depositing his own. Isn't that special? And she produces zillions of eggs which develop into nymphs and then morph into adults with four sets of wings. Four sets of independently functioning wings. That's how they can hover and fly backwards. Can you imagine the programming, the variable control?"

"Hang on," Tom said. "Let's get back to the dirty bits."

"They can fuck in the air."

"Oh."

"They do the wheel. He has this clamp thing on the end of his body, and her head has the groove – "

"You're making this up."

"No, really." Sebastian reaches out to touch Tom's head. "Docking is high risk."

"What?"

"It's how they find each other. The clamp and groove configuration is species specific."

Tom starts laughing, his arms reaching for Sebastian, who joins in laughing.

"Say it again," Tom says. "The tongue and groove is what?"

"The clamp and groove," Sebastian said, "the configuration is species specific."

When they stop laughing they are cuddling on the couch. Their warmth mingles and pools and Tom thinks, *He smells nice what is that?*, and Sebastian thinks, *I'll have to ask him not to wear fragrance.*

The smell was a barrier to mating.

Out loud, Sebastian completed his thought. "Prevents different species from interbreeding."

"What does?"

Sebastian frowned. "The clamp and groove."

"Oh that." Tom really wasn't paying attention. The most he had ever read about bugs were the instructions that came with a dark green bottle of killer shampoo. Tom decided not to mention how long he thought crabs were *public* lice. Scurrying home with his little green bottle, he felt infested and risked permanent nerve damage leaving the shampoo on twice as long as recommended, his skin crawling from the assault. A week later, he repeated the entire process to kill any babies. He felt itchy just remembering. Tom hoped, with a strong sudden surge of passion, that Sebastian was not going to pull out any crab sex photos. His glance rested again on the praying mantis. He was starting to find it creepy.

With little encouragement from Tom, Sebastian launched into this huge controversy surrounding praying mantids because sometimes the female will grab an approaching male and chew off his head. "It's so unfair really," Sebastian said. "The fact is, they are programmed to ambush. That's how they do things, how they hunt, how they mate. And the ambush reflex operates from nerve bundles separate from the brain. In fact, the brain is there to second-guess the ambush reflex, to cut down on mistakes. The brain is a filter, not an originator."

They slipped down a little on the couch, their heads lolling towards each other.

"Mantids are also interesting because they are the only insects that can look over their shoulders. Poor little guys. Males try to avoid the ambush reflex by approaching from behind."

"Really? Could be fun."

"She still might grab him and chew off his head."

"So much depends on mood, doesn't it?" Tom whispered.

"And you know what? A headless male can still manoeuver his body into position and carry out the mating. *More* evidence the male brain really is not located upstairs."

Tom laughed, and slid his hand up Sebastian's thigh.

"So the head is just a decoy." Tom pressed his lips against Sebastian's cheek. "A distraction," he said, then drew back to consider Sebastian's wide-eyed expression. "How much work would it be, to chew off a head?"

Sebastian grabbed Tom's head again in his hands and brought his face towards his own. For a moment, a long delicious moment, they both disappeared.

Andrew Ramer

The Birthday Party

I came to the door naked. He came to the door empty-handed, his crooked smile a little more crooked. My disappointment must have shown, because he shoved me back inside, closed the door, and gave me a long wet kiss. Then he pulled away, grinned, and said, "Try my jacket pocket, baby." I unzipped it but it took a while to get to the pocket, because he knelt and started sucking on my cock, with three fingers jabbing up my asshole. Finally I shoved him on his back on the floor and pulled a small white envelope out of the inside pocket. Neatly folded up inside a square of tin foil was a chunk of hashish, my favorite. To thank him I climbed on his chest, grinding my butt on his cock, and started sucking on his nipples through his shirt. Then I peeled his shirt off and slid down his body so that I could yank down his pants, the good black jeans he wears on special occasions. As I was tugging at them something fell out of his back pocket. A little box, wrapped in turquoise paper. I ripped it off and found a tiny silver Buddha on a leather thong inside. I slipped it over my head, gave him a long "thank you" kiss, then finished pulling his pants off. What a sight, his fat cock jutting up through white jockeys, the front already stained wet. And his white socks. His dead-white skin. Brad is one of those men who have incredibly hairy legs and arms, and his hair is jet black, but he doesn't have any on his belly, chest, or back. I like that. But I wanted him totally naked. And that's when I found his final gift. He was wearing two cock rings. "One for each of us, Danny." They were brass. "Remember, you told me how every weekend when your were little your father would take you and your sister to an amusement park, and how she sometimes got the brass ring on the merry-go-round, because she was older, but you could never reach it? And then, just when you were big enough to try, the place burned down."

It was impossible to get my ring off him while his cock was still hard. So we took a break so it would go down, and went into the kitchen to eat breakfast. Finally, between bites of mushroom and asparagus omelets, he was able to slip mine off. But I was hard again watching him do it, so we had to eat some more until my dick got soft again and he could get the ring over my balls. Then we fucked on the kitchen floor, he coming first, on my stomach, in long ropy splats, and me coming all over his big balls and his fat red cock. Which was how I turned thirty. Wet, on the old linoleum. Our cocks jutting up from brass rings. A silver Buddha dangling between us, smiling.

Colin Thomas

Four Faggy Moments

#1: Mama

Driving from Vancouver to Utah to go hiking, we stop in Idaho to camp for the night. Stephen tells me what to do as I help him to assemble the latest of his five tents. It's a miracle of spring-loaded poles and taut nylon. I ride Stephen about being a gear queer, but it looks good on him: the durable shorts and sturdy boots frame dancer's legs that mere minutes outside the car today have turned the color of honey.

Unexpectedly, I transform. When the sun drops beneath the prairie horizon, it drags my heart with it. In that moment, my whole body understands what it means that my mother will die one day. I collapse. I drain. A landslide in my body chemistry tumbles me into an instant depression.

Stephen is inside the tent zipping our sleeping bags together. I creep in and explain that my heart has fallen into the dust. Softly, he reassures me that he will always be there. So calm. So quiet.

When we crawl into bed, I wrap myself around his hairy back. We both smell slightly sour from hours in the car, but I breathe him in until I fall asleep.

#2: Art

Two days later, we wake up in Monument State Park and hike off to rock formations called the Devil's Playground. As we enter the area, there's a huge sandstone wall on our right-hand side – red with delicate cream striations. The color and form are overwhelmingly pure – like a painting by Mark Rothko. I weep with joy. I am such a fag.

Stephen smiles indulgently. Sometimes I think I live his emotions for him.

#3: Sex

Days later, we're heading for the North Rim of the Grand Canyon when we spot a tiny sign: "Grand Canyon closed due to snow." This is May.

Pissed off, we head west towards Las Vegas and Death Valley. Las Vegas is like bad drugs. All of the fake façades, all of the mirrors and gold, start to freak me out. I'm hungry and losing control. I start to panic. I'm afraid they're going to have to cart me out of there in an ambulance, screaming.

We eat. We escape. Sort of. It's 130 degrees and we're driving the only car in Nevada without air conditioning. I put my hand out the window and it feels like it's being barbecued.

By the time we reach Death Valley, Stephen and I are annoying each other with every syllable. But it all shifts once we decide to spend the night there, in a state campsite, among a few scrubby willows. When we stop fighting the heat, it becomes strangely sensual. We move slowly, making ourselves creatures of this climate. Our limbs are heavy, but full of mystery.

Night falls. Clicking sounds come from the desert. We swim in the pool at the resort nearby; there's a rattling in the bushes near our feet as we leave, but our flesh is bursting with sensation and the fear of a rattlesnake just adds one more level of giddy thrill.

We crawl into our tent, which is just mesh; we've left the fly off so that we can see the stars, smell the early-blooming cactus. We writhe like slugs in slow ecstasy. We've been together for almost twenty years and Stephen's athletic body still turns me on: the girth of his thighs, the sweet-scented power of his chest. And his fresh cock, curving up to hit him in the belly. I dive for it and soon he's doing unimaginable things to my trembling dick. I find out later that he's been rubbing it, like he's been trying to start a fire with a stick. The sensation is so unpredictable that it drives me crazy. So does his ass as he moves his knees to either side of my face. We've been together since we were boys, mostly inventing our own sexual culture, and I have never licked his butt. But now I can smell the sweet tobacco scent and yearn for the taste on my tongue. He humps his hips further and further forward. I am amazed that he's going to let me do something so dirty. But I reach with my tongue and he delivers his puckered, fragrant hole. At first I just lap like a hungry dog, savoring the dark taste. Then I wash his whole undercarriage – long, flat strokes. And I relish the delicacy of his bud – and the possibility of a sharp point of contact – as I plunge my tongue as deep into him as I can.

Nothing has ever felt so intimate.

This becomes my favorite sexual practice.

#4: Opera

Five years later, Stephen leaves me without warning for another man. He moves in with Dieter the night he tells me we're through. Six months later, they buy a house together.

A few weeks after he has walked out, Stephen and I are having a friendly chat in my apartment. We share custody of our two dogs. I still hope he will come back. We talk about Dieter, who hasn't been out of the closet for long. After the first time they had sex, Stephen told me, "You're still the best, baby." Although an interior voice warns against it, I joke: "I bet he doesn't lick your asshole." Stephen shoots back: "Oh, yes, he does!"

Fury hurls me out of my chair and onto my feet. I am going to attack Stephen. Instead, I charge upstairs and storm back and forth in the hallway. I want to roar. I fly back downstairs and, in a breathless growl, tell Stephen to get out.

The door shuts behind him. I lurch around the living room. We had been drinking water and twice I vault across the room; my body wants to grab one of our glass tumblers, hurl it at the door, hear it smash.

But I realize this will not call him back.

My mother is ill now and will die soon.

R.W. Gray

All That Summer

All that summer, weight gathering around the careful wait of desire, not knowing what to want as the heat pressed in, blurring the sight lines, the careful gather then release of tired tired tired, holding on to the already rather than reaching out in this thick of it, even to the width, the breadth of that boy's wide wide back. Sometimes shelter looks good. Even when it hides you from the night-water breeze.

Decreasing measure of the tide erasing its line and redrawing it in surges until it's at our feet and us sitting here on this short log that surely won't float.

The first date you told me about the sensation of rain falling on your bare back as you swam lengths in the outdoor pool, and I told you about the sleepy pain with which a surgeon opens your body.

Asked you what your favorite scar was and you told me about a boy you once were riding alongside a barbed wire fence in the dark and . . . the punctuation of scars all up your side now, like brail for the love lost. The first time holding someone in so long I read you so carelessly, my fingers forgot to look for those pauses, those ellipses. Much later now, I want to read back, be more careful, but we only had that once so it's all left to my fumble-touch-sleep thoughts.

You were gravity from the first, the way sink holes open in the streets while we sleep, pulling whole cars in. I think we have these hollow pockets where we store empty till they fall in on themselves, stare us in the face all open-mouthed.

Back to not wanting to sleep, back to filling the day with nothings, waiting and hiding so I'll see the sinking when it comes.

If I hadn't lost you to fear, I would have lost you to the water, you, the boy who does laps like some people swallow. In the pool by the ocean (because you like the word *ocean*, one syllable slipping into the next like undertow) wondering how to talk to someone already underwater.

Some whales beat the surface to communicate across large distances, but I don't want them to think I am drowning. I'm not. Just sitting in the shallow end, knowing it's only a matter of time – longing pulls you out into the ocean a little more each moment. And me pulled along by the leaving, wondering what you see out there, pretending I don't know.

Rachel Kramer Bussel
Silence

I never speak to Billy when I'm fucking him. That's just the way it's been since the beginning. There's no need for words with us, never really has been. In fact, that first time we met was the most electric. I saw him across the room at a boring party, and our eyes connected, then our cocks. I beckoned him over, but when he came towards me and was about to speak, I held up a finger, silencing him. I pulled him along to the host's bedroom, locked the door, and threw him onto the bed. And that was the start of a very beautiful but twisted relationship.

So now that's our way of life, even after five long years. It works out well, even though sometimes Billy's friends don't understand the nature of our relationship. They're not jealous so much as threatened by the lack of words, perhaps because they secretly desire such a way of communicating but don't know how to achieve it. But it's not my job to tell them; it's our secret world, and to explain it fully would take away from it, and would be impossible anyway. We communicate on so many levels, I feel like I know Billy better than anyone else. We do talk, outside of bed, but there's really no need for us to have long, involved conversations. We get enough solace from each other's bodies that words would be superfluous.

There's too much noise in my life as it is. I want to escape all of it when I'm with him, and he wants it too. Sometimes I see his mouth open, see him about to ask for something, and instead his mind churns, his body moves, and he shows me what he wants, instead of telling me. We both rise to the challenge of this silence that engulfs us, forcing us to make our needs known clearly.

I remember the week his mother died. After the funeral we arranged to meet at our usual spot, a seedy hotel where we could get a room for fifty dollars for the night. His eyes were red-rimmed and all he did was grunt hello and pull out a flask of whiskey. He took a few swigs, then passed it to me. I put it on the bedside table, and motioned for him to get down on the ground. He did, then looked up at me with the sweetest, saddest expression. I think the way he was poised underneath me, and his obvious need, brought out the (com)passion and cruelty in me. I kicked him and beat him, slammed his mouth against me and made him take my cock over and over again. I used the crop on him, working his ass till it glowed bright red, then smacking it with my hand. I let him cry and heave and moan, let him roar at the unfairness of both his beating and his loss. I held him against me long after the sex ended.

Once I made the mistake of telling a friend not just about Billy and how wonderful he is, but about how we don't speak when we're fucking. He didn't understand. It was a big mistake, to think I could confide in someone else. I confide in Billy plenty, every time my cock slides into him, every time I sear him with a look that commands and consecrates. To me, the silence adds to my power over him, and for all I know that's how he feels, but we never get around to dissecting what we have. In a way, it's too special for that, or maybe it's not special enough, but either way it's what works best for us. It forces me to watch more closely for other cues, to see the way his fists clench, or his feet unfurl, the way his cock trembles. He can read my mood in an instant, knowing if I'm feeling playful or angry or just plain horny. Sometimes he's better at knowing how I really feel than I am.

Over the years, we've settled into a pattern, though sometimes we deviate from it. We usually meet at the same time, Thursday evenings. Sometimes we have dinner first, but usually we're too frantic to feel each other to satiate any other hungers. It's a challenge to read each other only with our hands and tongues and cocks, but we do. It seems routine in some ways, but our sex is never routine. I remember one funny time when he'd just shaved off his hair, leaving the faintest of buzz cuts. It looked totally hot and I threw him down on the bed and started stripping him. When I reached for his head, I found that I had nothing to hold onto. I had to improvise with the scruff of his neck, and I couldn't get enough of the smoothness of the fuzz.

Right now, he's curled up against me, letting me stroke his hair. Every minute doesn't have to be about domination and submission. Sometimes the silence soothes us back into ourselves, lets us breathe against each other, breathe life into each other. We drift off and finally wake up for good around midnight. When I stand and point for him to get down on his knees, I see his cock hard and firm and ready. He doesn't need words to know what I want, as he turns around and nuzzles my ankle. I'm tempted to force his head up and mouth the words " I love you," but I don't. I think by now he knows that already.

Linda Little

Cass Hutt

What Cass Hutt remembered was how the man touched his face with alarming tenderness and kissed him on the cheek. This thing so intensely shared was the reason for all the rest. He knew that now. No matter what else was true, the touch said, you and I, without names or pasts or futures or circumstances, are both true right now. "Come," the man said. And Cass went. He learned to give the man what he wanted, was willing to pay for. He learned to draw the pain out of the man's eyes, wind it up for him, hold it for a while. He reached in to touch, just for a second, that diamond hole in the centre of the man, to hold that bead of solitude and slip a thread through the centre of it, tying it to his own.

The man said to call him Bill. Bill gave him an expensive pair of high polished boots. Cass wore these all the time, looked down at their black authority, marveling at the size of them. When he walked he felt the length of his stride, the heft of his footfall on the pavement. Bill gave him a leather jacket and Cass felt the proud weight of it settle on his shoulders. He watched himself in store windows, glaring at the reflection, taking in that picture of the man who had grown around him. Six-foot-two, broad and flat with a dark steady stare. The dirty stupid boy who lived inside him slumped in relief.

That was twenty years ago. Cass had no idea what had become of the jacket or the boots, long since worn out or abandoned or lost. Cass worked steady now at the One-Bar-None Ranch, kept himself mostly upright, mostly sober. Nothing really bad had happened for a long time. He was pretty sure this was what people meant by happy. He was doing okay. But from time to time an angry loneliness welled up inside him, a feeling of dislocation and restlessness. Desperation itched like a rash, bred the fear that he would fall off the planet, that he was not attached, that gravity had no reason to hold him. Urgency, a kind of survival imperative, overcame him. When this happened, he headed out for Calgary or Edmonton.

City men. Cass never refused money if it was offered though it wasn't their money he was after. It was their need, desperate and demanding, that raised him up, that fed him. In those seconds of ultimate passion they loved him like a god and like a son – like salvation. In these seconds Cass wallowed in their unconditional, total, and infinite love.

They wanted him lean and raw in jeans and dusty boots. They spotted him propped up against a bar, a bus shelter, a tree, with his Stetson in his hand. They met his eyes, hovered, looked away. When they glanced back, they were his. These men always had a place in mind. They were men who planned. They had money, expensive haircuts, clean soft hands, bodies rounded with success, bones well padded with luxury, warmth, hearty meals with rich sauces and slabs of pie. They had strong teeth, shirts with cuffs, big cars.

They all wanted Cass in charge, to feel his muscle mount their will. They all wanted to loose themselves in him. And Cass loved them all, their cleverness, their clean creamy lives – beautiful lives made perfect in an instant by a visit from a dirty cowboy who could ride them like a bull. He loved them for their perfect sad ignorance, the way they loved him to the center of his soul and down through the core of the earth, fleetingly and utterly, though of course not at all.

Many men he met only once or twice. A few were regulars. He collected all their pictures in his mind, gave them names. The one he called Puppy always loosened his tie slowly, pulling it out from his neck, letting the knot fall askew several inches from his Adam's apple. His wrist always twisted right around when he opened his collar button, creating the little vee at his throat. The tie was navy with red cartwheels. Or green with yellow arrowheads or red flecked with chocolate. He never took it off, always left it hanging like a leash around his neck. Another one hung his jacket on the back of a chair, smoothed it down and patted it. Harris Tweed, the man had said the first time, and Cass, thinking the man had introduced himself, answered with a name of his own. He remembered the rich confidence of the laugh, of the explanation, of the introduction almost, to the jacket. Harris Tweed, wanted spurs and he kept a pair hanging on one of the bookshelves that filled the room from floor to ceiling. He thought of those spurs hanging on display, winking at Harris Tweed over the heads of serious men, guileless friends, acquaintances, the cleaning lady. After a visit with Harris Tweed the smell of ink and paper and furniture polish sat in Cass's nostrils for hours. The one he called

Butch drove them out of the city in a four-by-four to his father's section of wheat and crouched there naked and whimpering, begging for the lash of the belt. Butch always called him Sir and paid him so much money Cass couldn't spend it without feeling the burden of the guilt it carried.

How they loved him, a strong good man. Like a saint, they loved him. A day or two, perhaps a week, in the city would do him. Before he left he made sure the last one touched his face and kissed him ever so lightly on the cheek. Cass always returned to the ranch whistling.

Mark Wildyr

Six-Shooter Sex

"Sandy! Sandy Bails!" Rowley hailed the Rocking-Bar-Seven ranch hand, happy to see a familiar face. This was enemy territory to Rowley Cooper, a Grange troubleshooter, and Sandy was as welcome a sight as a lariat to a mud-bogged steer.

In the twilight that comes after sundown, buggies and hansoms and riding mounts crowded the grounds in front of the big ranch house. Old Man Jemsen was throwing a hell of a party. Rowley dismounted and ground-hitched his blue roan.

"Howdy, Rowley," Sandy sidled over to give him a peculiar look. "Ain't you kinda pressing your luck?"

"The invite says everbody's welcome," the young Grange man answered, referring to handbills plastered on every fencepost in the county.

"You figger that includes a Grange hired gunman?"

"I ain't a hired gun no more'n you. I ride the farmers' fences and try to head off trouble. Now, you gonna jaw all night, or do you want a drink? I got hard liquor in my saddle bags."

"I wouldn't mind a little hooch," Sandy allowed, glancing around as Rowley rescued two bottles from his saddlebags. "Don't wanna share, we best go down past the barn. They's a hot spring down there a piece," Sandy volunteered, taking liberal swigs from the bottle. "Good grassy spot. We'll polish off the booze and go look us up a couple a gals."

Rowley laughed harshly. "They all took by now. Shit, Sandy, they's ten cocks to ever hen in this country!"

"Yeah," Sandy answered, looking up the neck of the empty bottle. "But I figger we the best looking fuckers around this countryside. What the hell happened to all the whiskey?"

"You drunk it up," Rowley said, opening the other bottle.

"I figger I'm the best looking of the bunch," Sandy continued his line of thought.

Rowley halted dead in his tracks. "*You?* Shit, Sandy, I got you beat a mile! You probably second, though."

Sandy rounded on Rowley, all loose-limbed like he was feeling the liquor. "Ain't neither. I am! And I got the biggest cock, too! Hell, I got the biggest pecker in the county."

"We'll just see about that!" Rowley said, unbuckling his holster and dropping his shooting iron. He hopped on one foot and then the other, tugging at his boots and worrying off the rest of his clothing.

Sandy turned around and looked at him all slack-jawed. "Shit, Rowley, you ain't gotta strip nekked to prove your cock's big."

"Not big. Biggest!" Rowley said, pumping his rod.

"Fuck you say!" Sandy started shucking his garments.

The two nude young men stood face-to-face awkwardly trying to figure out how to measure cocks. It wasn't easy in the dying daylight even if they were both painfully erect.

"Lay down," Rowley finally ordered in exasperation, drunkenly making a pallet out of their discarded clothing. When Sandy planted his ass on the pile, Rowley flopped on top of him. Propping himself up on one arm, he pressed the undersides of their tools together. Then he placed his balls on top of Sandy's and moved his hand up and down the length of the cocks. "Shit! They the same size!"

"Lemme see!" the cowpoke said, brushing Rowley's hand aside. He grasped a handful of cock, moving his fist and masturbating them simultaneously. "Crap! That feels sorta good."

"We ain't here to play," Rowley complained. "Shit, that does feel good," he acknowledged when Sandy continued to pump up and down.

"Yeah. Too good to quit."

"Hell, man, leggo my cock! You ain't no woman."

"Don't need no woman," Sandy answered, beginning to pant a little. "Ain't you never done it with a man?"

"Fuck, no! You?"

"Yeah," Sandy answered, closing his blue eyes a moment. "Willis Handy, he done it to me once when we was on a drive."

"Well, shit, Sandy! Turn over and I'll – "

"Don't need to," the blond said, raising his legs and spreading them.

"You can do it this way?" the Grange man asked incredulously. "Fuck! I guess you can!" he added as the tip of his cock poked Sandy's ass.

A shudder ran through the cowboy as his sphincter parted to admit

Rowley's big cock. Surprised by the smooth, sensual entry, Rowley quivered like high 'c' on a fiddle.

"Oh, shit, Rowley! That feels like a hot poker!" Sandy grunted.

"You want me to quit!"

"Fuck, no! I want you to get busy."

Glorying in the warm, wet welcome of the good-looking cow hand's channel, Rowley moaned. "Uhmmm. Yeah, man! Yeah!" The handsome, dark-haired Grange man began to slowly pump his hips. "Oh, shit!"

"Yeah," Sandy answered, cupping his hand behind his partner's head and pulling him forward.

Rowley jerked away as their lips touched. "Hell, Sandy! We fucking, not making love!" he exclaimed, setting up a steady pace, pulling his big cock in and out of the wet hole, thrusting, driving.

"That's it, Rowley!" Sandy cried. "Fuck me! Fuck my ass! Throw me that cock! Harder! Oh, man, fuck my shithole!"

The flesh on Rowley's back puckered in the night air as the buildup began. The back of his thighs prickled. His buns clenched. His balls drew up. His nerve ends charged, discharged, shattered. His balls delivered his cum. Suddenly, Sandy shouted as his own orgasm hit.

Panting, Rowley rolled off the towhead. "Man! That was some fuck!"

"I'll say," Sandy panted. "You done it lots better than Willis. He didn't fuck the cum outa me like you done. Ain't it grand? Now we can do it anytime we want!"

"Yeah," Rowley answered sourly. "As long as we don't get in a six-shooter fight over a strand of barbed wire."

"Or some stray beef. Well, it don't worry me none," Sandy said confidently.

"You ain't no better shot than me. Now bring that big cock over here. I got something else to show you!"

Wes Hartley

Hockey Buff

The number one perk in the male escort racket has got to be the paying customer who fleshes out your wetdream so totally that you'd bang his boybutt anytime he wants it no charge. If you're a pro of course you try not to let these perfect chemistry scenarios interfere with the hardcore business of sex-for-cash. With certain too-good-to-be-true superstars, however, business as usual can get tested to the max.

My steady regular Janko the teamsport jock is the prime example. He's a perfect fit. Janko tells me I'm his Mister Perfect. He found out my big one fits perfect. I find out I'm the stuntdouble for Janko's real Mister Perfect. Janko is queer for a certain pro hockey teamcaptain he believes I resemble to an eyelash. As a longtime shinny stickhandler and hockeyrooter I'm totally typecast. I embody Janko's hockeyporn fantasy sweaty flesh and solid bone. My uncanny resemblance to Janko's hero has been extra hard on my workingstiff dick and seriously hard on my fan's cash account.

Janko's not one of your regulation athletic supporters, he's an extreme jock. He lives and breathes contact sports of all flavors, but hockey is the game that turns on his redlight and racks up the numbers on his scoreboard.

Janko's a musclejock. His winner thighs are downhill skijock and his bulging pecs are weightroom gymjock. His abs are sixpack and his deltoids are brickshithouse. Janko's boybutt is Olympic gold medal. In my pro career riding bucking buttboys, Janko's humpy powerpeaches take the buckle every rodeo. Janko's jockbutt is trophy.

My gymtoned steady regular is twenty-nine. He's five years older than I am. He's kinda cutelookin'. Janko's a hardworking bottomboy. He likes certain bodycontact close encounters and fuck positions. He's got a couple of equipment enthusiasms and hockeytalk fetishes that keep our ongoing sexconnection cuttingedge. Porno hockeytalk revs Janko's engines bigtime.

My superfan introduces himself at a sportsbar during the Stanley Cup playoffs. He approaches my barstool cap in hand with a look of stunned disbelief on his pug Slavic mug. Janko thinks I'm his hockey hero the captain or at least the forward's twin brother. Janko's hockeygroupie stammering and blushing get my bone's attention right away, even before his tied tongue can ask for my autograph.

When I notice my fan's sporty masculine equipment flexing in the crotch of his hockeysweats, I know professionally speaking that I've got a former first round draft pick knocking on my front door. When I get to check out Janko's world champion trophybutt, my big one jockeys for position, comes on strong, puts the move on his goalcrease, and the rest as they say is hockey history.

Unlike Janko's hetero teammates at the sportsbar who are clueless, I know right away that my first round pick is a queer bottomboy. I can spot a jock bottom in a crowd of rooters at a tiebreaker seventh game during *O Canada* in French when the rink is dark as six inches up the coach's butthole. Jock bottomboys are my favorite workout.

After the big game at the sportsbar, I tell my new admirer I'm ready to faceoff at his centerice if he can handle my signing bonus. Stickhandler says he can handle it. Janko's got the cash and he proves to my complete satisfaction that he can handle every inch of my big bonus.

My gameplan gets finetuned after a dozen periods of major icetime. Janko plays hardworking rookie to my no-nonsense veteran.

Saturday night, hockey night. I arrive at Janko's homeice with my hockey equipmentbag. His backdoor is cracked open. Inside, I get naked and climb into my game uniform. Shoulderpads, elbowpads, kneepads, jockstrap, gloves, helmet. I lace up my skates. My stiff big one and lowhangers poke through the stretchedout hole in the crotch of my hockeyjock. I grab my stick and head down the hallway to the rink.

Janko waits for my big entrance sprawled in front of his XL-size TV on the giant red mapleleaf. Hockey Night In Canada theme music blares from huge speakers. My rookie opponent is facedown on homeice under the spotlights. Janko is psyched for the big home game. He's wearing his hometeam whites. Shoulderpads, elbowpads, kneepads, jockstrap, gloves, helmet, skates. His legs are spread wide, his spotlit sweaty jockbutt is humped up gameready, and his gaping goalcrease is wide open and unprotected.

He's teasing me with that wideopen fivehole. I make him pay for it. I slap a few practice pucks into his crease. He spreads his legs wider tempting me with his vulnerable slot.

I come on strong in Janko's home territory. I plan to take away his homeice advantage. Janko follows my lead like a starstruck contender. He plays right into my hands. I've got him right where I want him. I call the game like a veteran colorcommentator.

The Captain goes out hard. He wants it bad. He takes it to the rookie. He jockeys for position. He gets in close and gets a piece of him. It's starting to get physical in Homeboy's goalcrease.

The Veteran upends him and takes him hard to the ice. Great bodycheck. Took him right off his skates. Extra power behind that stiff check. Nothing wrong with that hit. He's showing his stuff. He's making him pay for it.

Dark Jersey hangs tough in the crease. It's getting real crowded in there. He battles for it. He's looking for trouble. He gives him some lumber. The big guy got his stick up. He's having a hard time keeping his stick down.

The Forward gets in tight. He's hot on the scent of it. Close quarters. Working it hard and heavy. Rookie all tied up by the Veteran. It's a one-on-one. Number Ten's feeling lucky. He drives hard to the crease and tries to poke it in. It's a matter of inches.

The Playmaker keeps up the pressure. He's real aggressive in the crease tonight. He's showing tenacity. He pokechecks him in the slot. Getting chances. The big guy's looking for an opening. Waits.

The Captain makes his move. He really hammers it. A hard one right where he wants it. He buries it deep and gets right in there for a big one. A gamewinner for the Allstar. Give him six inches and he'll put it in every-time.

John Shandy Watson

Navel Grazing

Sid's turned on by navels. Innie, outie, it doesn't matter, just don't call them belly-buttons. He tries to brush past them with the flat of his hand on a crowded bus, imagines licking the cum out of them after the guy's jerked off.

He could spend the whole night licking around the rim of a navel, probing it with his tongue, tracing the tiny folds with his fingertips. If he could find someone who would let him do that, he'd be happy never to have to get off again.

Raves were the perfect excuse. Everyone tripping and touchy-feely. If he didn't stay with one person too long, it was mighty fine. But he hated it when they called him a freak. Just keep moving, tease himself a bit by groping breasts or cupping baskets before he zeroed in on their navels. He'd tried Ecstasy once, but it was all too much. He'd just wanted to spend the whole time in a dark corner, feathering around his navel with his fingertips, jerking off with his free hand. A few guys had come up to him, over the course of the night, dangling their cocks in his face. They'd let him run his hand across their stomachs, trace circles around their navels as he had spiraled in towards his target. But they'd gotten pissed off after a bit, realizing that he wasn't going to do more than give their cocks a few cursory licks.

* * *

Sid gets back home and lies in the dark. Images of stomachs seen and imagined. The shirtless guy coming out of the pub, his abs stretching his navel taut; at once an imperfection and a glory, it breaks the smooth lines of his torso. Sid touches himself, thinking about the shirtless guy, imagining the ridges of muscle, the lip of his navel that his tongue hesitates over before tracing the sunken star of flesh. And after the guy comes, lapping it up from that natural little bowl....

He gets off on this, but it's one of the nights he shoots too high, feels a couple of splotches land on his chest, the last bit to the side and below his navel. He sighs, reaching for a tissue. Give it another shot in the morning.

* * *

The bus is crowded, but Sid has a seat facing into the aisle. His favorite spot, confirmed again by the man standing in front of him. Full frontal. The bulge in his pants – he must've taken care, his cock is so obviously well-placed for maximum appeal. Has to be a fag. But Sid's already past the bulge, his eyes already tracking above the belt-line. The shirt hangs loose – Sid quivers – but too low to see anything of his stomach. Sid's about to close his eyes, let his imagination draw it out for him, but the guy shifts. He reaches for the bar to steady himself, his shirt lifting like a wave breaking along the line of his muscles. Smooth stomach and . . . the treasure trail. Sid follows the wispy hair upward, imagining what lies under the hem of his shirt – probably the only fag in the world who wouldn't be following the trail southward, trying to follow it to the riches below. Sid thinks he sees the lowest edge of the guy's navel, and almost bites his tongue to stop himself from letting out a moan, but then the moment is lost. Just a slash of skin is now visible.

Sid looks up. Goatee, earrings. He's smiling down at him. Sid shudders, his mind going into fast-forward. The bus stops and Sid looks down again, stares hard at the crotch in front of him. The guy takes advantage of the people pushing to get on the bus to move his bulge closer to Sid's face – would have smacked him in the mouth with his cock if it had been free. Sid looks up and the guy is grinning. "How's it going? It's Dave, isn't it?" Sid asks.

The stranger stares at him, then clues in and says, "Mike? I didn't see you down there."

"What are you up to these days? Still spending much time at the gym?" It was Sid's favorite set-up line.

"Yeah," the guy says. "Finally getting my body nice and hard."

Sid feels a concurrence within his own jeans. His balls tingle as he commands, "Lets see those abs," and begins to lift the stranger's shirt before he can respond. Sid runs his other hand from the belt upwards, his fingers exploring the beveled edges of the guy's six-pack while his thumb traces the spray of soft hair up his midline. He lets his thumb slow as he reaches his navel, caresses the arc of it lovingly with the side of his thumb.

Then, bold impetuous stupid, Sid leans forward and licks his navel. His tongue digs a bit, like an animal rooting in the earth, searching for traces of the delicate scent of cum. It hides there, Sid knows, even after a shower.

"Hey, knock it off," the guy says.

Sid feels his balls crawling back down. He looks up with dread. The guy is still smiling and leans over as if to kiss him. But he whispers in Sid's ear: "There's a park at 38th if you want to get off there." Oh yes, Sid thinks. The guy continues: "But don't lick my belly-button – I fucking hate that. You're lucky I didn't knee you in the face by reflex." Sid can feel his nascent hard-on dissolving already. Still. Sometimes you gotta do what you gotta do.

Blaise Bulot

Baggies

Some brothers with ugly faces sure have beautiful bootie. It's the best part of them. I guess you've guessed; I'm an ass man myself. Love them round, firm, chocolate asses! Shame to hide 'em under baggies, wearing oversized pants with the crotch way dowm to the knees. Can't see anything, front nor back. Can't see what the boy's got. Whoever invented such a dumb style anyway? Prison wardens? I'll be glad when it goes away. And baggies are a pain in the ass, so to speak. They keep slipping down and you have to hoist them up. Or walk with a straddle. Some dudes cheat. I've noticed hidden safety pins. But that's not cool. Frowned on. Baggies do fall. I've seen 'em fall a couple of times as I happened to be walking along in back of some dude. But they all wear boxer shorts underneath so you never see anything, never a get a treat. Chicken if you ask me. I'm told some kids don't wear nothing underneath and drop 'em to scare the girls at school or moon the bus. Wish they'd try to scare me. And you sure can't run from the cops in baggies.

My wotey, Tyrone, he wears baggies. Way down. You should see him all decked out. He sure lets his nuts hang out. He's one bling-blinging, big-timer, big-baller. He's got so much fake gold around his black neck, I guess it's fake – chains galore, crosses, medallions – if he ever fell into the river he'd sink and drown for sure. And on his nappy head, a dewrag and a soldier rag. Although he ain't no soldier. Wouldn't be a wotey of mine if he was. I met him on St Claude and I says, "What's up, wotey?" He say, "I gotta get me some cheddar." I says, "What else's new?" He says, "I gotta job." I says, "On the real?"

Old man Johnson, can't get up a ladder anymore, over in Treme going to pay Tyrone to fix a window the kids busted with a fly ball. We get the ladder and put it up in the dogtrot against the side of the shotgun. Long way up for me, so Tyrone he climbing up and I hold onto the lader. Tyrone, he got the hammer, putty and points in his pockets and the piece of glass in one hand, the other holding on. Stuff in his pockets heavy. His baggies start to slip down. Don't ever try to climb a ladder in baggies. Every time he try to get his foot up onto the next rung his baggies get pulled down a little farther. Between his shirt and pants I can see a strip of brown skin. The strip gets wider and wider. Ooooo-eee! I can see the top of his crack. No shorts! That bad boy ain't got on any underwear. I like what I'm seeing real good. Tyrone, he tries to step up to the next rung. Whoops! And them baggies of his slip right down to his kees. That boy is all hanging out and I do mean all of him. His whole ass. Why, he's practically butt naked. I'll say one thing for my old wotey, he sure got one mighty fine butt. I've seen it before but it looks better than ever this time. Two perfect, round, firm, brown buns. I gotta get me some of that! He's only up the ladder a couple of rungs so I reaches up and puts my hand on his ass. Feels good. He doesn't object. Guess he must like it for I see his cock stiffen and stick out like a pole. But me, I like bootie better than cock, so I stick to his ass. I feels his buns with both my hands. Feels real good! They are so nice and firm and smooth and warm. I slip my hand between his legs and feel his crotch and the back of his nuts. Getting warmer. Then I slip my hand between his bus and into his crack. Hot in there!

I run my fingers up and down his crack and push them in deeper and deeper. Ah, there it is. His tight asshole. I rub it. I run my finger around its edge. I push my fingers up against it. It resists. For a while. Then I can feel it relax and loosen up. I push my finger in. Tyrone groans and wriggles on the ladder. I push it in as far as it will go. Tyrone drops the glass. I step up onto the first rung of the ladder so I can reach. So I can kiss his sweet ass and lap his perfect buns. Oh I kiss and laps right into his crack. I push my face right in there. I spread his cheeks and I get my eager tongue right in there. He's a little sweaty but not real funky. Perfect seasoning. I grab hold, not of the ladder, but of his slim hips. He has reached down through the ladder and is beating his meat. I push my face up into his crack as hard as I can. I push my tongue right up his old wahzoo. Push it up as far as I can I reach around, grab his cock and pulls on it. He's groaning and wriggling: the ladder is shaking and rattling. Then all of a sudden he yells and my hand is all set and sticky. He's come. A big load right into his baggies. But sheee-it! I can't laugh. I've come too. Right in my pants. I'm all wet. My baggies are slipping and I ain't got any underwear on neither. Now my bootie's hanging out too.

Daniel Collins

I Had a Dream Last Night and You Were in It

Hey, I had a dream about you. We were traveling in an open roof car, not a conventional convertible, but something like a jeep or an SUV. It was a hot day in a foreign country and you were driving. Two young men were in the back seat – Logan, that model I told you about from the drawing class who always got a hard-on and once came without touching himself, and Roger, another straight model, that hot guy with a lisp who I introduced you to when we were at that breeder bar the other night for Michael's reading. Anyway, an army truck passed us, full with soldiers in the back under a rolled-up camouflage canvas, and their prisoners, about a dozen or so male enemy children, about ten or twelve years old. The boys were looking out at us with eyes full of pain. I stood up and yelled, "War is not healthy for children and other living things!" The truck slammed on its brakes, cutting us off and forcing us to stop. You said, "Now you've done it." Rude and ugly soldiers came over and hassled us but our papers were in order. We were all Canadians, eh. They let us go after a bit of your ass kissing. From the back of the truck, serious dark-eyed prisoner boys looked upon us the whole while. The army truck drove on and we continued to our destination, an abandoned and ruined church. The windows were all empty, the walls bare and battle-scarred, the floor full of rubble. Amidst the debris were small, carved *putti* figurines, beautiful broken stone cherubs that lay about like dead birds. We went down a spiral staircase into a hot springs grotto, where we bathed naked and lolled about. You and I went ashore into a tunnel of sorts, around a bend and began to make out. I was laying down on my back, jerking you off while you were bouncing up and down, impaled on my erection. We spent some time stuffing a string of walnut-sized plastic pumpkins up my ass like ben wah balls only they were orange pumpkins with smiling black jack-o-lantern faces on a thin rope, sort of like Halloween lights. They slipped into my anus rather easily and we'd crammed a lot of them into my rectum. So we were fucking and unbeknownst to us, around the bend, Roger, as a joke, not seeing where they ended up, lit the string of pumpkins, which turned out to be connected by a fuse that hissed as it burned and zapped the pumpkins, which began to explode one by one. By the time we realized what was causing the noise and smoke, the pumpkins were exploding inches from my asshole and the heat was intense. Our fingers got burnt as we frantically pulled out the pumpkins one by one so they wouldn't explode inside me. There were so many inside and the heat from the explosions was so close. That's when I woke up, raging hard, of course, and closer to a wet dream than I've been in years.

O. Spleen

Pseudo Masochism

An Account of a Dream

I am at home, expecting no one. There is a knock at the door and I open it to find an old friend – an acquaintance, really. His face – probably irrelevant – is nondescript, like an average suggestion of all those characters who exist on the borders of one's social past and present, and who, in my case, tend to know me better than I know them.

With an embarrassed and nervous tone in his voice, he tells me he came to confide in me. "Something's been upsetting me and I thought you would be the only person who might understand," he says, his head hung low. "The thing is . . . " He pauses and takes a deep breath as if his words require great strength to force out. "I have a tendency to be an extremely sadistic and masochistic person." With a brave face and a sense of relief from the burden of his long-burning secret, he looks me straight in the eye, hoping for some glimmer of recognition, something more than empathy, a deeper understanding. I return his gaze and smile sympathetically, then reach out my arms to comfort him. "That's okay," I say. "I don't have a problem with that. It's not uncommon."

As I embrace him, I am unaware that he is reaching into his pocket to retrieve something. I feel a movement slice across my face, my arm, my leg, followed by a stinging, intense pain and look to see great white chunks of flesh fall from my body, cut with a razor-sharp metal object, not unlike a cheese grater. I am horrified and swiftly back away, gawking in stunned silence. He lunges toward me and despite the agony of my fresh wounds I fight with all my strength to prevent him from tearing me apart with nails, teeth, and whatever else is at hand. I grip his head in both hands and with my thumbs I push his eyeballs deep into their sockets. He just grins maniacally and, with insane vigor, strips away at the skin of my back with his fingernails. I try to crush his windpipe as he gnaws away at my right cheek. I attempt to knee him in the balls but somehow miss. There seems to be no way to stop him. I am growing weaker, losing blood (by now, through some means or another, we both seem to be naked). He has somehow acquired a kitchen knife, maybe a reincarnation of his previous weapon. It is just as sharp, and with ease it severs three of my fingers. In my fear and terror, my degenerating body musters a last internal burst of strength, enough to wrestle him to the ground and pull the knife from his hand. Sitting astride him, trapping him, I thrust the knife deep inside his back, conquering him with a release of all the anger and pain I have ever known. As the knife penetrates skin, flesh, and muscle tissue, splintering bone, he lets out the most unearthly, high-pitched, lamenting wail of orgasmic pain, followed by silence. He then turns to me – laying exhausted on the floor – and asks, matter-of-factly, "Was it as good for you as it was for me?"

He reaches into his pocket for a packet of cigarettes, then lights one for himself and offers me one. Drained, I cannot respond. "You know, I'll have to give you my number so we can meet up again sometime." He finishes his cigarette and jots down his phone number on a piece of paper which he places in my hand. I remain in stunned silence. He gives me a friendly goodbye kiss on the cheek and shows himself to the door. Leaving me, a huddled traumatized wreck, bleeding and sick to my stomach.

G. Merlin Beck

A Cut Above

"You're going to kill me," I said, gasping.

"Perhaps."

Daddy stood in front of me, big and bulky, making me feel like a slender little boy. I looked down, cold and shaking, and wished he would put his arms around me. Instead, he grabbed my hair, pulled my head up, and stared into my eyes. Pinpoints of light danced around his face, making his grey and black beard sparkle. I'm going to faint, I thought. He must have seen it coming; he let go of my hair and slapped me hard. My face exploded with a stinging, gritty pain that made the little lights vanish. I looked down, and saw him close the pliers onto my nipple again.

I felt a burst of rage, and tried to pull back. My naked ass pressed against cold grey cinderblock. The pliers bit down, and my rage melted into a rush of fear. I screamed and danced. Wrists and ankles pulled against the cuffs bolted into the wall. My ass scraped across rough stone. The pain made my stomach heave. I stood on my toes, pushed upward by the searing white heat from my chest.

Daddy let go and stood back. The pain died gradually. My tears spattered on the concrete floor and on his scuffed black boots.

"That looks like it hurts," he said. "Want me to stop?"

It took me a moment to understand, but I finally managed to nod yes. Something felt like it was coming loose inside me, and I couldn't stop crying.

"Okay. Tell you what I'll do." He talked louder, to be heard over my sobs. "I'll release one of your hands. You just have to jerk off."

"That's it?" I looked at him through my tears. My jaw trembled. Relief flowed over me like warm rain.

"That's it. Oh, except for one little thing." He held up both pairs of pliers, and grinned. His big forearms flexed as he gripped the handles.

"I can't," I said. He stared at me, his expression fixed. "I can't! I can't! Aren't you fucking listening? I can't do that!" My voice was breaking.

Daddy's face went red. He slapped me, making my head whip around. I screamed, "No!" and he hit me again. And again. I clenched my teeth and bowed my head. Go on, I thought. Beat me to a pulp.

"You will fucking do what I tell you!" he shouted in my face. I smelled whiskey and sweat. I was quiet. Daddy's breath was hot against my forehead.

"Suit yourself," he said, his voice a growl.

I opened my eyes, just in time to see him reach for my nipple. This time, he held pliers and a big, gleaming knife. The pliers sunk in and he pulled, yanking my nipple into a tight point of flesh. I went up on my toes again. He put the edge of the knife just behind the pliers, and cut.

"No! Don't!"

I felt the bite of the knife, and then warmth. Blood was flowing. I couldn't look. Panic rose inside me. I fought it, hyperventilating. There was more cold metal, more blood.

"This is going to be good," Daddy grunted, teeth clenched, sawing. "Maybe I'll make you eat it after I cut it off."

He was serious, he was really going to do it. The panic broke through, and I lost control. I screamed. I struggled. The world became a blur as my head whipped around. My body had taken over, and was trying to escape, yanking and pulling at the cuffs that held my wrists and ankles. I felt the knife parting flesh again. There was the sound of water; I was pissing on the floor. From far away I heard a high, childish voice scream:

"I'll do it!"

My right arm was released; it flopped onto my thigh. I looked down, expecting my nipple to be hanging by a thread. There were a few scratches, a little blood. No worse than you would get rough housing with a mean cat. Daddy smiled at me. He put his hand under my chin, lifted my face, and kissed me. His teeth sank into my lips and tongue, making me moan. Gratitude and love welled up and made my head swim. My moans turned into giggles that threatened to become sobs of hysteria. He shoved me away.

"Do it."

Still choking back sobs, I grabbed my cock, trying to make my muscles respond. My hand was clumsy; I felt like I was being jerked off by a corpse. But my cock quickly stood up. Its heat warmed my fingers. I masturbated fast, hoping to come as quickly as possible.

No such luck. The pliers closed down on both nipples. My cock stiffened. The pain built up quickly. I clenched my teeth, pumping hard, racing against the agony. Time slowed. I could feel every vein in my cock, every tiny ridge of skin in my hand. My cock was filled with heat, fed by the fire in my nipples. I was shaking, melting from the crotch outward. I looked up. Daddy was staring at me, his eyes wide, drinking in my suffering. Cut off my nipples, I thought. Kill me. Please. And then I went over the edge. Pleasure exploded upward from my cock and burst into my head. I lost control; my body flailed and slapped against stone. For a brief second I knew that I was dying, and pleasure became terror. I screamed out my anguish. There was a confusion of arms and legs, leather and metal. And then it was over.

I found myself kneeling in my own piss. Daddy rubbed my face on the ropes of cum that had landed on his belly, then buried his cock deep in my throat. It took only seconds for him to fill my mouth. It tasted like hot whiskey and tears, with only a hint of blood.

Jordan Mullens

Tofu-Desire

I arrived at the all-meat sex-buffet carrying a small Tupperware container full of tofu. I kept it hidden in a blue plastic bag.

I knocked tentatively, then pushed the door open.

Before me, six men stood behind a table laden with a stack of steaming chicken legs, a prime rib ready to be carved, hamburgers piled in a pyramid, and a gigantic, aromatic leg of lamb.

The men had undressed and were eyeing each other.

The biggest guy, a hairy, barrel-chested man with a bushy goatee, turned and stared at me.

I heard my tofu sloshing about in its container. I placed it on the table and took off my jacket.

Suddenly the only blond-haired guy reached forward and lifted a slice of lamb into his mouth, making a loud, sucking sound. His teeth tore into the meat; he lifted his head, jaws moving, as strips of lamb hung from his lips. Blood-red juices dribbled down his chin onto his clean-shaven chest.

Two men beside him then grabbed burgers that they stuffed into their mouths. Both their penises thickened and rose. The blond's hands soon began throttling their thick, reddening dicks. Another guy knelt and pressed his face against the blond's asshole. The men continued eating, throttling, and sucking; the more food they ate, the stiffer their dicks got, and the harder their dicks were, the hungrier they got.

The giant, barrel-chested man was now right beside me, still staring.

I quickly undressed.

The other men now stood in a row, fucking each other, their skin slapped together as they pounded each other like animals, their asses, dicks, and balls covered in beef fat. The guy on the end had a chicken leg sticking from his butthole.

The giant knelt before me, closed his eyes, and opened his mouth.

It was then that I reached for my Tupperware container and snapped off the lid. The beige rectangle of gelatinous tofu floated in a murky sauce and gave off a vague, sulphury smell. I tore off a piece. It felt cold, wet, half-sponge, half-slime.

I said, "Ready, dude?"

Eyes still closed, he opened his mouth wider.

I immediately shoved the tofu in, and then, with both hands, pushed his jaws shut and held.

His eyes gaped wide in horror. He retched but I held his mouth so tight he had now choice but to swallow.

He sat back breathing heavily.

Then the change came over him.

Slowly at first.

His ferocious look softened.

The sharp glint in his eyes faded to a warm glow.

His dick was still hard, but when he spoke, his deep voice was now more mellifluous, almost musical.

"*Mon amour*," he said. He looked at me for a minute and then suddenly cried out, "Your hair is like a field of wheat gleaming in the sun."

Then he took me in his arms and together we began slow-dancing about the butt-fucking men.

One of them noticed and cried out, "What the fuck's with you two?"

My new friend turned and gazed back. He spoke softly. "All I can say is: You have not known desire until you've known tofu-desire!"

The other men glanced and went back to what they were doing.

"C'mon!" he cried. "Try it! Just once! Aren't you even curious? Or are you a bunch of cowards?"

No one likes to be called a coward.

Each man finally took and swallowed a small piece of tofu my new friend offered them.

Then everyone stopped moving.

A minute passed.

Suddenly the blond started crying, and the other four men looked into each other's eyes.

"You are the most beautiful man in the world."

"No, *you* are the most beautiful man in the world."

They all proceeded to make love, but quietly, tenderly, hands wandering over skin that now seemed so soft to the touch, the men couldn't believe they had never noticed before. Somewhere violins started playing, and the blond, finding himself left out, sat in the corner where he got out a pen and began scribbling love-poetry on the wall.

My friend's mouth and hands were all over me as, weeping, he called me "my angel without attitude," "my buttercup without butter," "my sunbeam without carcinogenic effect."

When it was over, all seven of us lay in each others' arms, sated, our appetites appeased.

Since then, we all meet regularly for tofu parties. We lay in perfume-laden beds of roses, as orchestras serenade us, and everyone ejaculates amidst exclamations of "Your sperm is like an ivory rain falling," "Your cum-drop is the liquid jewel Diana offered Zeus," or "This scat is a perfumed emerald dropped from Paradise."

Our sex acts are no less carnivorous than before, but the scent of meat can no longer match the arousing sulphur-smell of tofu.

Sean Meriwether

The Bathroom Rebellion

Robert quoted *Fight Club* like it was the proletariat's bible, and got us hooked up with cater-waiter jobs to begin our own revolution. Though we never pissed in anyone's food, we did fuck in their houses, and with every ejaculation we asserted ourselves as gay men and exorcised the homophobic karma of the building.

I know this because Robert told me.

The first time was in a starkly-lit utility room – nervous kissing and a quick, unsatisfying mutual jerk-off session; but Robert was so turned on by leaving his rebellious spunk on the washroom floor that we fucked for hours afterwards. *Vive la révolution.*

The subversive sex was good for a month's worth of catering gigs. We'd hook up in the fifteen minutes between entrées and dessert, then leave some physical evidence of our two-man revolt: a used condom in the toilet, a splash of cum on the tile, the unmistakable musk of anal sex. But Robert grew dissatisfied with leaving room for doubt – he needed for them to *know* we'd been there. He left gay stroke mags between the towels, AIDS prevention pamphlets in the medicine chest, dildos under the sink. Robert kept a detailed list of each skirmish – what we did, where we did it, and what we left behind – until it filled a notebook.

The gay agenda can't move forward until we reclaim sex from the religious right who've infected it with puritanical guilt. By fucking with abandon, right under their turned-up noses, we conquer the internalized homophobia they've laid on us and embrace our true sexual selves.

I know this because Robert told me.

He paid the boss off to ensure we got every political gig in DC that our company catered, and we bathroom-battled the homophobes with enough sex-positive sorties to rival Chi Chi LaRue.

Robert called me before a gig with the enthusiasm of a boy who'd gotten his first blow job. "Trent *Fucking* Lott," he said. Our moment had arrived.

Trent Lott's D.C. home was exactly what you'd expect from a misogynist-racist-homo-hater; it was big and gaudy. The house was chock-full of politicos so uptight that they could have been replaced with cardboard cutouts without anyone noticing the difference. The man himself swaggered through the party like a bull elephant, and the sight of him made me want to take Robert right there and assert our carnal independence.

After we served the main course, and all those right-wingers had their mouths full of broiled swordfish instead of bullshit, we made our way upstairs.

Trent Lott's private bath was typical; masculine, marble, and a countertop littered with prescriptions and squished-up tubes of Preparation H and Ben-Gay; not exactly dick-inflating, but I dropped my pants in the name of queers everywhere.

Robert lubed me up with one hand and pulled a condom on with the other. With only fifteen minutes between courses we had to be quick, but the thrill of getting caught, of putting a curl into some evangelist's lip, always made it intense.

I braced myself against the marble sink as he thrust into me. We watched ourselves in Trent Lott's mirror as Robert waged our campaign in the crack of my ass. I pictured the dour face of the Mississippi senator if he had walked in right then, discovering us doing, under his very own roof, one of the acts he'd love to abolish.

I screamed out my independence from sexual tyranny and sprayed the marble sink. Robert, equally fervent, drilled his spunk into his condom, then dropped it into the sink next to my cum. We congratulated each other on our victory with a simultaneous piss on the counter.

Robert dug a silver Sharpie out of his pants' pocket and said, "This calls for something special." He wrote across the mirror, in indelible silver letters, *We're Here, We're Queer, We Fucked in Here*, then turned to me with a savage smile, "Now for phase two."

Danny Gruber

A Matter of Pride

"My nuts are bursting, man. Does it always take you this long?"

Two men are standing above me, whispering to each other, jeans bunched down around their ankles just inches above the dirt. A drop of precum hangs from the tip of one's dick, shimmering in the moonlight. I want to reach over with my free hand, scoop it off, and apply it to my own aching cock, but I don't dare break the rhythm I've worked up on the other. He's gone soft on me twice now and my jaws are starting to hurt.

"Maybe it would help if you played with my balls," Greg suggests to Frank.

"Fuck no," Frank says loudly, his refusal echoing off the tall pines surrounding us. "You know I don't get into that shit."

I smile to myself. Another straight guy. My friend Curtis says there is no such thing as completely heterosexual men and that "straight" really just translates into "straight to bed." Taking Greg's suggestion to Frank, I abandon the attention I've been giving my own cock and cup his balls with one hand and work the other hand between his asscrack.

Greg starts to back away but I roughly squeeze on his nutsac and insert my middle finger up his butt in one quick movement. I hear him gasp as his butthole clamps down on my intruding finger and give his cockhead just a little pressure with my tongue. My finger finds the hard knot up his butt that it seeks and I massage it gently. I can feel his cock flex as warm, acrid cum jets into my mouth. Works every time. He grabs the back of my head and keeps bearing down, forcing his cock deep into my throat, until he has dried and is starting to go soft. I can't help but gag, however, and hear the two of them laughing above me.

"Finally, dude! Move over, it's my turn."

I'm sorry to see Greg pull up his jeans and go because I want to tongue his ass, which is like two globes of ripe melon, but the guy who is on his knees in the park is not the one calling the shots. I know they need me too, but the dudes offering to be cum dumpsters outnumber the tricks most nights. We don't get paid from these mostly married guys, but it's a matter of pride for some of us to see how many we can bag in a night. My record is nine, one that I can't seem to get past, but more men are coming to the park all the time so it might happen soon.

Jeremy, a wiry young guy just out of high school, has the record with thirteen, but we think he counts the guys that fuck him, too.

The sight of Frank's cock before me makes my own instantly jump two levels of hardness. Guys like Frank don't want to see the dick of the guy blowing them, so I have to be content with beating off when I'm between guys or, sometimes, when I get home. It's lucky for me he doesn't make me stick it back in my pants, something I don't want to do since it's dripping thick gobs and probably won't stop until I relieve myself onto the ground later.

Frank's silky cock is making short, quick jabs in my mouth. He has a hairy gut so I cautiously let a hand travel up and lightly rub his belly. He doesn't pull away, so after a few strokes I venture a little further and my fingers find a nipple. He's pierced and I grab the heavy steel ring and twist it slightly and hear him groan in a low, guttural way.

"Dude, can I fuck your ass?" Without taking his cock out of my mouth or even letting up on my mouth pressure, I shake my head no. He just grunts and picks up his tempo.

My first week here in the park I let a bodybuilder with a really thick cock fuck me and while he was stretching my hole out and having the time of his night, I couldn't enjoy any of it because I was afraid someone was going to catch us in the act. I think that just made it all the more exciting for muscle boy because he shot his load deep inside me in about ten thrusts, leaving me hunched over in the dirt with his jizz running down the back of my legs and a sacful of cum. After that, I vowed never again.

I first heard about the park when I was in junior college, but was always too chicken to try it out. I worried about getting VD or having some psycho come after me with a knife. A year or so later I was on a date with a guy who told me he went there all the time, so after splitting a sundae at Dairy Queen, he took me down to the park and introduced me to some of the regulars. It was then I decided to skip dating altogether.

The rest, they say, is history.

Frank pulls his cock out of my mouth so fast that my teeth rake across his cockhead. "Stand back," he barks. I feel warm droplets of cum hit the front of my shirt and fall on my arm. I squat there, mesmerized, as his load is mostly wasted on the ground before me.

After Frank buckles up and takes off, I take off my shirt and suck the jizz off it. The ground below me shimmers with his cum and I pick up a river rock with a nice glob on it and lick that off as well. I am satisfied that I got enough of his juices that I can add him to my count for the evening.

After all, I have my pride.

Antonio Ruffini

The Way of Empty Hands

We are training in the park when the *Sempai*, the senior black belt, calls upon Nadal, a brown belt, to demonstrate *Heian Yodan*, *Kata* number four. Nadal, lithe as a neophyte ballet dancer, can show us the grace we must aim for. Yet in contrast to Nadal's meticulous fluidity, his frayed off-white *gi*, the pajama-like outfit of a *Karateka*, is far from pristine. Like me he has grown up doing Karate, and perhaps has forgotten that a laundered *gi* is a sign of respect. When he thinks no one is looking, he surreptitiously plucks from his crack the intruding cloth of overly tight grass-stained pants.

Though he choreographs the simulated combat of a *Kata* with a precision that even the black belts envy, Nadal is too willowy to effectively display the pugnacity appropriate for a *Karateka*. His *kiais*, the cries intended to terrify an opponent, are perfunctory, question marks rather than exclamations. The absence of aggression from the pit of his stomach convinces us less that he is mercilessly destroying an imagined enemy and more that he preens for our benefit. High-arched footwork, annealed attenuate muscles stretched over femur bone, and clenching crescent arse aside, it does not help that Nadal's stances emphasize the bulges of his crotch. His threadbare cotton pants squeeze his gonads a little uncomfortably, surely. Yet it takes me an eternity to see what I of all people should have noticed before; a dry pearl-amber stain centered on Nadal's groin, completely separate and disparate from the grass smears concentrated about knees and shins.

"Choose partners," shouts the *Sempai*. "You will carry your partner on your back up the hill towards the *dojo*. At the halfway mark, swap over and continue to the top."

Nadal seeks me out, as eager to choose me as I am to choose him, neither of us wanting to carry someone heavier. As I bend my back for Nadal to mount, I am jolted by the sharp earthy scent of stale ejaculate. His groin heats up my neck and I imagine how only hours earlier he was frantically rubbing his itching glans inside his *gi*, luxuriating in the outcome, deciding he will clean himself up later but instead daydreaming an imaginary lover, then falling asleep.

At the *dojo*, the waiting *Sensei* instructs us to do stretching routines. Nadal sits on the sandalwood floor, back against the wall. I squat before him, and pull on his umber belt while my feet push against his thighs, forcing his straightened legs as far apart as elongated groin muscles and tendons can extend without tearing. Nadal can almost do the splits but I sense in the way he grimaces, in the sharp concavity of his stomach, that even his flexible joints are dangerously overstressed. I should ease up but am distracted by his hardening penis, the stained taut cloth making it as blatant as a streaker at a football match. Sweat slicks his endomorphic sternum where his *gi* has fallen open.

"Don't worry, it is supposed to hurt; no pain, no gain," he says. "Keep going."

The *Sensei* glances down at Nadal, and raises an eyebrow at me. My face must be as flushed as Nadal's but at least my *gi* is loose and voluminous. Nadal has to be aware that any watcher can't help but notice his erection outlined against soiled cloth.

Last month a senior brown belt pointed him out, "He's a wanker." I know what I risk by partnering with pretty olive-skinned Nadal.

A ripping noise like escaping air breaks my concentration apart and just as rapidly the color bleeds from Nadal's face. He hastily shows me the tear in his pants to ensure I have not mistakenly interpreted the sound. Nadal flinches as I readjust my cold grimy foot to greasy olive skin where the cloth has peeled away from his inner thigh. Amazed at his high and distinct tan line I study the arteries and ropes of flesh that transmute across the juncture of inner leg. I even catch sight of some stray pubic hairs that have escaped still invisible, obviously very brief, underwear.

The *Sensei* says we should not restrict ourselves to one discipline. We will supplement our Karate skills by practicing Judo throws and wrestling holds. Of course I have realized by now that no one will contest with me to partner Nadal, who gamely ignores his torn pants, as a *Karateka* should, a minor inconvenience. In the seconds during which we bow to each other before we begin to fight – begin *Kumite* – I peek through torn pants at revealed skin, at the sybaritic chords of his body flowing over bird-alloy bones.

Nadal is the only person in the *dojo* against whom I have some weight advantage but he moves so rapidly that in trying to gain a handhold I clumsily overbalance, pulling open the front of his *gi*, exposing his thin, pectoral-coated ribcage. I trip both of us up in trying to keep my hold, clutching at torn cloth. His damp intractable penis sears my wrist. No underwear! While I am scandalized into immobility, Nadal writhes, slithers to hook my neck with his calf and knee, to pin my arms. My free hand is trapped under his haunches, and it is being bent the wrong way. I should concede but am desperate to avoid the embarrassment of such a rapid defeat. I twist my fingers hoping to find a nerve, anything that will weaken his hold.

I don't know which of us is more stunned by what happens next. Two of my fingers already beyond the barrier of rent cloth pass equally unhindered through his surprisingly yielding anus, into his rectum, into his body cavity. His hold breaks. Nadal's mouth opens in shock as his jism spills onto the wooden floor at the *Sensei's* foot.

Christopher Lucas

Park & Ride

Once again there he was, as if waiting for me. He quickly, silently led me into the thick bushes, to a weedy, person-sized clearing; a bed used by wild animals. In the near-light he turned, grabbed me, and we hit the ground, his hand down my jeans groping and his face in mine, an instant stubble-burn across my lip as he explored my mouth with his tongue, canvassing my teeth and sucking our spit. He was ravenous, as if he'd been driving a semi for weeks and was furious for the rough touch of another man. He slid his arms under my T-shirt and ripped it over my head, then peeled off his own palm-stained tank and wrapped his arms too tightly around me, nuzzling his nose and lips into the back of my neck like we'd shared a savage love for years. I'm not a small guy, but I felt small in his enormous presence. Suddenly smothered, I inhaled his highway sweat mixed with grease; my cock already hurt pressing against the button of my jeans. His soft matt of thick chest hair, forming a "Y" between his nipples and descending blackly down to his belly, caressed my back and chilled my spine.

This time, there was just enough light to make out a fading black/blue tattoo splayed across his upper left pec with stylized curlicues that read "Tony". I wondered if Tony was his name, or the name of a current or former lover.

From behind he stripped off my shorts and massaged my ass with strong calloused hands. Before I could move, a warm tickling ooze dripped into my crack where he spit. Then his mouth took over and he licked the outside of my anus. I curled, fetal. He lapped my ass like water, and pulled my cheeks apart so much they hurt, but his motions were quick and final and I closed my eyes. I yearned to touch the coarse, scattered whiskers on his face, or run my fingers along the wet line of sweat along his back. Instead, I breathed him in deeply and looked beyond the chain link, to the morning traffic zooming past, an asphalt shoulder away.

When he eased a finger into my ass, he expanded my chamber and before I could adjust on the matted weeds and dirt, a second and third finger slid in and instantly gyrated around as if searching. My teeth clenched and I squeezed his muscular arm, struggling in vain to get a clear look at his dark face in the dull light. Soon my ass became accustomed to the probing and I buckled as he played. I felt like falling, but he held on tightly, as if letting go might send me flying into traffic. The more he explored, the less aware I was of my surroundings – a busload of Albuquerque commuters could have been watching and we wouldn't have known or cared. I became mesmerized by his probing; I barely noticed minutes later the crinkling wrapper, the roll of latex, and then the "thwapt" as he spit on the condom. Then he spooned me as he shoved his penis energetically into me, instantly fucking me as if behind on a deadline.

Taking a break without pulling out, he turned me onto my stomach, held my arms above my head, and pounded me like he was doing push-ups on a gym matt. I felt his weight as he let himself entirely down on me, his breath heavy on my neck, then he'd pull up and come violently down again, grinding my torso into the dirt. Sweat from his forehead dripped onto my cheek while he kissed my neck, then lapped my wet armpits with his tongue.

Most of this time, my engorged cock was rubbing fiercely in the dirt. Without warning it exploded beneath me, lubricating my stomach and thigh. The friction from the dirt and leaves burned my prick, like someone forcefully rubbing the tip with both hands. Tony reached down and stroked my red-burned cock, smearing cum around my shaft and squeezing my balls.

After coming I never want to continue being fucked, but Tony didn't get off me. He persisted, holding my sweaty ass-cheeks together and continued to pound me from behind. Moments later his muscles tensed and the thin sheath of sweat we shared between us became more liquid. After I felt his cockhead expand inside me like foam spray, I heard the snap like a rubberband as he yanked the latex and then, sweat dripping from his chin onto the back of my neck, a hot stream of cum exploded across my back, raising goose bumps and sending chills wherever it fell. Tony collapsed exhausted on top of me, knocking the breath from my lungs. Again I had his dead weight pinning me down. Then, he pulled us sideways and quickly stroked my hard-again cock. Within seconds I shot across the bushes with more cum than I thought possible for the second time in ten minutes. When I finished draining again, I closed my eyes and absorbed the warmth of his large slippery body as he tightened his arms around my chest.

I awoke to the heat of the sun burning into my back and legs. When I moved, my back felt tight from congealed cum stuck to my skin. My hair was also stiff where it met my neck: more of Tony's gift to me.

When I sat up, I stared into the face of a little girl with a bright-white poodle sniffing my dirty toes between my sandals. "Melissa!" someone screamed from the parking lot. "Get away from that man!" The girl stared for another brave second, then ran back across the grass dragging her nervous little dog with her.

I slid my ripped T-shirt over the cum blotches on my back and stood up, staggered to my car and continued driving south, basking in the early-afternoon sun.

Harry Matthews

Park Way

It wasn't difficult to tell the hot from the hungry. There was a row of cars parked by the restaurant, and another row across the parking lot, facing the woods. Signs announced trails for hiking and cross-country skiing, but it wasn't those attractions that drew me, nor the others on the "odd-side" of the lot. This particular "service area," on a bluff overlooking the Hudson River, was known for a special kind of service.

I sat for a moment behind the wheel, wondering if Friday was the best evening to visit and whether this was really the best way to adjust to the change from city to suburban living. Then I heard a tap at the passenger-side window. It was a young Hasid, red-haired, blue-eyed, and eager, his face framed by the ritual braids called *payes*, a scrawny beard, and a broad-brimmed hat. "I do you a *mitzvah*?" he asked.

"What kind of good deed?" I replied.

"I give you a blow job, you get to suck a really big cock," he replied bluntly. My new neighbors, I thought, have an admirable distaste for euphemism.

"In the woods?"

"No, no! Why get our clothes dirty? We can take off our pants and get in the back seat."

While drivers of the adjacent cars would be, I assumed, sympathetic, I was not totally comfortable with the idea of witnesses for this particular exchange. "There's no privacy in the back seat," I replied.

"Picky! Picky! You *goyim* are so hung up on privacy! The kid next door and I brought each other off under the picnic table at a block party and no one was the wiser. Are you cut?"

"Well, uh, no," I stammered, a bit stunned by his query.

"Okay, for something exotic, I'll get some leaves on my shirt. Get out, lock the car, I'll show you a place."

I obeyed his orders and then followed him into the woods. We walked a few minutes along a well-trod path before he veered off into the underbrush. Pressing through a row of small trees and bushes, we reached a clearing where the grass had been tramped down by many previous visitors. The clearing was scattered with condoms and even an empty KY tube. My host meticulously picked up the litter and piled it neatly at the base of a tree. "Now you see why I wanted to stay in the car," he remarked, then proceeded to take off his shoes and socks, folded his pants on top of them, and crowned the pile with his hat, leaving his white shirt, black vest, and a respectful *yarmulke*, hair-clipped in place on his head. He knelt in front of me and announced, "The zipper pulls my beard; take off your pants."

I followed his example, neatly stuffing my socks in my shoes, and piling my folded pants on top. I stretched out on the ground and he vigorously went to work, licking my tits, balls, and cock, then sucking with vigor, while stroking my body with unexpected gentleness. Before long, I was writhing in delight. He locked his arms around my hips and went down hard on my cock, taking the load and swallowing contentedly. After my breathing returned to normal, he smiled and said, "Now it's your turn!"

He grabbed me by the shoulders and rolled me on top of him. Refusing to be kissed, he suggested I warm up on other parts of his body. I was just getting into it when I heard a loud rustle in the bushes behind me. Maybe the back seat would have been more private. A plaintive voice addressed my companion.

"Yaakov, what are you doing here? *Mammele* is waiting! You're supposed to bring the wine, not the salt. As soon as I saw your car, I knew you were wasting time again!"

"Moshe, we're almost finished."

"Finish fast! It's sunset in half an hour."

"*Oy vey*, in Jewish families, each of us is his brother's keeper. Moshe is right; I have to go. We can't drive on Shabbas." Yaakov had sprung up and was quickly putting his clothes and shoes back on. "Next time, remember, you owe me!" he said, with a wink.

"So sex is kosher?" I asked, in a conversational gambit.

"How do you think we've survived for 5,000 years?" he replied with a laugh as he rushed off through the woods.

Marshall Moore

Certain Shades of Blue Look Green, Depending on the Light

Sanjay lies in the median of Interstate 80, looking up at me. Traffic whizzes by, yet we are invisible, shielded from view by the v of our impact-spliced cars. We are somewhere between Vacaville and Davis, California. Nothing for miles in either direction: flat fields, distant farms, the blue suggestion of hills off to the west. Oleander shrubs tower over us: toxic leaves, lethal pink and white blossoms. Only deer can eat them without dying.

It's too early Sunday morning for heavy traffic. What timing.

I cradle Sanjay in my arms and smile down at him. He shouldn't have left me. I will make love to him again. I will convince him to stay. If it's the last thing I do.

"Fancy running into each other like this." Through his pain, Sanjay looks happy to see me. I find this strange. Couldn't he tell I ran him off the road? But he is a generous soul. He may not suspect I did it on purpose. He is injured, perhaps severely; my presence comforts him. He tries to put his arms around me, but winces: something inside him is damaged. A grimace contorts his face, and sweat gleams on his brow.

"Don't talk," I tell him.

Doctors would caution me against exposing myself to the blood now dribbling down his chin, but so what? I have swallowed how much of his semen? Had him inside me how many times, raw? I wipe the blood away from his mouth with my shirt sleeve, then kiss him. Copper electric taste on my tongue. Him.

"I've missed you," I tell him. "I've missed you so much. I never would have wanted something like this to happen."

"Have you called 9-1-1?" His voice is weak.

"Yes," I lie. "As soon as I recognized your car."

The lie doesn't matter. Someone else will have made the call. Any minute now, a highway patrol cruiser will screech to a stop next to our wreckage. Maybe a fire truck, maybe an ambulance. This is a busy and well-patrolled expanse of nothingness. It won't take long for help to arrive.

"Sanjay. I love you so much. Stay with me," I beg him.

The tears welling up are sincere. I do not want to lose him. It would feel like losing a part of myself. Which is why he should not have left. He should not have said he'd leave first thing in the morning to stay with friends in Sacramento until he could sort everything out, that maybe we ought to take a break from each other.

"How badly are you injured?" I ask. I gently unbutton his shirt, red linen, red like the blood on his face.

"I don't know. Everything hurts."

"Stay with me, Sanjay," I tell him. "You'll be all right. Everything will be all right. Help is coming."

I undo his belt.

"What are you doing?" he asks.

"Checking for bruises."

He nods and lets me unzip his pants.

What few cars are on the freeway at this hour do not stop. This is good. I slide Sanjay's black jeans down his hips, exposing his cock.

"You're fine," I tell him, unable to take my eyes off it. I want to take him in my mouth, but he's not hard. He is trembling. "You're going to be fine. I think it's just a concussion."

He looks confused. I suspect he's okay. His skin tone is healthy – maybe a shade or two off his rich Indian tan, nothing more.

"Stick out your tongue," I tell him.

I caress his cock, his balls. Soft heft. I would taste their salty authority here and now but the cops will arrive any second. Myself, I am aroused to within an inch of my life. Sanjay, in my arms again. I didn't let him get away. I'm so hard I hurt.

It's now or never.

Sanjay has bitten his tongue. I lick the gash made by his incisors – that coppery taste again – and I'm thinking, *This is what men really taste like*, as I slide my own pants down and lower myself onto him. When his cock touches mine, waves of pleasure course through me, intense as the tremors of an orgasm.

"*So handsome,*" I whisper.

There's no time to penetrate him, not here, not in the median with cars whizzing by. I grind against him. He probably thinks he's dying. His dick stiffens against me, anyway. We grind against each other, me expecting the cops any moment, my pleasure spiking from the danger of getting caught, him probably too dazed to question making love right here of all places, right after I've run him off the road.

We come in unison, dicks jammed together. Supernova of the flesh.

"I love you," he says. "You're always there when I need you most."

Only that's not how it happened.

Sanjay drives a blue Accord and so does this woman lying on the pavement, coughing up blood. Okay, not blue. More green. In the blink of an eye, my vision of Sanjay vanishes. I was frantic to catch up with him, talk sense into him. Then there he was next to me on the freeway, surprise. I just caught a glimpse. The long hair. The dark skin. Late-model Accord; even the license plate numbers are similar. Only the paint color is different. Certain shades of blue look green, depending on the light. And it's not Sanjay.

"I'm so sorry," I whisper to the dying woman at my feet, the woman coughing up bubbles of blood.

She looks through me. Sirens, in the distance, coming closer. For a long moment, I stare at her. Finally, she stops moving. Dead, glazed eyes are fixed on some point in space.

Oh god. What the fuck have I done?

Without another second's hesitation, I rip a handful of leaves off the poisonous hedge in the median and start chewing.

Robert Labelle

Père Grâce

Grace was my mother's name. She died of pneumonia when I was an infant, a common enough occurrence in the pre-antibiotic days of rural Québec. The aunt who took care of me attached her deceased sister's name to the one my mother had originally given me, Jean-Joseph. The mystery as to why everyone began to call me Père Grâce upon my ordination can no more be explained or rejected than the kind of grace which is bestowed upon us by the Lord. It was accepted like the duties I perform each morning for my old ladies, the dwindling mainstay of the congregation of Eglise Immaculate Conception, duties which also include my daily walk. The act of walking out alone along the street used to be part of our way of "keeping in touch with the community," but I now fear I appear like a lurking, almost sinister figure – especially with the recent newsworthy stories surrounding the hidden lives of many Catholic priests. I cannot speak for them and the crimes they have committed, only for myself. For that, there is only one incident, one story to tell, something I consider both a shadow and a gift – a gift of grace that has accompanied me throughout my lonely years.

The incident I speak of happened on another walk taken long ago back at St Jean de Dieu Collège Séminaire in Trois Rivières. On Saturday mornings after early mass, we senior students were given three hours of temps libre. While others sequestered themselves with hidden, proscribed books or cards, I wandered out alone along the streets which curved and descended away from the seminary house. The way naturally led me to the edge of the St Maurice River and its huddled parcels of cramped, clinging buildings. One of these was Chez Claudette, a small diner serving up quick and hearty meals to "working men."

After several visits, I began to notice one of these men who habitually occupied a table facing mine. What first impressed me about him was the way he read his imported *Journal de Montréal*, twisting himself into profile to hold the paper outstretched to the side of the table. But it was only on the morning when the chair blocking my view of his lower half was removed that his body so utterly gained my attention. It may be hard to believe that even an innocent seminary student, one who was now coming of legal age, could possess an awareness and experience as narrow as mine. Oddly enough, the two legs beneath the table, set apart in their thoughtlessly confident way, reminded me of a pair of muscular cattle, as seen on my aunt and uncle's farm, cattle occupied in the common goal of digging for feed at the trough. The trough itself was, in spite of the shadows, embossed with the soft, empty folds of his blue workman's pants and hard-looking, rounded bulges. These seemed to communicate to all the world (or at least to me) an insistent, classically heroic presence, bringing to life certain finger-worn pictures I'd found in the classical art books of the seminary's Bibliothèque des Ètudes Latines.

When my gaze returned above the table, I perceived a flicker of recognition in the man's eyes, a recognition I equate to this day with the ringing of the bells at the Elevation, the moment of the Mass when bread and wine are turned into the body and blood of Our Lord.

My working man friend soon finished his meal – more quickly than usual, I thought – and left. To accuse me of following him out of the restaurant would not be quite fair. I waited for some time, though this "some time" may actually have been only about a minute or so, for as I came out onto the busy street, I could see he'd progressed only a few paces away. That I did not turn and go the opposite way was a defeat for my gathering, remembered cloud of "Thou shalt not's." At the turn at every street corner, the same decision was repeated. The last of these came at the bottom of a long, spiral, staircase outside an old brick tenement house, the door of which had been left ajar.

Up I climbed, finding another inside staircase which led to rooms set on the third floor, one story higher than the surrounding buildings. The door here too had been left open, and I had to blink a moment to adjust my eyes to the bright sunlight that flooded the room. Somewhere between the doorway and the bed, which lay within the same pool of warm sunlight, I believe I was lifted, or at least felt lifted, only to tumble again onto dishevelled sheets. The spot was warm from the sun, and warm, I assumed, from where the man had lain the night before. Clothes were shed and cast to the side of the bed, and his large, solid body arched over me. My face nuzzled into the valley of a hard, rounded chest, while his sex, swollen and straining forward, grazed heavily, rhythmically over mine. Through it all, two great arms, hard set on either side, did not force me to turn, to push me into obeyance of his pleasure alone, but seemed to follow the course of another rising feeling, protecting and framing me in something I perceived as love.

I cannot recall this moment coming to an end, only that the sun eventually, reluctantly shifted its gaze away from us. I must have gotten dressed, retraced my steps, returned to St Jean de Dieu and my books at the Bibliothèque. Somehow the incident was never repeated, and the course of my life proceeded like a long denouement following a brief explosion in a one-act play. It is a play filled with repeated actions: taking my walks, listening to the confessions of old ladies and the raising of the Host at the Elevation to hear once again the ringing of the bells.

Trebor Healey

Jimmy in the Bath

I found Jimmy on a subway platform in Oakland, complete with a bicycle, and loaded down with pannier bags over both wheels, because he'd just ridden cross-country.

He had the too-long look on his face too, and it was aimed at me.

Lanky Jimmy, like an overgrown puppy, with bony shoulders and knobby knees, a grown-out dye-blond with roots as black as engine grease. It never crossed my mind not to take him home.

And so we came up from underneath, the subway tube under the Bay delivering us from the womb of earth at 16th and Mission, ground zero for the lost youth of America – all coming to San Francisco.

I had roommates, but I offered him a place to stay anyway. The previous roommates had all brought someone home at one point or another. They'd all fallen in love and been driven out by the others who didn't want a fifth or sixth to share the bathroom with and to clean up after. There were always plenty of friends waiting in the wings to take their place. Now here I was, and he had a bike with him too – and panniers. They'd know when they saw that rig; they'd see he was no one-night stand.

"I don't know how long you can stay, but at least a few nights before they turn on you," I sheepishly told him, rounding the corner, anticipating furrowed brows and general passive aggressiveness that wouldn't go full blown until mid-week at the earliest. It was a tolerant city after all. Tolerant until it wasn't, and then you were cooked good.

The shower was broken in our apartment so everyone had to take baths, which was ridiculous because baths take time, and four or five people with one bathroom don't have time. But I couldn't think of a better thing than bathing Jimmy. I'd never bathed anything but a cat, but like how I felt on the platform, it never crossed my mind not to bathe Jimmy. Jesus Jimmy. I needed to oil his feet.

We parked the bike in my sad little windowless room and I marched him grinning into the bathroom, which was miraculously empty. I turned the lock behind us and ignored what came to six knocks during the course of our bath.

Jimmy let me pull his shirt off and unbutton his trousers. It was no lusty come-on kind of thing. It was me bathing Jimmy. But I got all bunched-up and heartbeat giddy when I had him down to his shorts, and out dropped his horsedick in a mess of Sicilian pubes, the trail to his belly like a church spire. Then, with sighing smiles, we looked straight at each other and kissed long and crazy. I don't remember how the rest of our clothes came off, but they did and fast, with the water making a racket filling the tub behind us. And then Jimmy had me up on the sink, and the next thing I knew every mile of America was flying out of him and onto me, and without a lot of choice in the matter – in bodily enthusiastic courtesy – I gave him back my own paltry travels, which dripped off him like tears.

Then it's Jimmy in the bath, and the wet dark roots under his yellow hair and the muted green of his pale skin – and how dark he is under his arms and at his waist. And his horsedick bobbing hard again up in the soap bubbles, forcing me to go diver down to rescue the sinking ship. And the thing about a bath is that it gets filled up with all kinds of stuff that has no way of getting rinsed away. But I didn't want any part of Jimmy rinsed away anyway.

I dried him off as he shivered, arms tucked close against his chest. I got a little carried away drying his cock and balls and hairy ass-crack, and before you know it, Jimmy was inside me. I was up against the door, my hands pressing into it as someone on the other side knocked furiously in perfect harmony with Jimmy.

"See, you fit right in here, Jimmy. You already got the groove."

Jimmy and his say-nothing smiles.

That night, Jimmy scrunched up smaller than I ever seen anyone do in my little single bed. He curled up into a ball, right in the pocket I made for him out of myself – my heart the deepest part of it, where the best and shiniest coins were.

Jimmy was frisky by morning. Before I wiped the sleep from my eyes, my calves were up on his bony shoulders and the horse was through the gate, and I'm hanging on for dear life as Jimmy flew through me like an acrobatic stunt pilot.

* * *

Tanya had her hands on her hips in the hall, glaring at the bike. She said, "Hi," real firm-like, and Jimmy said, "Excuse me," and walked right past her, me hot on his trail, giving her a wink. In the bath again, I sponged Jimmy's back, and scrubbed away the endless miles, and pulled semen from him like long ropes that promised somewhere out there beyond in the fog a big ship was coming into harbor.

Traveling Jimmy, who said he'd be right back, clumping in a half-run down the steep Victorian stairs, forcing Tanya to clutch the wall and glare.

* * *

Two weeks later she says: "When you gonna get this bike out of here?"

"One more week, Tanya. Give me one more week."

I scoured the city, peering under piers and freeway overpasses, rifling the dumpsters of Mission Street, and foraging among the clubs and tea rooms, hoping for a second coming. One more week to walk by that empty cross of a bicycle. He left everything. His treasure is not of this world. I know that. But I still need to oil his feet.

Barry Webster

Enough

On our first official date you looked deep into my eyes and said, "You really need to go shopping."

"Shopping?!" I said. You smiled at my baggy shirt-front. "What? Is there something wrong with my clothes?"

"Something wrong?" you asked, grinning. "When I first met you at the beach, I never dreamt you'd look like a sock-puppet when fully dressed." You squeezed my hand.

I have never noticed what I use to cover my body.

I wear loose, floppy cotton that doesn't hug my shoulders or vise my armpits but allows my muscles to shift and settle. My slim thighs and calves are curtained by tent-trousers. My sex can hang in this pant leg or in that, and air-bubble shoes safely shield my soft soles from the hard earth I walk upon. Because I live in a body, don't I? Blood surges through my veins, my heart pounds like a fist in a cage, and sweat appears on my hairline and pours down my face. The first time we made love back there in the bushes by the beach, something in the very center of me exploded, my lungs fluttered, my limbs trembled, as my wet lips wandered over the rock-surface of your skin, and I thought your body was enough. Isn't it? Aren't our bodies enough?

"You're going to have to start dressing better," you said, "if you're to be seen with me in the village."

And so you took me by the hand and led me to Holt Renfrew.

Beautifully folded shirts on racks like soldiers at attention; mannequins and clerks pointed and preened. You handed me an olive Versace shirt with seams trimmed with herring-bone stitching, gold-studded jeans that clutched my butt cheeks as if they were two golden apples that could never be allowed to fall.

When I looked at myself in the mirror, for a second I was not sure who this was. I was not really in my body but outside it, watching. I studied the spiral-embroidered cuffs from which sprouted two pale-skinned hands – yes, I recognized them, they were my own. For I lived in a body, didn't I? Wasn't that enough?

Oh, how you chattered and laughed in the restaurant afterward. "You look beautiful in that shirt," you said, and I began to notice your clothes, the lustrous tie flowing in undulating waves down your denim shirt that puckered subtly at the armpit seams whenever you reached for the salt shaker.

But later in your bedroom, things started going wrong. When you removed your clothes, your body suddenly seemed less shapely than the fabric that had covered it. I huddled naked on your mattress, equally ashamed of the single-tone coloring of my skin and the randomness of the moles and hairs scattered across my torso. We touched each other with vague, hesitant gestures while all around heaps of multi-colored clothes throbbed with a life you and I now lacked.

The next morning, we woke and quickly got dressed.

"Now you've got one good outfit," you said, "but a fine, urban gentleman needs several."

And so you led me further: through boutiques specializing in mercerized golf shirts, sleek Dino Baldini business suits, jaquered, boxer shorts, or hand-spun, Ermingeldo Zegna neckties; a tide gathered, and I was soon lost in a sea of whirling fabric where sleeveless, Dolce and Gabbana sweaters and knee-zippered, Diesel slacks spun in whirlpools, Cerruti shirt-cuffs floated in dizzying eddies, Oscar de la Renta wing-collars gleamed like coral, and Gucci goat-leather belts thrashed like snakes in fast-moving streams of money.

When we walked in the village, men turned their heads at us from car windows, their eyes riveted on the lama ensign on my shirt of an eighty-twenty blend of lycros and camel hair.

But at night, our bodies again lay lifeless on your bed as all around bags overflowed with Dada Damani jeans and turquoise Ascot Charez shirts; San Rafael blazers bulged through closet doors and print boxers spilled from dresser drawers too full to close.

I did not know what to do with this body lying next to me. I shut my eyes, listened closely but could no longer hear the sound of my heart beating. I pressed my nose into my bicep, inhaled but smelled nothing.

When I woke in the morning, I turned to speak but you were at the mirror, already dressed.

"Coming?" you asked.

"I'm not feeling well. I'll stay in today."

You stared at me. Then took your credit card from the desk and smiled as you walked out of the apartment.

I did not put on any clothing. I spent that afternoon on the balcony hammock dozing.

I did not hear you when you returned. I only awoke when I heard the gasp of a man about to reach orgasm.

I raced into the bedroom where you lay naked in a pile of new clothing, a silk shirt-tail grazing your nipple, an Armani tie wrapped round your genitals.

Your eyes met mine and your forehead wrinkled.

"Is it okay?" you asked. "Is this all right?"

"It's perfect."

I dumped bag after bag of clothes over his now-thrashing body. You licked at labels on shirts, sucked price-tags like lozenges, stuffed a pant sleeve in your mouth while rubbing Banana Republic chinos over your penis. Finally, only the $2,000 Hugo Boss silk suit was left. I let it fall on your face and immediately heard you exhale wildly. You'd ejaculated. I was freed. I ran naked from the apartment.

Blood pounded through my veins, sweat streamed from my pores, as I raced past fashion boutiques where people shouted and jeered. Inside the entrance of Holt Renfrew, I leaped, pulled down a mannequin clad in cargo shorts, and smashed its head on the floor. And amidst screaming shoppers, fainting salesclerks, and security guards rushing towards me, I thought: Is my body enough?

And it was.

Robert Thomson

The Chair

"Happy birthday," Mario smiles, tucking a roll of cotton inside the collar of the smock. My eyes dart sideways, glimpse the thick, dark hair covering his arms and hands. Patches of them on his knuckles. I feel my cock stirring.

"I'll give you a special birthday trim today," he says.

I close my eyes and take in a deep breath. I hear scissors, Mario stepping towards me, and the silvery snip-snip of the scissors being worked by his thick fingers. My hands grip the armchair. He moves in closer to me, his crotch an inch away from my grasp. I feel his breath on my cheek as he trims the hair around my ears. And then I feel it. His crotch presses up against my hand. I freeze.

I remember as a teenager visiting the barber shop and my horror at feeling exhilarated by the touch of the barber's crotch against me as he cut my hair, so close, so intimate. This would explain my weakness for Italian men. My barber all through adolescence was a dark-haired Italian man in his forties named Testino.

I do not pull my hand back as I used to when I was a teenager. I don't move an inch. Mario moves in closer. I can actually feel his penis pressed up against the tight-fitting fabric of his pants. Is it my imagination, or is he getting hard?

My index finger trembles, moves slightly, an invitation. The clipping of the scissors continues. Mario's eyes are on my head. His hips move ever so slightly upwards and then foreward, placing the bulge in his pants right on top of my hand. I curl my fingers back and press my knuckles against Mario's hardening cock. Without a word, without eye contact, my fingers fumble for the zipper of his pants and slowly pull it downwards. His thick hairy cock springs to life in my hand, but before I can do anything with it, Mario places his comb and scissors down on the stand beside him, then turns back to me and lifts the smock up in a grand sweeping gesture.

Soon his hands are unfastening my belt and pants. I squirm, lift my hips up as he jerks my pants down. One hand grasps my cock, already hard. The other hand makes its way to my face, its thick, hairy fingers parting my lips, probing my mouth. I suck on them so he'll know how good it will feel on his cock when he drives it between my lips. But first the wet warmth of his mouth spreads over my engorged cock head. His bushy moustache an added sensation as his lips glide up and down my shaft. Oh fuck. My barber is sucking my cock and doing an awesome job of it. Mario encircles his thumb and index finger around the base of my shaft as he continues sucking, making a deep-throated growling sound as he does. The noise vibrates through the flesh of my cock.

"Please," I say, sounding depraved.

Mario looks up from my hard cock in his mouth, holds still, then pulls back. "You don't like it?"

"No, I love it, but let me suck you now."

He stands up, pulls his pants down to his ankles, and steps forward towards me. Then he reaches his hands out and takes me by the shoulders, pulling me down to his cock.

There it is, a second away, so thick and hard, a pearl of precum peering out between the folds of his foreskin. "Take it," is all Mario says before plunging his fat cock down my throat. He thrusts his hips forward, immediately establishing a face fucking rhythm and sending his cock in and out of my throat. "Oh fucker, take my cock, yeah. Swallow it all, baby."

I close my eyes, feel his rigid cock penetrating my mouth, his hands bracing my head, the gyrating of his hips, his growing need. The throat fucking is interrupted. Mario pulls his thick, fleshy cock out of my mouth, backs up, and motions for me to stand. I do as he directs me. He turns me around so my back is to him. Once again, he pushes my head down and forward.

Behind me I hear shuffling, probably Mario removing his pants from around his ankles. I keep my eyes closed bending forward onto the barbershop chair. I hear what sounds like a condom wrapper being torn open, then the unmistakable sound of a rubber being rolled down. Everything else is silent. The world outside has stopped. A hot stream of adrenaline rushes through me. If my ass had a tongue, surely it would be salivating right now. And then I hear the soft mechanical whirr of the shaving cream dispenser being activated.

Footsteps move in close to me. I feel Mario just a heartbeat away.

Then a hand pulls my ass cheeks apart. A warm, wet froth gets slathered all over my hungry hole, Mario's fingers working it all over my ass.

"Are you ready to take all my cock?" he grunts.

I cannot speak, I want him so badly. I simply grind my ass into his erection. I tilt my head back and catch Mario's handsome smiling face as he shifts his hips, lining up his swollen cock head with my puckered hole. Then he slides it in.

A smack on the face, lightly, on my right cheek.

"Hey, mister, you better wake up if you want a safe shave," Mario says, holding the straight razor up in one hand, and moving the other hand – covered with warm shaving cream – towards my face.

"Sorry. I must have dozed off."

Mario spreads the shaving cream all over my face and neck. Brandishing the gleaming razor in his left hand, he moves in very close to me. And then I feel it. His crotch presses up against my hand.

Michael Wilde

Rob Story

When I enter the bathroom Skye is telling Rob that she doesn't have breasts yet because speed keeps her from gaining fat and that's what breasts are. She says she takes the hormones anyway because of the other changes it makes to her body. He asks her if she's had a sex change. She tells him no because she's not a woman trapped in a man's body, her sexual identity is a union of the sexes. He's confused but in time he'll understand.

I flick the needle a few times again to make sure there are no air bubbles. I've got butterflies in my stomach. Hitting someone is a very intimate thing. I never let anyone hit me. I've always done it myself. It's hard for me to let down my barriers. I'm always scared to get hurt.

Rob won't let anyone hit him but me. It's a brand new needle. I won't risk a cleaned one. He's HIV-negative and I plan to keep him that way. He told me earlier that he wanted us to try and start a relationship and I'm scared. I love him a lot and I'm afraid to fall in love with him. I don't know if he can handle the stigma of having a man as his lover. I'm afraid of losing him if we do pursue this as a romance. He says he loves the person regardless of their sex and he thinks I'm the one. Maybe the butterflies are fear: fear of him not liking my intimacy once he's tasted it.

He has these big beautiful arms even though the rest of his body is sort of thin. Veins bulge everywhere. The thought of blood coursing through his veins begins to arouse me. Thoughts of him letting me have access to them, and through them, his whole system. Shooting up is so sexual. He doesn't want to do it himself. He can but he wants me to do it.

I can still feel his arms holding me when I think of them. He holds me tight unlike other men. They go weak in my arms and I protect them. I like to do that. But his arms tell me that I can relax, he's holding me. You can let your guard down because I'm going to protect you. That's something I need. Someone who will protect me for just a while, so I can relax and know I'm safe. He makes me feel invincible. I want to make him feel invincible. To protect him so that he can be weak for a while. We all need that sometimes.

He asks me if I'm okay. I don't do speed anymore and he knows that I don't want him to. I want him on my wavelength. But he wants to and I don't believe I should tell him he can't. He doesn't do it that often, every three or four months. Sometimes not even that. I want him to notice me right now, to look at me in the way that feels like his arms. I'm really feeling needy all of a sudden.

I kneel before him where he sits on the toilet. I run my fingers along the veins in his arm. There's no need to tie him off, you couldn't miss these veins in the dark. I recommend a tie for the sake of controlling the rush. He declines. I can feel his pulse just by tracing my finger. I want to kiss him so to taste his mouth and feel his breath exhale onto my face. I want to feel his body like he does.

I'm notorious for being able to hit the smallest of veins so I suggest an inconspicuous spot but he says not to bother. Right in the crutch of the arm will work just fine. I'm not going to argue because this is all for him anyway. I like him the way he is and want no changes. I want him to come to me freely.

I angle his arm right and lay the syringe on his forearm aiming for my target. I begin to get a slight erection. The rush of speed is much like the rush you get the moment of orgasm, except it lasts an hour or two. No wonder it's so addictive. I want to give him that pleasure. I want to give him any pleasure I can and wonder where I will draw the line when it comes to what I will do for him. I don't want to have to protect myself with him. Anyone else, but not him. I wish he was holding me now.

I hold the vein in place with my left thumb and push in with my right hand, slow and precise. I feel the needle pop the vein and I know I'm in. A steady hand is crucial. I pull back the plunger ever so gently. Blood flows in and I've registered. Perfect. His pulse races under the heel of my hand. Securing the rig in place I count down while the plunger injects the fluid into his body. I pull out gently so I don't make the hole larger. He looks into my eyes and begins to leave me. I tell him to hold his arm over his head so that the rush hits harder. He does and the rush comes over him. His body quivers. I know the pleasure he's feeling and it's wonderful. I'm so glad he's feeling good. It's still a new feeling to him and he can't describe it. Don't talk just feel it, I say. Isn't it wonderful?

In ten minutes he's adjusted. He's jabbering with everyone else and I'm ignored. I'm not on his wavelength right now and I understand. Tomorrow he'll be strung out and wishing he hadn't but we know that we'll think that way the next day. Tomorrow he'll want my company again and that's okay. He's happy now and that's what's important.

Darrin Hagen

Circle Jerk

Whatever happens, don't let them see you watching.

Hey, call the guys over.

Whatever happens, don't tell a soul.

Hey, check it out. And there's more where that came from. Let's go grab the rest.

Whatever happens, don't get caught.

Aw, c'mon! Your old man will never know.

pages of bright shiny skin seduce like sirens images memorized for fantasy later pretend you don't notice the hardness the tension in the room it's just sex right?

. . . right?

if he touches himself, so can you

if he pulls it out, so can you

as long as eyes never meet

Why can't I watch him?

Whatever happens, don't stare.

a secret society every day after school far enough away from adults everyone relaxes you're not really buddies until you've cum while he's there we're all men right?

... right?

High Society Penthouse Playboy Chic Hustler stacks of glossy pages all tell the same story:

That belongs to me someday.

Look at her, man. What a fuckin' slut. Oh, fuck, she wants it bad.

Sex-Hungry Sluts Who Can't Get Enough Cock: page 29
Nympho Bitches Spread It Just For You: page 41
So Horny It Hurts: inside
"I never thought the letters you printed were true, but now. . . ."

I keep the magazines because that way I get to be there every time it happens.

Meet me by the road.

sitting in tall grass the dogs will warn us if someone's coming spread magazines out conversation stops the world shrinks to that spot on the page the light the pose it all points to the same spot *Man, if she were here right now. . . .* cuz they all want it right?

... right?

Hey, I have the place to myself today. Bring the porn.

A masturbating teenage boy is a thing of beauty. All self-consciousness falls away leaving a man in ruthless pursuit of his own pleasure.

Whores Who Like It Hard: page 97
Shaved Schoolgirls Show What's Under Their Uniforms: page 108
Make Her Beg For It: page 20

"I never thought it would happen to me, until. . . ."

. . . until it happened to me.

I am already initiated into the ways of men, have already learned how bad the fags want it; lured them into back alleys where they fall to their knees and do whatever I tell them to do, just because I'm fourteen.

I watch my buddies and their tall, lanky, easy, casual grace; I realize I want them just as bad as the fags want me. One day in class I find myself writing one of their names on the inside of my binder over and over and over

watching him watching her stroke for stroke breath for breath waiting for the moment he turns to me instead of her that second you know this is the time it's just getting off right?

. . . right?

Ya know . . . I could take care of that for you.

Whatever you do, don't touch back.

I memorized his touch. I had watched it happen enough times that I knew exactly what he wanted: where to stroke, when to pause . . . mind you, by that time he was so close all it took was something warm. Seconds later, muscles tense and release, an embarrassed tucking back into the underwear, then. . . .

Fuck, if she walked in right now, I'd show her what she needed.

Pretend it never happened.

We're all in that teenage delusion that some day a hot horny adult woman with a craving for cock like those chicks in the magazines will seduce us and lure us into their bedroom and fuck the living daylights out of us, cuz that's what we read night after night after night. They all want it. So how do you get it?

I am the first of us seduced by an older woman. The retelling of that tale becomes my seduction of them. Somehow, me getting laid gives us all permission to relax, stop hiding the hardness from each other. We're all men. There's the proof, spraying all over the shiny naked glossy pages. One of us had passed the test by getting laid. It was just a matter of time before we all got to be the one. The man. And men need to get off.

I don't mind helping a guy out.

They wait their turn. One at a time. For all of them, their first real blow job. For all of them, their first time shooting into something other than the air.

For all of them, a secret they will probably take to their grave . . . because we're all men.

I'm not a fag. I didn't suck any cock.

Cock Craving Cuties: page 9
Bitches In Heat: page 27
Are You Man Enough?: page 84
"She licked her lips and started caressing my rod. . . ."

as long as I'm looking at her when I get off there's nothing wrong with me that doesn't make me one of those because I'm a man the proof is that he's sucking *my* cock right?

. . . right?

They approach me later, one at a time.

Let's meet when the other guys aren't around. Just you and me.

And the next day, in school, when I'm watching you at your desk and remembering the way you tasted and writhed and tensed and released, pretend you don't know what I'm thinking. Pretend you don't remember. What happens in secret stays a secret. That way, the next time it happens, we can play the game again: the game of not knowing what's coming, the game of me seducing all over again as if it were the first time, as if we don't know where this is heading, as if the only reason you're letting me touch you is because there's no women around to do it.

Pull out your magazines your hardness all your stops.

Hey, what do I look like, some kinda fag?

Only when your cock is in my mouth.

David Greig

Hey Straight Boy

I see you there, buddy. Oh yeah. You know that I do.

Stocky and proud and hairy and handsome. Lording it over the entire workplace. Striding about like the king of the mailroom. One-time high school football jock. World on a string. Calling everybody "dude." Sly smile. Cocky bravado. Ass like granite. Cropped hair and big feet. Overgrown boy stud. A purebred puppy.

I see the way you see me seeing you. Oh yeah, I do, buddy. And you know that I do. You can't fool me. You hide it well, but I see it's there. You pretend to be all straight and shy and cast down your eyes every time I catch you leering at me for the hundredth time since I started working as your boss last week. That fake shyness turns the key and I begin to picture your tree trunk thighs and firm fuzzy ass straining grey cotton. Boxers that cup your straight young cub-basket like a Daddy's hand.

Bring that ass over here and let me lick it. Let me shove my tongue into that virgin hole and prepare the way for your heart's desire. Jesus, man, your face is so handsome it turns heads. Black brush cut. Thick goatee. Lips swollen as if they've been bitten. And eyes that sparkle with spunk and defiance. Let me lick your face and feel the roughness of your beard's stubble. Then bend over for me so Daddy can die a happy man.

Don't worry. You and your buddies can still shoot pool. Your straight boy pals with straight boy names. Like Otto and Ahmed and Randy and Jim. They're all here now, drinking beer and smoking weed. Way out beyond the highway at my place. And they've all got the same need as you.

Get ready, buddy. It's show time and you're on. I want you to slowly peel off your clothes. Start with that denim shirt. Unbutton it gently. Undrape that shirt as if it were a veil. Oh yeah. That's it. Lightly-haired chest and bull-thick neck. Small, hard nipples, stiff with cold. Deep black forests of bear cub pits. Smooth shoulders, weightlifter thickened. Muscled forearms covered in ink. V-shaped back. And a firm waist with just a hint of belly. Nice, buddy. Very nice.

Now pull off each boot. Harley-Davidson's. You're too much. I can smell your feet as you slip them off. You redden and grin when you see that I do. And now the jeans, buddy, slide them down. I love the way they get caught on your feet. Just stand there in your socks and underwear.

I see you're losing your shyness, your hesitancy. You're starting to get off on this. I know you are. You like being the object of a Daddy's desire. You're starting to enjoy my enjoying you. You're starting to enjoy being on display.

Now pull down those boxers and show me your ass. Now all the way. Pull them right off. Then turn around and show us what you got. Oh, yeah, there it is. Not very big but rock hard. The head of your cock is slightly purple. It's even a bit blue near the piss slit. The head's almost square and really spongy. There's scar tissue where you were circumcised. The shaft is thick and heavily veined. Your cock sticks up parallel with your belly.

Your buddies are all staring at your hard-on. You're embarrassed by your erection. You're embarrassed that your pals are watching. They see you can't control your boner. They see you're excited by Daddy watching you strip. They see you're excited by all of us examining every inch of you. Naked straight boy ogled by handsome straight guys.

Now take off your socks while standing up. Lift your legs slowly so we can scrutinize your asshole. Your asscrack is coated with black hair and sweat. Bend over and pull apart your butt cheeks. Give us all a good long look at that hole of yours. Oh yeah, buddy. That's the way.

Your pals can see that your face is red. Blushing and naked and hard and exposed. Masculine and vulnerable and beautiful and proud. Just stand there fully exposed in front of us. In front of your leering handsome buddies. They're all staring at you. Sizing you up. Comparing your body with their bodies.

Caress yourself as we sit back and watch. Run your hands through your chest hair. Pull on your nipples. Stroke your cock. Pump it like you do each night in secret. Run your fingers along your nuts. Reach back and push a finger into your hole. We hear you moan as you shove it deeper. Blush as we watch you finger your ass. You were once the captain of the soccer team. Big-shot, straight boy, high school jock. Now you're stripped naked in front of a bunch of horny guys. Completely nude and fingering your asshole.

Now grab your cock even tighter and concentrate. Pump it, buddy. Pump it till you spurt. Jerk yourself off. Shoot your load, buddy. Shoot it all over your chest and beard and face. Oh yeah. There it goes. Your head snaps back. Your mouth hangs open. You let out a long groan and lose yourself. We watch you lift your spunk into your mouth then savor and swallow your fresh cub juice. Your own straight, bare ass, jock-boy cum.

Oh yeah, I see you there, straight boy. I see you getting off on us getting off on you. You know we're watching you, little buddy. Tough, swaggering virgin-ass straight boy. You've had a taste now, buddy. And you want more.

Scott Johnston

Moe

It's not that he is especially attractive. Moe has a generous belly and wears Bermuda shorts and white tube socks stretched up his calves. But he has broad shoulders and muscular legs and a head of shiny, thick black hair.

He appears to be straight, except for the fact that he's in his early forties and has never been married. I know this because I asked him just after I moved into the building, when he dropped by to look at the outlet above my sink – which was all he did. He told me that he was engaged once, but changed his mind. He did not elaborate.

Maybe it's the foreign thing. He's clumsy and shy due to a lack of confidence with the English language. But you can tell he'd get down and dirty in the moment – and I've imagined the moment.

Sometimes, he comes to fix the outlet above the sink once and for all. I watch him from behind: his thick hands unscrewing the plate, the bulk of his thighs as he squats in front of a toolbox searching for wire-strippers. We chat about nothing in particular as he works – the weather, the apartment, other tenants. Then, he begins to rub himself through his shorts. I wonder what he's doing, what I'm supposed to do, but he acts as though nothing unusual is happening. I excuse myself to the bathroom to clear my head, to rub myself. When I return, he's leaning against the counter – his shorts around his ankles, his socks around his calves.

Other times, I don't have enough money when he comes to collect the rent. He counts the bills in the envelope, then looks at me and smiles once he's decided on a way for me to earn my stay. He grabs one of the belt-loops on my jeans and pulls me toward him. Then he places his warm hands on my shoulders and applies firm, even pressure.

We flirt with each other. At least I think we do. Little things, really. The way he smiles at me when I open the door, or the look he gives moments later as he waits for me to ask him in. Once, after he'd stepped inside, I offered him a glass of iced tea, then apologized for not having beer on hand. He said it was a good thing I didn't because he forgets things when he drinks. He did not elaborate.

I've started to wear as little as possible on the first of each month. Usually a T-shirt and boxer shorts – the flimsiest I own, that do little to disguise my arousal, which is entirely the point, I suppose. It surprises me that I can be so obvious, but the thought of waiting another thirty days for the next opportunity provokes ostentation. And it works, to some extent. Moe's eyes dart from my face to my shorts and back to my face as he stands outside my door. And he stays longer than usual, asking questions he's asked before, like "Is the pressure of your shower water good?" and, "How's your electricity bill like?"

On the first morning of this month, I woke early to get ready. The apartment was immaculate, my boxer shorts were just so, and more than enough beer was chilling in the refrigerator. To create the optimum environment, I turned on the television and readied a porno in the VCR. Once I had him seated, I would reach for the Power button on my remote control, so that we could speak in peace, but I would press Play by mistake. Oops.

"You want to come in for a beer?" I asked, as I opened the door.

Moe did not answer right away, his eyes watching the deliberate movement of my thumb, which had found its way under the material of my shorts. "No beer for me," he said, finally. "I take medication for cyst on the groin that does not heal." He did not elaborate.

R.W. Gray

Waves

I've never slept with a whale trainer before. It makes me trust you somehow. The way you must love something so much bigger than yourself.

Do you miss her? No, that's not what I was going to ask, I was just thinking about her under the water, floating there, so immense and heavy, yet floating. In the quiet. Yeah, I guess it's probably not all that quiet. I wasn't imagining the screaming kids. I guess what I was wondering is if she thinks of you, wonders where you are.

I was just thinking of her floating there. She must know there's a world outside of the screaming kids and the quiet water, you know, must know that you've gone there now, someplace she can't follow. I sense it all over you. They say a grown man can stand and walk through the chambers of a grey whale's heart.

When I was just a kid I worked in a corner store. There was this man who came in every Monday to buy groceries. The scent of salt. Of fish crusted to wooden docks. He was wearing big gumboots. The cashier, she thought he was a fisherman, just like her ex-boyfriend. But I knew differently. I saw it in the way his eyes crinkled in the corners and in the thickness of his gristled hands at rest on the counter. I knew he too had left a whale behind somewhere.

A whale's song can be heard for miles. And there's barely inches between us, you and me.

And you see, there's something I feel certain of – it's all over you. That it's you who's out here trying to pretend there's something besides the smooth water and the way she is always drifting towards you.

Maybe that's the way it goes. Some people spend their time pretending they're always about to leave and some people pretend they have to stay. Both heavy and floating.

Just like you lie here pretending you're sleeping, and I lie beside you pretending that this is the accident. The sleeping man in my bed who smells faintly of fish. That this wasn't what I was looking for. It all comes down to stories, I guess. How you'll leave in the morning and how I'll pretend that all I hear is the quiet water as I drift.

Kyle Faas

Sweater

That sweater you borrowed when you came over to my apartment that night somehow feels warmer.

We were all sitting watching a movie that night – eating pizza, smoking up, mostly silent, but jumping in now and then with a remark or two. Earlier, you and I had stumbled over glances, but had said very little to each other. Now on the couch we were touching inadvertently and noncommittally. I considered all of the people between us. You were seeing my best friend Mike who, I was pretty certain, liked you quite a lot. I was seeing someone I thought I liked well enough, but then again. . . .

I sat there with the two of you, and because I could not look at you and not stare, I searched for clues intermittently in Mike's eyes instead. He returned my looks quizzically and uncertainly. Sharing you with Mike had never been an option, I thought. We had shared many things other than men, but as the evening and the silences grew longer, I thought less about sharing you, and more about

You kissing me urgently, my hands sliding down your body and my arms closing around you, holding you hard. Getting you naked, out of your loose T-shirt and jeans. Your hands gripping mine, my tongue licking yours, you pressing into me. You hearing me groan and me feeling you now taut against me. And then. . . .

Mike raised his eyebrow, seeming a bit bewildered. I didn't see him right away – I had gotten caught again in your glance-turned-question. The movie had ended. Mike kissed you on the neck, and wrapped his arms around you so you laid back onto him. You both just stared at me, saying nothing at all.

I had slept with Mike in the past. That was how we'd become friends. But after so long being friends, would we now be sleeping with each other again? I sensed things would become messy rather quickly, and I sensed you sensed that too. So I left, walked home and went to bed and thought of

You again in my arms, gently and firmly taking my head in your hands

and raising your lips to mine. You and your smile and your eyes warming and softening as you spoke volumes about yourself in your silence. You and your hand I have only shaken, pressing into my upper back. You in my arms and my breath and me touching you finally, and me trembling to be close to you, to be kissing you, to be loving. . . .

"I think I love him already," Mike said to me the next day. "I don't know, but I get all excited when he's coming over." He took a sip of his beer, and asked, "What do you think of him?"

I lit a cigarette, sat back and thought for a moment. "He's nice, Mike." I finished my beer, and added, "I like him. I have to admit, I'm a little envious of you, actually. Where do you find them?"

"I don't know. I bitched about the same thing to you last winter." He sat back on my bed and smiled, "But he thinks you're cool too."

I choked. What?! Why stop there? "*Cool*" is like "*interesting*," it means nothing at all. And then I smiled, because "nice" and "envious" certainly didn't commit to much either. Okay, I'll wait, but then what? Mike is too important to me, but then again, when did I ever feel like this? I nodded at Mike and held up my empty bottle in a toast, "Well, at least one of us is happy."

Later that night after Mike had left, I was sitting at my desk thinking about you, when the door opened. I could hear two people come into the apartment. One of them was my roommate Jeremy, the other was you.

"Hey, I ran into Jeremy on the street, and thought I'd drop by for a bit," you said.

I had no idea how to respond. Jeremy went into his room to check his voicemail, and the two of us stood staring at each other and then glancing away, shyly.

"It's nice to see you again," I ventured.

"You too," you said softly, then turned and looked at Jeremy's closed door. "You too," you repeated, reaching out to give me a hug.

I hugged you back quickly but firmly, turned and went into my room for no apparent reason. You followed, standing beside me as I sat down at my desk. Jeremy had decided to call someone back, for a change.

"Where were you headed?" I asked, nervous and overwhelmed and excited and horny and hoping.

"Nowhere near here, actually." You smiled. "Hey, can I borrow a sweater? It's kind of cold in here."

I pulled one out of my closet, handed it to you, and watched hungrily as you took off your shirt and pulled on the sweater. Then I closed the door. "I have to do some stuff. . . ." I started, turning towards my desk, then

You took off the sweater and stood there, shirtless, looking into my eyes. No question, no fear, just you in your jeans. You reached for the edge of my shirt and pulled it over my shoulders, and I stood there not believing it.

You reached for the edge of my shirt, and pulled it over my shoulders, you pressed your bare chest into mine, you drew my arms around you and looked up at me and kissed me once softly and laid your head on my chest.

We stood together and shivered for a moment, and then you pulled away and pulled the sweater on again. I could hear Jeremy coming back too now.

"I have to talk to Mike," you finished, and left the room.

Mattilda

All Faggots are Fuckers

I meet him at Basic Plumbing, when we finally touch there's a charge to it. He kisses me and I suck his tongue into my mouth, hold onto his neck with my hands. His tongue is pierced, he keeps sliding it up against the roof of my mouth, and then he grabs my head and our tongues reach deep into each other's throats. He pulls my shirt off then slides his hands all over my chest while I hold him against the wall, right at the hips. He runs his hands over my face, usually I freak about that because I think I'm gonna break out. But this time it turns me on, like he's blind and trying to know me.

We jerk each other off in the corner of the back room, people are watching and on most nights I'd be watching them too, but this time I don't even notice anyone else until after I come. It's so hot in there that when we're done, we're covered in sweat so thick that it feels like cum. I lean up against him and we start kissing again. I ask him if he wants to go over my house and take a shower. We walk home in the rain, make out in the shower. Water gets in my contacts but it feels okay. He asks me if he can wash my face, I've never let anyone do that before. My body, sure, but not my face. It feels so intimate. I wash his face too and then I make tea.

We hold each other on the sofa and then go to bed. I can't really sleep because I've taken too many herbal energy pills and only half a Valium, but it feels good to have his arms around me. At some point in the morning I hear him putting on his clothes and that's cool, then he goes into the bathroom, and then I hear the door to my apartment open and close. All the sudden I'm wired. I get out of bed, look around, and I don't see his number or even a note. I mean, all I wanted was a kiss goodbye or thanks or see you later. Anything but nothing.

Clayton Delery

No Man Over Thirty

I'm in Billy's living room when, all of a sudden, he opens a box on his coffee table and starts rolling a joint. I think, *Christ, this is all I need. If Jerry finds out, he'll have a fit.*

* * *

Jerry has always hated marijuana. Whenever he found out somebody was smoking it, he'd go ballistic. When I'd ask what the big deal was, he'd say, "It's illegal! Isn't that enough?"

I'd nod like he made good sense, but inside I'd think, *In this state, every time we have sex it's illegal. Are we gonna stop fucking?*

So for seven years I didn't smoke any. It was no big deal. I was never hooked on grass, if people even call it that anymore. Maybe at a party somebody would pass it around and I'd take a drag. Giving that up for Jerry was nothing. But two or three times over the years, Jerry and I wound up where somebody was using it. He never said anything until we were alone, but then he'd blow his top. Once we'd gone to see *Trick* at the only place in town that still shows independent films, and somebody behind us lit up. On the way home, Jerry acted like it was my fault. "How could you bring me to a place like that?" he demanded.

We never again went to a movie unless it was in a suburban multiplex with Julia Roberts on at least one screen.

* * *

I look at Billy again. He takes some small puffs to get the joint going. He holds it out to me, but I shake my head. "I'm going to be driving."

He shrugs and takes another puff, his black eyes half-closed.

* * *

I knew Billy before I knew Jerry. It was his eyes that first caught my attention. Black, but sparkling, like he was always about to laugh. I was talking to him, working up the nerve to flirt, when his boyfriend, John, joined us. I was disappointed to find out Billy was taken, but the three of us became friends anyway. When I met Jerry, I hoped the four of us could do things together, but something was always off. I thought maybe it was John. Later, when they broke up and John left town, Jerry and I had Billy over a couple of times. It wasn't any better. After every time, as soon as I was alone with one of them, each one would say the same thing: "I always get the feeling he doesn't like me."

❦ ❦ ❦

Billy's head is tilted back and his feet are on the coffee table. His legs are spread, and I can see all the way to his crotch, because he's wearing shorts. That's the problem with living in Louisiana. It's three days before Christmas, and I'm wearing a new sweater so I'll look nice for Jerry, and it's warm enough for Billy to be in shorts.

I'm always out of step. Take the break-up with Jerry. We were having a rough time, but I figured we could work on things. I mean, after seven years, there's going to be some tension, right? Well, I guess he was tenser than I was. First he starts spending all his free time with some guy named George. Next thing I know, Jerry says we're broken and can't be fixed. He makes me move out. I ask if it has anything to do with George, and he gets this holier-than-thou look and says, "We're just friends. And I resent you implying otherwise." So I move out and for two months we have almost no contact. Then Jerry calls and asks me to lunch. Twice. He's really flirtatious, and when the second lunch is over, he kisses me goodbye in the parking lot. In seven years he never once showed affection in public, and there he is, kissing me on the lips, where everyone in the Pizza Hut can gawk at the two queers.

Today Jerry calls and says, "*Let's go Christmas shopping,*" so I cancel a lunch with my mother. Then Jerry stands me up. I wait for three whole hours in the mall, until Billy walks by and sees me swilling my fifth cup of coffee. I tell him I'm just killing time, which isn't exactly a lie, and he invites me over to his place. He gives me some herbal tea to help flush the caffeine out of my system, and he lets me use his phone – twice – so I can call Jerry. No answer.

Now Billy asks, "So who's George?"

"Just a friend of Jerry's," I say.

Billy takes a drag on the joint. "I heard he moved into your house."

"They're just roommates." That's what Jerry tells me, and I know better than to imply otherwise.

I look at the cloud of smoke in Billy's living room. The marijuana smell is strong, and I wonder how much has gotten into my hair and my sweater. I think about going to Jerry's house – formerly ours. I wonder whether, if I drive with the windows open, the smell will go away before I get there. And then I hear that character from *The Boys in the Band* saying, "No man's still got a *roommate* when he's over thirty years old."

I look at Billy again. More specifically, I look up his shorts. And I think, *What the hell am I doing?* I mean, Jerry dumped me. Then he raises my hopes and stands me up. Why the fuck do I care what he thinks?

I go and sit on the coffee table next to Billy's feet. I grab the joint, take a drag on it, and say, "You know, for the first time since we've known each other, we're both single." I take another drag as I slide my hand along Billy's thigh. "If you ask me, this has got possibilities."

David J. Cheater

Elf Lust

I had been looking forward to this event ever since I had been a youngling. I remember the first time that I had read Bilbo Baggin's story, "There and Back Again," and his adventures with the Elves, and Dwarves and Humans. I always wanted to have an adventure like that, and to see the people that I had heard so much about. I also wanted to meet Elves, who sounded so elegant and beautiful, unlike my own short and slightly chubby little self.

So, after years of waiting, it finally happened. My friends and I had come to this event, a long anticipated gathering of Dwarves, Halflings, Humans, and Elves. I felt a little shy and anxious over my clothing and general appearance, especially my ears, even though I had spent hours getting everything just right; us Halflings are just not as elegant as the Elves.

My nervousness faded away when I saw my friends, a mixed bag of Humans and Halflings, but none dressed half as fine as I.

Then I saw him across the room, and he was perfect – and he was looking at me.

He was definitely one of the High Elves from Lothlorien: silky, blond hair hanging halfway down his back, flowing, saffron-colored robes, and gracefully swooping hand gestures punctuating his speech. He was the lone Elf in a group of Humans. Every couple of minutes, he would glance my way.

I had to meet him. I had studied a little Quenya, the language of the High Elves, the previous year. I gathered up my courage, and my memory, and made my way across the room to this vision of grace, careful that none of the Men would step on my big feet.

He smiled at me as I drew near and I cleared my throat and said in a confident voice, "*Elen síla lúmenn' omentielvo*" (a star shines on the hour of our meeting).

He laughed joyfully and threw back his hair. "Whoa! Your costume is *excellent*, you've got the ears and the big feet and *everything*."

"Thanks," I said. "The feet are actually a pair of 'bigfoot slippers'. You look amazing. Like, every other Elf who's in line to see the movie looks like they just sewed up the drapes à la Scarlett O'Hara. But your robes are perfect. Where did you get them?"

He posed and spun around. "I ordered them off the Web. They're actually Vulcan ceremonial robes. I got the ears at the same place."

"Cool."

We talked and flirted while waiting in line to see the movie. My friends came over and we all had a major geek-out. The Elf's real name was Trevor but he told me that I could call him Aranathon. I managed to prevent myself from saying that his user-name sounded like a villain from *Mighty Morphin Power Rangers.*'

We sat together in the theater and had one hell of a good time. We both shrieked at the scene where Frodo sat on Sam's chest holding a rather phallic sword.

After the movie, I offered to walk Aranathon/Trevor home. I changed into boots and a parka but Trevor hadn't brought a change of clothing with him. (We did put his wig into my knapsack.) Fortunately he didn't live far from the theater but let's just say that men dressed up in long robes at two o'clock in the morning tend to have trouble getting taxi rides. On the walk to his home we chatted all the way about our fave scenes and whether the Powers-That-Be actually intended to make Legolas look gayer-than-a-tree-full-of-monkeys-in-buttless-chaps-singing-Somewhere-Over-the-Rainbow.

When we got to his house, I decided to go for it. He'd invited me in to warm up, so I put my arms around him. He was freezing, as it turned out that he hadn't bothered putting on warm underwear.

It was so hot, sucking him through his robes. The pseudo-silk was smooth and cool but thin enough to feel and even taste *everything*. He was a bit worried about the cum stain on his costume, but the stain didn't set.

We are looking forward to the new *X-Men* movie coming out. I've grown out some mutton-chop sideburns and have been practicing spiking up my hair. I got Trevor a pair of wrap-around sunglasses. Just as soon as we can buy the leather uniforms on line, we'll be ready to make the world safe for all who are different.

V.K. Lem

Potato Queen

I'm not *sticky-rice*. Call me a *potato queen*. When I visit my favorite bar, I stroll right past the Asian men hanging out together in a dark corner and head straight to the pool table at the back. I like to lean up against the wall and watch the guys set up the rack of balls and get down to work sinking them.

There are usually one or two cute white guys hovering around the table. I like to watch their moves, reaching one arm forward to steady a cue, bent over the tabletop, thereby offering me first-rate views of great asses in tight jeans.

A blast of sulfur fills my nostrils as I strike a match and light a fag. The first drag always tastes the best. Soon a light haze of smoke hangs above me. A freshly pulled draft rests on the shelf near my elbow.

It's still early. There's a new guy playing pool solo this evening. His shirt-sleeves are rolled up revealing dark, hairy forearms. I note the firm contours of his butt as he lines up a shot. When he moves to the opposite side of the table, I spy the jumble of hair protruding from the open neck of his plaid shirt. A flash of heat surges through me and I stumble one step forward before I can regain control of myself.

My face feels flushed. The new guy sinks a shot, then looks up at me. I smile and stare into his cocoa-colored eyes. He smiles back, and winks.

My heart is pounding now, and my pants are suddenly too tight. My eyes slowly travel down the length of his body, to the impressive bulge at his crotch. My gaze lingers there before returning to his handsome, clean-shaven face. Returning to his game, he fails to sink his next shot. He mutters "*maudit*" as the ball bounces off the side of the table. With a shrug, he straightens up and saunters over to me.

"I haven't seen you here before. Can I buy you a drink?" I ask.

"Sure," he says. "I'll have whatever you're drinking." Then he extends his hand and continues, "My name is Michel. I just moved up from Ottawa last week."

His grip is firm, but his skin soft, just like the purr of his voice. Quickly I blurt out, “You have a great smile.” My face reddens again.

“I can tell that you like more than my smile,” Michel laughs.

I grab a server’s attention and order Michel a draft before we sit down at a nearby table. I recall the horoscope that I read earlier in the day:

Nothing ventured, nothing gained. Be prepared for a change. New opportunities will come your way.

What good fortune. I’ve met too many white guys here who are only turned on by other white guys. Tonight, I’m feeling lucky. I can’t wait to skin this potato. *Yum.*

Billy Cowan

Monster Lust

I don't really fancy my older brother Joe, but then again I don't really *not* fancy him either. My feelings for him have always been ambiguous.

As a kid, I looked up to him and hated him in equal measures. I admired his masculinity. His powerful arms and thighs were twice as thick as mine. His voice was deep and seemed to vibrate the house whenever he spoke. My voice was so thin and squeaky like a girl's.

I especially loved to watch him get ready for a hot date. In front of the bedroom mirror, he would strut and pose like a rock star. I found it strangely arousing when he would grab hold of his package and exclaim, "Wait till she gets her hands on this monster." I wanted to get my hands on his monster as well.

Yet, when he was grabbing me around the neck threatening to knock my block off if I didn't tidy his room, I'd really hate him.

I can still remember a dream I had. I must have been about thirteen years old. I'm walking to the toilet when I hear some groans coming from Joe's bedroom. The door is slightly ajar and I peep inside. Joe is lying on the bed. His hand moves up and down inside his shiny boxer shorts. My dick grows hard in my jeans. I feel guilty for watching but can't seem to move away. Suddenly, he looks at me. I jump back.

"Hey, Michael. Come here, you little fruit."

I walk into the bedroom, head lowered.

"Get a good look, did ya?"

"I didn't see nothing."

"Like watching your big brother toss off, do ya?"

"No."

"Come here."

"Wot for?"

"Just come here or I'll kick your crap in."

I move over and sit down beside him. He takes hold of my hand and drags it over to his crotch.

"How about finishing me off? Go on, take hold of my big monster."

He places my hand inside his shorts, and I wake up. A sticky mess in my pants.

For months after the dream, I couldn't look Joe in the eyes. I was convinced he would see that I was not only a fruit, but that I had incestuous tendencies as well. It was at this point that I decided to push any thoughts of him and his big dick out of my mind. I spent the rest of my teenage years fancying other boys, usually famous footballers like Kenny Dalglish and Emlyn Hughes.

There were times when I even convinced myself that I hated Joe more than anything in the world. I hated his arrogance and his crap taste in bands like Johnny Hates Jazz and Go West. I hated his taste in girls who wore cheap plastic earrings and pink lipstick. I hated the stinking Denim aftershave he drenched himself in, and I hated the thin burgundy leather tie he wore when he went to discos.

Yet, even when hating him, there was still part of me that was ashamedly attracted to him. Why? Because he possessed something I didn't – a roughness of character, a manly physique? Even though he was my brother, all I knew was that I still fantasized about getting my hands on his monster to "finish him off."

To my utter surprise, my hidden lusting was fulfilled in the most unexpected way last Thursday night. Nothing good on the box. Bored, I switched on the PC, connected to the internet, and logged onto Gay Chat UK. I typed:

Any web cammers wanting 2 toss off with GL 25 yr old?

A whisper from Hermann: *U got cam?*

Yeah.

I sent him my IP and quickly undressed as I waited for his networking invitation to pop up. I pointed the web-cam between my legs and started to stroke my cock.

The invite from Hermann popped up. I accepted.

It took only a few seconds for the video window to appear and then there he was: my supposedly straight brother Joe, sitting in his shorts. Immediately, my dick went limp. I panicked, and was about to cut him off when –

Hey, great bod. Why don't u let me see ur face?

I sat back down and watched as he stared at my body from the screen with his hands inside his shorts and a big grin on his face. I couldn't resist.

Can't. Have 2 be careful. Married man. :(

How easy it is to lie on the web!

That's ok. It's not ur face I'm interested in. lol

Oh yeah. . . . .

It's ur cock. R U going to play with it 4 me?

My cock struck twelve straightaway. Joe pulled open his shorts and out popped the head of his monster.

Take ur boxers off, I typed.

Joe stood up and took a step closer to the cam. He slowly lowered his pants and his monster sprung fully into view.

Ummmmm. . . . nice. R U going to toss off 4 me?

U bet.

We both started to wank. I soon forgot that it was Joe in front of me. He wasn't my big brother anymore, just a hot guy on a screen on my computer.

I'm gonna blow – put the cam closer so I can see the spunk fly out of u.

He didn't have his arm around my neck but I obeyed his instruction anyway. We both blew at the same time. As soon as it was over, Joe severed the connection.

When I woke up the next morning, it felt like I was thirteen again. Nothing had changed. I still fancied my big brother and tried to convince myself that I didn't. And I knew that when I saw him again, face to face, I wouldn't be able to look him straight in the eyes – though I would be tempted to ask him if he had a friend called Hermann.

Tom Lever

Greek

INSTANT MESSAGE: Just saw your profile on Gaydar. Was that you in the info center at the weekend? Hugs. Nik

REPLY: Yep! That was me. Tom.

INSTANT MESSAGE: Glad I found you! Was just surfing. Hot man! Wanna meet up sometime?

❦ ❦ ❦

Friday nights are taken up by volunteer work at a gay information center. The plus side of the job is I get to meet lots of cute guys – Nik being a notable example. The down side is that as a professional volunteer, I would never dream of taking advantage of my position. In this case, however, there was no conflict of interest. He found me. Out of office hours. And all thanks to the wonders of modern technology.

The first of the photographs came quickly by email. Nothing raunchy, but some nice topless shots – showing off his muscular body, hairy chest, and tatts.

"Nice pecs," said my huzBear, Bill, looking over my shoulder. "Maybe we should invite him over."

"Well, he's keen enough," I replied. "I'll send him some pics of us. See how he reacts."

❦ ❦ ❦

INSTANT MESSAGE: Cute boyfriend! Is he on for a threesome? Hugs, Nik

REPLY: Ready when u r! Tom.

* * *

The next weekend, Nik was at the door. The apartment was ready. Clean. Condoms by one side of the bed, sex toys on the other. Bill was horny as hell. Me too. Whether Nik decided to stay or go, it was guaranteed to be a fun evening.

Dinner over, we retired to the lounge. Nik asked if we had any Bear porn. Turned out he'd never seen any. Video on, we relaxed on the sofa. I was stiff as a board. Fucking hot, hot, hot. I could tell that Bill was feeling the same way. But Nik appeared to be more engrossed in the men on the screen than in us. What was going on? Maybe he was just nervous. I knew he hadn't much experience, was, in fact, still closeted.

After the second beer, I put my arm around his shoulder. His reaction was startling. In seconds he was plunging his tongue down my throat. Licking my lips, sucking face. Like he couldn't get enough.

"Bed?" I asked, without waiting for the reply. I took him by the hand and led him to the bedroom.

Undressing together, I watched him strip. His muscular, hairy body . . . and that cock! Big. A big fucking cock. Nine long, thick inches – *Trust me, I measured it!* – hard as a rock and pointing skyward. And him standing there, hungry, on fire.

Bill stood behind him, and gently bent Nik's face backwards to kiss him. I knelt before him and squeezed the head of his cock. A bead of precum oozed out. I licked it off. Running my tongue around the rim. Sticking my tongue into the piss slit. Taking his cockhead into my mouth. Centimeter by centimeter. Wetting it with my spit. Feeling its length as it slipped down into my throat. Cock. Penis. Dick. Whatever you want to call it – it feels great to have a man in your mouth. Especially one like this. Big fucking Greek cock. The smell of manmusk. The taste of precum. Shaved balls cradled by my fingertips. Reaching back to explore his ass, his cock reared in my mouth as I ran my fingertip around his asshole. *Fuck, yeah.*

Bill was still working on the top half. He now stood facing Nik. Kissing face to face, his hands working the two erect nipples. Nik moaned. Cock, tits, balls, ass, mouth. Where does one body end and the next one begin? Where does one man's pleasure give way to that of another? It was a circle of lust. Desire. Worship. Three men, each bent on the pleasure of the other. Each with only one desire – to see that spurting white fuckjuice.

Pumping. Throbbing. Straining. Technology has its place, for sure, but at moments like this you realize the full value of hands-on experience.

I was so engrossed in cock-worship that I hadn't noticed Bill on his knees beside me. His mouth was filled with Nik's balls. Licking, slurping, rolling those hairless orbs over his tongue, burying his nose in the hair at the base of cock. Smelling his musk. Licking. Running his tongue around, between, beside, over, balls and cock. The two of us worked between Nik's legs, sparring with each other. Swapping over Nik's cock and balls. Hungry for one and then for the other. Nik moaned his pleasure. His fingers worked his tits. We concentrated down below. Cock and balls and ass. All melding into one cycle of pleasure. One rotating, spinning out of control. Nik was grinding his hips. His ass pushed back onto my finger. I slipped one inside, then another. His ass hungry. His cock bucking.

Me on the left, Bill on the right. Each fighting to take the cockhead in his mouth. Our tongues licking, slurping, kissing each other with cock-filled mouths. Nik's dick glistened with spit. Our tongues basted it. Moving up and down. Slick. Two mouths. One cock, sliding between them. In and out. Fingers in ass. Massaging. Willing. *Come on.*

My own cock was throbbing. One hand worked Nik's ass – the other pumped my own cock. Bill was doing the same. Three men. One goal. Cockjuice.

Nik's cock was plunging frantically now. Pumping in and out. First one mouth. Then another. Then between them. Sliding his cock back and forth. He was hungry now. Hungry to finish. His cock pumped. And then he threw back his head, his ass squeezed tight and he began to spurt. Ropes of white cum. One after another. Shooting out. Spraying our chests. Our beards. Our faces. Cum. Fucking Cum. Fucking Cum.

* * *

INSTANT MESSAGE: Thanks for the WILD weekend guys! Can't wait to do it ALL again. Filiakia to you both, Nik. (*Filiakia* means kisses in Greek!)

REPLY: Filiakia right back at you, sweet Bearcub. And then some. Tom & Bill.

Daniel Collins

Malabar Spice

Pradeep and I clamber into a battered three-wheeled auto rickshaw and careen down Calvatty Road, past spice warehouses exuding an intoxicating bouquet of cinnamon, cumin, cardamom, saffron, pepper, and turmeric, the exotica enhanced by the veil of darkness and the warmth of the dark-haired boy at my side. As we turn down Rose Street, behind St Francis, the oldest church in India, I wonder if there might be a problem at my lodgings. My room is on the ground floor on the walled courtyard in front and the yard lights won't be on now because of the brown-out. I've already paid my bill since I'm leaving tomorrow. Pradeep calmly moves my hand from his thigh as the taxi slows to a halt in front of the Delightful Guest House.

I pay the driver and turn to see, not the gate-boy Shaju whom I've befriended and am expecting, but the wife of the Christian proprietor staring out the gate. In my ten days here I have never seen her down at street level or even outdoors at this time of night.

"Good evening," I say cordially. "We've just come by for a Coke."

"I can't allow it," Madame says, "Only paying guests." She looks at Pradeep, up and down. I become aware of his dark complexion and her much lighter skin. "We used to allow that and it was too much."

"Well, then, we'll go get a Coke at the Elite," I say, mentioning the competition. "Their drinks are colder anyway. Good night, Madame."

At the restaurant, Pradeep orders curried vegetables and I have curried shrimp. He blanches and covers his plate with his hands when the waiter attempts to serve him seafood. He drinks two Cokes and has no dessert.

After dinner, we go for a walk by the waterfront in Port Cochin, killing time before Pradeep must catch the last ferry back to Ernakulam. The evening's brown-out has been prolonged into an unscheduled black-out and the streets are conveniently dark. As we walk into the first of many shadows, he surprises me by slipping his hand into mine. He lets go quickly when we're back in the glare of emergency lights. In the next shadow when he takes my hand again, I try to kiss him. He resists and says, "Someone comes!" No one is but he is nervous and says, with mock earnestness, his teeth gleaming in the dark, "Not showing, Marty, not showing."

Down by the water, he finally relaxes long enough for a hug but hears footsteps on the boardwalk and breaks free. "Chinese fishing nets," he says loudly, pointing seaward, my tour guide again. He indicates one of the only artificial lights shining far off in the black sky. "And this the lighthouse on Vypeen Island," he says with a smile.

I play along. "Is there a ferry there?" I ask a little louder than necessary as a couple passes by. On our way back to the jetty, he says, "Not showing, Marty, not showing!" several times when I try to hug him, but now giggles when he says it.

Down on the darkened jetty, he leads us to the middle of the dock. We lean against one of the two poles the ferry ties up to, between two separate groups of men. One group is smoking by the rotting public urinal about fifteen feet behind Pradeep and the other is about twenty feet behind me. The women and children are up in the sheltered waiting area, out of sight.

Pradeep again falls into his tourist guide role. As he speaks of the dark islands in the harbor, he gropes me with his free hand and gestures over the black water with the other. "The Taj Malabar," he says, indicating the bright lights of the luxury hotel, obviously with its own power source, on nearby Willingdon Island, while his hand cups my crotch. "And this Bolgatty Island and Bolgatty Palace," he says, squeezing my swelling cock and pointing out a few more dim lights in the darkness.

I gesture with one hand while rubbing his crotch with the other. His cock springs to life. "There?" I ask, pointing. Meanwhile my left hand slides up under his shirt to caress his nipples which harden at my touch, causing him to smile broadly and look around to see if we are being noticed. We aren't. I slide my hand down his smooth belly into his pants and find the tip of his erection poking out the top of his underwear. I squeeze it gently. "Is there a ferry there?" I ask.

"Yes, tomorrow," he says, smiling as he squeezes my cock extra hard.

"Okay! Okay!" I say gently and look down. I slide his foreskin down and blow onto the exposed glans. He grins, then looks around and stops me. We concoct a plan while fondling and gesturing. I'll leave my room in

Fort Cochin early in the morning and find a room in a hotel by the train station in Ernakulam where I'll change my ticket for the next day. We'll meet back in the park at four, after he gets out of school.

Soon the lights from the approaching ferry attract other passengers to the jetty and we disengage. Pradeep has one request. "Do you have something for the ferry?" he asks. "And maybe for a movie tomorrow?" It doesn't register right away about when he would have time to see a movie between school and meeting me and I say, "Of course. No problem."

I give him the loose change in my pocket, about double the ferry fee, and twenty rupees "for the movie," although I know ticket prices start at two rupees. He shoves it quickly into his shirt pocket.

The ferry docks and everyone, as usual, jams the entrance. Pradeep, like many of the other men who can't be bothered with the queue, jumps in through the window. The loaded ferry turns around and chugs off. Pradeep comes out alone onto the open stern deck. After checking around to see that nobody else is watching, he pulls up his shirt to show me that he still has an erection poking out the top of his pants. His beaming smile retreats with the diesel fumes and slowly fades into the dark night like the confident grin of a Cheshire cat.

Gerke van Leiden

Gourmet's Heaven

Since I had just survived a borderline shock experience – two hairy bears competing in a David Copperfield-sex-contest: "Look, my butt can make an arm disappear"/"Look, mine can make two arms disappear" – I was in the mood for some harmless kissing, cuddling, maybe a suck job. What better place to look for one than in an elegant restaurant with a menu full of unpronounceable dishes, cloth napkins, and people who find it natural to clean their fingernails?

I headed for Chez Patrick, which was one of the most swishy-sounding places on the map of Sitges, one of Europe's gay meccas. Big golden frames encase sunset-colored walls. Drapes are hung dramatically in places where they are least needed. Depictions of the sea with lost seagulls, pondering seamen, and lonely rocks complete the setting.

"Good evening, sir."

I looked up at my server, whose sharp eyes held the promise of crispy sheets and a strong cup of coffee the morning after. "Nice place," I said.

"Thank you. I did this all myself, you know," he replied.

I had found my mate for the night. Instead of wasting my time with smiles and winks, I decided to take the direct approach: "May I have you for dinner?"

Looking self-consciously around at the other guests, he said: "You're kidding." Then he blushed.

"Never," I grabbed his hairy arm and felt heat surge through his skin.

"Listen!" he said, lowering his voice, "I work so much, that I can't remember the last time I had sex. I am not even sure that I still can."

His French buns had made me horny already, but the prospect of having sex with a practicing virgin gave me an instant hard-on. I let my hand drop from his arm onto the table so that it fell close to his crotch. It's firmness gave me a taste of the French that would soon pour forth from him. "I will be back by the time you close," I said, and then ordered.

* * *

Patrick leaned out of a window on the second floor and buzzed me in. Inside, we started the usual game of checking each other out. To relax him, I pulled him into the darker corners of his apartment where I found his bedroom with only a mattress on the stone floor.

We undressed and I laid back to watch the show: the play of muscles in his thighs and on his pelvis. I grabbed his balls and pulled them slightly. He sighed. I pulled harder, squeezing them in the process. "Ah, that's good!" he screamed, his body rocking. His eyes closed tight and a second later, he shot a major load all over my chest and face. But no, it wasn't just his cum; I had gotten off too without even touching myself.

"I haven't come this hard in a long time," he said as he went down to give my oozing dick a French polish. There was something else on my mind: I had to pee, but Patrick was doing his job so compassionately, that my dick wasn't inclined to go down.

"No problem," Patrick said, and pushed my head back onto the pillow, dribbling a good portion of saliva into his hand to grease his butt. Then he straddled me and heaved himself onto my boner. "Now you do it!"

The idea of peeing into his ass made me almost shoot another load. How could I relax enough to leak? But soon I felt a trickling sensation in my lower abdomen, then heat rising in my stick that pointed straight up to heaven, and eventually a soft tickle around it, comforting, enlivening, thrilling.

"Good boy," Patrick said as he pushed himself deeper into my lap, his eyes closing in ecstasy. He held me tight, fell on his side, and started to move back and forth, my cock still inside. I felt his smooth little muscle-ring massaging me as I was going in and out. It was an eerie sensation, but it felt good. It didn't take much for me to come again. What an image: my sperm floating around like little fish in a sea of hot urine.

I pulled out and surely expected Patrick to take a French leave, but instead he turned around and threw me back onto the mattress to give me a deep and very sensual kiss. He was good, I had suspected it the instant I saw him. And how could he not? He ran a gourmet restaurant, his apartment, the way he dressed – the guy had good taste.

Then he sat upright on my chest and smiled. There was almost something dreamy in his eyes, and I was beginning to worry that he might be falling in love. At least until I felt this warm streaming sensation spreading quickly all over my chest.

Ron Suresha

Your Evening in Jerusalem

You pause, about to tongue a heavy, dark cock, and look up at the trim-bearded Semitic face, his deep-olive eyes wide in anticipation. You flew halfway around the world, disregarding imminent threat of war to appease family in Jerusalem, "city of peace," although peace has until now eluded you. You came although some of your extended "family" regard you as freakish, essentially because they know you're a cocksucker; it's warmer here than back stateside, and they do cook great falafels.

After excusing yourself from another awkward meal of unspoken suspicions and kreplach, you lurched through the cobbled Old City street, searching every hairy man's eyes for a lone ray of sexual desire, even the most religious-seeming Jews. Dark fur sprouting out the broad tops of tanks and tees, sweeping across thick forearms, draping down legs in shorts, tumbling down in curls like religious dreads. Bear-usalem. Bears abound in this Holytown, the hairy "navel of the world," except your gaydar doesn't seem to work here, and your most complicated Hebrew phrase is *Ani lo medaber ivrit.*

You wandered off alone and headed for Gan Atzmaut, the park where perhaps, even on this cool evening, someone could have helped you live up to your family reputation. You spied some single skinny muscleboys with military haircuts strolling nervously – none too close to each other – and you soon left, recalling a cozy-looking café nearby where you hoped an espresso would obliterate a portion of your jetlag and loneliness.

One step in the door brought a rush of warm food and coffee smells, and at two steps the security guard stepped right into your space, waving the scanner under your outstretched arms. So close as he patted you down that you could smell his weak musky cologne, it took a few seconds before you could notice the guard was bearded, handsome, barrel-chested. What at first seemed routine suddenly became alarming, as the guard, sensing no one watching this regular frisk, grunted in Hebrew, "You have a gun?" then pressed his hand against your crotch.

The brief squeeze so stunned you that, slackjawed, with your arms frozen outstretched, you could only grunt. He stepped back to look at you, frisking your eyes with his, and you blinked twice, thought that it *must* have been unintentional, and stammered in English that no, you don't carry a weapon.

You slumped into a stiff upholstered chair across the room. Next you knew, forty-five minutes later, mindlessly clutching the unsipped cold espresso, you realized you were still staring at the guard, trying to memorize how his perfectly trimmed medium-short black beard margins a row of pearly straight teeth. You shifted around trying to catch glimpses of his hands, backed with more fur than you have on your hairy ass, imagining him wiggling a handful of those chapped, hirsute fingers in your mouth.

Despite his apparent inattention to you as he stood at the doorway, occasionally checking entering customers – none frisked nearly as intimately as you, or rather as you imagined he did – you entertained every measure of fantasy about this stranger, whose swarthy good looks were indiscernible to you either as Israeli or Arab. You thought it best perhaps he ignored you – had he turned to look at you again as your eyes were fixed on him, the connection would have pierced your heart like a golden bullet.

You pondered the futility and stupidity of walking over and saying anything to him, with your terrible Hebrew, embarrassed by your transparent lust for him, the obvious hardness leaking down your pant leg nearly the whole time. After willing yourself unhard in order to stand up and relieve your bladder, you paid the check and asked the waitress for the men's room and she pointed to a hallway on the other side of the front entrance, just past the guard.

He stood with his thick arms crossed in front of his broad chest, his view outside the door alert for approaching diners. You weighed each step, trying not to fixate on the basket right aside his gun holster, almost trembling with desire. As you neared the door, he turned his head, regarding you coolly as you approached, with a friendly professional smile. You forcibly pulled your eyes up to his face, readying yourself to venture a seductive smile and say something, anything, when another security guard entered the restaurant, stealing his attention.

You hesitated, then walked past the entrance toward the bathroom. Your eyes cast downward, you realized the stain from your drooling cock was large enough for probably anyone looking at you to have noticed. A hot wave of humiliation washes over you as you entered the WC and closed the door behind you. You applied paper towels to the wet spot, then stepped up to the urinal. You let your long, sticky cock flop out and emptied your bladder, silently chanting recriminations at having wasted enough time tonight, combating a profound, unexpected despair that probably you'll never meet a gay man in Israel as handsome as the guard, who just then silently entered the toilet and locked the door behind him. He faced you holding his crotch, jerked his jaw to his left outside, and growled low, "Replacement."

You stood there, your astonishment in your hand, his eyes flashing with fierce carnality and fear of being caught as he opened his security uniform trousers and revealed a cock as stunning as the rest of him. You instinctively released yourself to grasp his heavy statue-like member and paused in grateful wonder. Clearly absent a second to waste, he pushed you to your knees, drawing you firmly toward the magnificent cock, his holstered gun dangling inches away. For a moment you paused, and he smiled, growled something happily in distinct Arabic, and a sweet passion and terror invaded and conquered you both this evening in this ancient city of peace.

Sandip Roy

Mourning Becomes Electric

1987, Bombay

"I am in town," you said.

"Really?" I whispered, astonished. It was the middle of the school year. You were supposed to be away in college, busy getting your MBA.

"Yes," you replied. "My father died."

"Oh," I said, and then didn't know what to say. I was never very good at saying polite things like, "I am sorry." "How did he die?" I asked.

"A heart attack," you said. "It was quite sudden. My mother called me. But it was all over by the time I reached home."

"Oh," I said.

"Do you want to come over?" you asked.

"Now?" I was genuinely shocked.

"Why not?" you replied. "Finally, everyone has left. Even my mother's gone to see relatives off. She won't be back till late."

"I don't know," I mumbled, never one to seize the day.

"I am going back to college day after tomorrow," you said persistently.

"So soon?" I couldn't hide the disappointment.

"It's the middle of the school year. I have to get back."

"Okay."

"Okay, what?"

"I am coming," I said.

I hung up the phone and went to the living room where my mother was watching television.

"Ma, do you remember my friend Vijay?" I asked her.

"No," she said absently.

"He was from my school and is now doing his MBA. I was talking to him about what kind of courses I needed to do for an MBA." Half lies, half truths. "Well, anyway he is in town. His father passed away."

"Oh!" she exclaimed. "What happened?"

"Sudden heart attack," I said solemnly. "I need to go over and pay my respects."

As I left I looked back guiltily at my father. He sat on the bed reading the newspaper. I turned away and ran down the stairs.

I knew you were in mourning but I was still shocked. Your thick wavy hair was gone. Your head was shaved clean. You weren't wearing the jeans and T-shirts you usually wore. Instead, like a good Brahmin, you had a length of unstitched cotton wrapped around your waist and over your shoulder. Your chest was bare. I could see the Brahmin's sacred thread in the filigree of hair.

I stood there nervously not knowing what to do. Your father's photograph sat on the table right in front of me. The garland of white flowers was still fresh. The slightly cloying smell of incense was in the air. You leaned over and kissed me.

Even as my lips opened, my mind was whirling. We weren't supposed to do this. This wasn't right. You'd barely finished the funeral rites. Your father's spirit was probably still hanging around. But I couldn't say anything.

I grabbed your waist to steady myself. The cotton was thin. And I realized you really were not wearing any stitched clothes just as Hindu traditions dictated. No underwear, no shorts. I could feel you hard and ready beneath the thin cloth. And I closed my eyes and took a deep breath and plunged wherever you were taking me to.

That was the first time we did it on a bed instead of in some dark park. That was the first time we didn't have to keep an eye out for cops, maids, or inquisitive brothers. I unraveled the mourning cloth from your body and felt you leap into my hands. Suddenly my clothes had too many buttons and zippers. I fumbled as I tried to unsnap, unzip, tug open. I felt your breath on my neck, your chest on mine. The wetness of your mouth on my nipples. The softness of the hair on your chest. The insistent, prodding hardness of your dick. The roughness of your shaved head scraped against my skin. I will always remember that. It electrified me with fear, shock, and longing.

2001, Bombay

"I am in town," I said.

"What?" you said astonished. "In Bombay? I thought you were in New York."

"I came last night. My father died two days ago."

"How are you coping?"

"I am okay. My mother is pretty upset still."

"Did you come by yourself? Or did your boyfriend come to? What's his name again, Ted?"

"Ed" I said. "No, I came alone."

"Are you going to stay in Bombay or will you come to Delhi to see me?"

"Just Bombay," I replied. "I can't go to Delhi now. I have the funeral and all that."

"Don't you want to get away from the relatives for a bit?"

"I do," I replied. "But I can't."

"Well, baby, I wish I could come to Bombay and be there with you."

"I wish you could too," I sighed.

"Do you remember when my father died?" you asked.

"I've got to go," I said guiltily and hung up the phone.

Once upon a time when I was a little boy I had told my father, "When you die I don't want to shave my head."

"Why not?" he had said, laughing.

"Because it looks funny," I said.

"All right," he laughed. "I am telling you now you don't need to do anything."

My mother remembered that and told me, "You don't have to shave your head. After all, you have to go back to America to work in a few days. Everyone will understand."

But I shaved my head. I watched the barber's razor move with swift smooth strokes. I watched my hair flutter down to the floor in black tufts. I felt the sudden cold sting of alum on my freshly shaved head. When it was done, I looked at myself in the mirror. It was strange how naked I looked. And all I could think of was you. The secret pleasure of that guilt sheltered me through the tears, the mourning, and the endless Hindu funeral rites.

Royston Tester

Service

Evensong was almost over by the time I made my way across Longbridge Lane to the church's side entrance; past the vestiary on the right and into the men's washroom. There were eight of them, overcoats in a welcoming row, ready for the picking.

There was always some spare change and cigarettes, the previous Sunday a wallet with fifty quid. It took only a few minutes.

Just as I was clearing out the last set of pockets I heard a distant squeak from one of St John's doors.

I rushed to the urinal, unzipped, and desperately tried to splash into the fragrant porcelain.

The washroom door creaked open. In walked Mr Ketland, one of the church wardens. He was a dusty-faced, stiff-looking Welshman – anywhere between forty and sixty – with an earnest manner and polished shoes. He had recently been promoted from assembly-line worker to factory foreman and was therefore newly converted to conservative politics not to mention exemplary religious practice, and neckties. The factory menopause like no other. He stood and watched.

"Evening, Mr Ketland," I said. "Damp night."

He nodded and put his hands in his pockets as though seeking guidance. *How do you supervise a church lavatory, O Lord?*

I smiled and looked away.

My ears felt hot.

"Arrived a bit late for choir," I told him, shaking my dick of non-existent pee. "Better get off home."

Mr Ketland was looking very stern. I was in for it.

It was time for desperate measures. So instead of slipping my cock back into my jeans, I let it flop out, then turned around slowly so he could see its uncut length. He stared at it, his chest rising and falling beneath the phony regimental tie.

I spat into my fingers and began massaging the head like I was soaping in the shower. With finger and thumb I pulled the foreskin back and forth. The old man continued to stare, passing a pale glistening tongue over his dry lips.

I offered him a lick.

Cheeks stained red, he grumbled something foreman-like but shuffled toward me, breathing hard.

Hit or fuck, I thought, patting the shaft of my dick left and right.

As he approached, I reached deftly for his groin and there, beneath his neatly pressed twill trousers, lay the stiffness of redemption.

I slipped his cock out from layers of cotton and began jacking him.

"You're bad news, Enoch Jones," he said hoarsely, pulling me against his jacket. He smelled of Old Spice.

"Aren't I," I replied, adjusting my grip.

He knelt down heavily then sucked me for a minute or two as I rested my hand on the old man's Brylcreemed head.

Eventually he struggled back to his feet.

"Sooner you're in Borstal, the better for us all."

"First line of a hymn, Mr Ketland?"

He started kissing me on the lips. I felt sick to my socks but liked the taste of flesh. Even his. How did he know about Blanchland House?

"The minute you and that mother of yours walked in here. . . ," he began, his throat straining.

I yanked the Austin prick harder and harder.

He buried his face in my shoulder.

"Oh, Jesus," he moaned, thrusting for eternity and God Himself.

Almost there.

"Jesus, yeah," I whispered encouragingly, steadying myself against a urinal.

"Trouble, I thought. You and that Vera Jones," he gasped, beginning a lengthy choking sound as he reached for my ass.

That's it, man.

"They're not from around here," he managed to say, trembling from tip to toe.

And he came – or rather, sputtered – over my thigh.

"You were right then, Mr Ketland," I said, squirting my own jism onto the tiled floor – something simultaneous to remember me by.

"Caravan runt," he spat, still gripping my elbow.

"Yeah," I agreed, fastening my jeans. "Not your sort at all."

"Next time you'll be reported," he said, zipping up and checking himself in the mirror.

"For bringing you off, like?" I asked, backing towards the exit.

"You know what for," he replied, turning a tap.

"Thanks, Mr Ketland."

"Scram or I'll change my mind," he said, with wet hands straightening his tie.

Before you could say Jack Robinson I was out on Turves Green, taking the back route home by the Carisbrooke flats.

Joe Lavelle

One Hour

The Curzon, 23:55

He wears: jeans, black leather belt, white crew neck, black boots. The back seam of his jeans follows his crack, emphasizes a small, pert, fuckable arse. His heavy balls and cock hang to the right. He is slim. The T-shirt hugs defined pecs and abs. His face is youthful, but manly. His jawbone is square. His lips are full. There's stubble on his chin. His complexion is tanned. Tiny scar at the corner of his right eye. Short-cropped brown hair, small ears. He is five feet nine inches tall. His blue eyes catch mine. I wink at him.

"What are you after?"

"Your arse."

Livingroom, 24:33

We're straight at it; kissing, groping, stripping off clothes. His body everything it promised. His rigid dick, short but thick, arches upward. His arse firm and pneumatic. A tuft of pubic hair and smooth flesh. Faint odor of beer and sweat.

Bedroom, 24:37

We collapse onto the bed. He takes my cock in his mouth, slowly working my cockhead with his tongue, exploring the ridge and piss slit. I grab his head and ease my cock to the back of his throat. He gags, relinquishes me, then returns his lips to my cockhead. Seconds later, he takes me in his mouth again. My cock yoyos in and out of him. Eventually, I lean forward, grab the cheeks of his arse and run a finger up and down his crack, tracing circles around his wet sphincter. I nudge a fingertip into him. He sighs. I push in further. Then insert a second finger. He squirms.

"Fuck me."

I withdraw my fingers and reach for the bedside cabinet. He straddles me, legs either side of my waist. Moments later, lube applied and condom in place, he guides me into him.

"Nail that arse!"

I grab his waist and thrust my dick into him. His sphincter offers some resistance, but opens enough to take me in. He groans. His hole is hot and tight. He pushes down and I thrust up, my cock buried within his warmth. I thrust deeper, then thrust again.

"Let me ride you."

He rocks back and forth, lowering and raising himself onto my hard rod. He grabs his own dick and works it with his right hand. We synchronize. His arsehole slides up and down my shaft. He leans forward, his warm breath mixes with mine. His tongue probes my mouth. I pull his arse cheeks apart and thrust deeper into him. He gasps. Our mouths separate. He raises his left then his right knee, squatting. I grab his waist and ram the head of my cock deep within his gut. He rides my dick. A new rhythm ensues. Eventually, I drag us to the edge of the bed. When my legs are on the floor, I sit up and wrap my arms around him. He devours my neck. I raise myself off the bed, standing upright.

"Fuck me."

Still inside him, I turn and lower him over the corner of the bed. He reclines back. I position his butt just over the edge. As I lean forward I feel his heels against my arse. I give long, hard, slow strokes. He raises his head and shoulders up off the bed then throws his arms around me, grabbing my back.

"Fuck me, fucker."

He kisses me and my cock thrusts deeper yet. My thrusts quicken, urgency takes hold. The headboard shakes.

"Go for it."

The bed rocks. His heels dig into me. I slam my dick further into him, pull him against it and hold him there. Gasping, I explode inside him. He spurts too. Some hits my chin.

Bathroom, 24:42
I pull the chain. The condom vanishes down the pan. He's at the door, dressed.

"See you then."

The Curzon, 24:55
His green eyes catch mine. I wink at him.

"What are you after?"

"Your arse."

Richard Andreoli

Desperate Times

Roland left for the bars three hours ago. I try to be outside when he's coming or going so I can say, "Hey Roland," and give him a look to show that I'm interested. I'm sure he knows, but he just smiles and nods.

Tonight he dressed in jeans and a T-shirt that tightly held his body like a uniform, but sometimes he goes out wearing chaps and a harness, and this one time I even saw him in hip boots with a leather jacket and jock strap. I couldn't believe he'd go out wearing that stuff, but he doesn't care what people think. That's what's so cool about him.

One time I tried talking to him. He'd parked in front of my place and I ran outside when I saw him leaving. I noticed for the first time that he had some grey hairs, in his stubble, too. It looks good on him because his chin is really strong, and his eyes are blue like a frozen bottle of Bombay Sapphire.

"Hey," I said, casual-like.

He nodded.

I wanted to ask him about his truck. I wanted to say, "I'm thinking of buying a car and wondered how you liked yours." I'd practiced it in my head, even thought about how he might respond and then invite me to ride with him sometime, but all I could do was look into those eyes. I felt like a junior high kid, all awkward words and limbs working against each other. I must've looked stupid.

As Roland unlocked his door and got in his truck I tried shouting, "Take me with you! I want to learn things, and explore things, and be like you! I want to service you and please you and prove that I'm not some stupid clone! I can handle it! I can!"

But all I could do was whisper it. While he started the engine, while he pulled out, while he drove away, I whispered, "I can handle it."

My problem is that I know he's messing with me. I've read books. I know Califia and Townsend and Preston, and I've studied how games are played. So when I see him come home at two in the morning, and he sees my light on, sees me watching, and then bends down and takes his spare key – his hidden key – to open the door, what else can it be?

Then last night he turned and rubbed his crotch in my direction.

That was my signal, I think as I cross the street and walk up his steps. *A Master's patience isn't infinite*, I know, *so I can't lose the opportunity.* I pop open the end of the hand rail and stick my finger inside, knowing the edge might cut but not caring. Then there it is. The key.

The snapping deadbolt is the loudest thing I've ever heard, and I quickly slip inside and shut the door.

I turn, slowly, my arms outstretched to embrace this sacred place. He has hanging plants in the living room! *Those hooks can be used for suspension play. . . .* A futon! *That probably has eyebolts on the back of the frame for bondage play. . . .* An extension cord on the table! *Oh god. . . .*

It's too much at once. I run into his bedroom, pulling off my shirt and kicking off my shoes. I dive on his bed and smell his sheets and imagine he's in there with me, watching.

I open his nightstand and find lube, a bottle of poppers, a leather cock ring. I take it and smell it, run my tongue on the metal snaps, desperately trying to know him. I unscrew his poppers and inhale as though they were smelling salts, and that's when I see it: his closet.

My legs are unsteady but I manage to stand and slide open the door. I run my hands through his shirts, suits, and pants until I come to a leather vest and jacket. Then I look down, because I know they must be there, and see his boots.

Another blast of poppers and I pick one up, glide it across my face. . . .

Then I spot a pile of his dirty clothes – his gym clothes – waiting to be cleaned!

I drag everything to his bed and lay back, licking the boot and pushing it onto my face because he wants them shined. With my other hand I grab his gym shorts and jock and shove them over my eyes and nose.

Yes sir! I'm your pig! Your cock boy!

I pull my cock out and spin over, humping his bed and madly grabbing the poppers for another hit. Then I toss the bottle and force the crotch of his shorts at my nose, shove his jock into my mouth, lick the straps that went under his ass, hump and hump, show him I'll do anything he says.

I shoot. Suddenly. Fully.

And reality crashes back home.

It's two a.m. He'll be back any moment.

I shove the clothes back in the closet, return toys to the nightstand, open his window to air the room, and quickly remake the bed.

Before I go, I hear his last order: *Lick it!* So I bend down and clean up my mess with my tongue.

Finally, I return the key and leave.

It's 2:30, and Roland hasn't come home.

horehound stillpoint

Backstory of a Bar Towel Cum Rag

"Where's the fucking bartender?" came a voice from the outer room.

"Blowing some guy in the broom closet."

Namely: me.

"Shit, I'll lick his ass if he'll get out here and make me a drink."

"Cool your jets. They'll be done in two minutes."

Hunh. I wasn't sure what that was supposed to mean. Anyway, the bartender smiled up at me, and his blue-collar mustache tickled my nuts. He looked like a car mechanic. Wiry guy, named Roger, with longish unkempt hair, very down-to-earth, and surprisingly comfortable on his knees.

The loudmouth back in the bar yelled something unintelligible. Roger's friend, the one who was keeping his eye on things, got louder in return.

"*Bitch*, I know you don't need a drink *that* bad."

Roger backed off my dick and stood up. I knew what was coming and it wasn't me.

"I better get out there," he conceded.

I started to put myself back together, but he wasn't having that.

"No you don't," he said, jerking my pants back down, all the way to my ankles. "I'll be right back."

Roger banged through the door and went out to confront at least one angry patron. A quarter of the people in the joint saw me, with a hard-on sticking out of my briefs. Some eyes rolled, others drank in the view, most guys maintained a cool unconcern.

Roger did not come back in a minute. Not in two minutes, not in three.

Pulling up trou and walking out with a sheepish grin on my face would have seemed like the most normal course of action, but that felt like admitting defeat. Not to mention busting the bubble on a nice little fantasy.

It's not every day a bartender offers to suck your dick.

And since I was about to move into the Zen Center, this kind of random, happy surprise was only more unlikely to occur in the future.

Besides, I wanted to go six months without sex. Well, part of me wanted to. This desire – and its half-ass nature – was one of my main reasons for moving into the Zen Center.

First rule there was you could not start up a sexual or romantic relationship within the building for the first six months. Theoretically, I guess I could fuck seven strangers a night in dark corners anywhere else or let them all fuck me . . . as long as I could get my tired ass onto the Zen cushion at 5:40 a.m. and sit for an hour without squirming.

That's hard enough to do, without dried cum cracking on your inner thighs and raw memories banging around in your head, after not enough sleep.

In preparation for my move, three weeks ago I had quit my evening job of many years, scrambled and found a new day job, pronto, and remembered what hell it was, adjusting to new conditions, new computer systems, new bosses, new co-workers, new hours. Change change change, hated it, hated it, fucking hated it.

I had come into the bar to let a little pressure off. To kiss some stranger and fall into his arms and let him kiss me and lick me and pull me off into a realm of forgetfulness.

So, naturally, I ran into an old buddy. He wanted the full scoop. What was I doing here, where had I been hiding? What was going on with my life these days?

I told him. Gave him the whole nine yards. Meanwhile, I could feel my desire for sex with a stranger seeping away. By the end of the conversation, it had all gone down the drain. I said goodbye to my friend, and then I took my beer back to the bar.

"I'm taking off," I told Roger.

"I guess you got what you came for, then?" he asked, with a smirk.

"Not really. I ran into a friend."

"Oh, you had one of those 'What are you doing here, I just came in for a beer' conversations."

"Nope. I told him I was here to get my dick sucked, and he still wanted to talk. Now I gotta be somewhere."

"You got five minutes?"

"Yeah, why?"

"Step into my office."

And he stroked his mustache in a way that said, 'This mouth is ready to be used and abused.'

Which is how I ended up in the storage area behind the bar. Alone. Waiting for a hot butch bartender with a few free minutes. With my dick and balls hanging out, feeling every single breeze.

Roger came back from the bar at last, dropped down without a word, and sucked me so hot and wet and shiny hard, I exploded in ninety seconds flat and it was a big wild messy shootout at the OK Corral. I came on his face and on the wall and on my shoes, dammit, and yeah, some of it landed on his mustache, to our mutual delight.

He grabbed a bar towel and cleaned my dick first – such a gentleman – then his face, then the wall, and finally the floor. He handed the raunchy, gooey thing over to me, and said:

"It's yours now."

I took it home and eventually washed it. In the daylight, it was obvious that rag would never be white again.

Luckily, I like to fantasize, and fantasies may be all that are left to me soon, so . . . I imagine the reader of this story (yes, you) getting picked up by some guy and going home with him and having a good old time and after you both finish, when he pulls out an rough, old, slightly greying bar towel cum rag, I hope you'll have a laugh on me. I hope you'll remember that sometimes the plainest things have a secret history. Because I'm giving it to the next guy who comes over.

Before I move into the Zen Center, I'm giving everything away.

Jay Starre

Fantasy Boy

I wanted to devour him. I shoved his thighs back against his chest and buried my face in his ass. I ran my wet tongue up his silky-smooth crack until I found his soft pucker-hole and clamped my mouth over it. I sucked with lascivious, noisy slurps. He moaned his answering pleasure as I stabbed my tongue deep into him.

"I'm all yours, Jay. Do whatever you want to me!" Malcolm gasped out.

With my face deep in his warm ass, I was in paradise. Malcolm's utterances were exactly what I had craved to hear for months now.

Malcolm was my personal fantasy boy. I had ached for him every time we ran into each other at the gym. In reality no boy, he was actually in his mid-thirties but his perfectly proportioned body and flawless alabaster flesh was boyishly fetching. Misty blue eyes and a constant smile completed the picture of perfection.

I lusted for Malcolm on a daily basis. My fantasies were myriad. In my dreams I had him in every position, and explored every orifice and body part with vivid imagination. Then, to my total astonishment, I had him. For real.

That day, sweaty from our work-out, naked and alone in the change room, Malcolm had whispered to me out of the blue, "I want to fuck you all night. Let's go to your place." I responded to his offer with my instantly hard cock.

In my apartment, on my couch, Malcolm and I stripped each other, fleshed pressed to flesh. Hot tongue stabbed into hot mouth. His body was so magnificently true to my fantasies. When I had him in my arms I was amazed at how solid he was, his entire frame tautly-packed muscle. I groped his naked butt while we struggled on the couch, locked in a deep kiss. His ass was like marble come alive.

Then I broke off the kiss and shoved him backwards, diving into his ass for my dreamed-for feast. I tongued and sucked his hot little hole. His softly muttered cries were music to me. My hard cock slapped against my belly, eager to thrust and dig and drive. I opened my mouth and slobbered over his distended hole, wallowing in it. But it wasn't enough. I wanted more. I rose from my wet meal and moved upwards, slurping up his hairless balls and wrapping my fist around his steely cock. The hard rod jerked under my fingers while Malcolm writhed around beneath me.

"Oh god, yeah! Do me! Fuck my wet asshole!"

I reared up. His eyes and mouth were wide open, his lips moist. He stared up at me, hungry. It was all I had wished for, and more. But it wasn't enough yet. I felt my cock quiver at my crotch. I lunged, impaling Malcolm on six inches of fat shank in one thrust.

"*Agghhh! Fuck my ass!*"

Yes. Fuck Malcolm's ass. Hard, fast, deep. I rammed into him, right to the balls. His slick hole expanded enough to accept me, but clung with moist heat. He was totally open to me. His eyes stared up into mine. I buried him with my body, thrust my tongue into his moaning mouth and fucked him deeper and harder. My cock was on fire, burning up as I plunged in and out in a furious panic to have him. It wasn't orgasm I wanted. It was all of him, to fuck and fuck and never stop.

He broke the kiss, crying out. "You're fucking the cum out of me!"

A jet of warm goo splattered my stomach and his. I drove my cock to the hilt, twisting it in circles to massage his prostate while he unloaded in a squirming mess beneath me. Then I pulled out, still hard and hot.

"Now it's your turn. I'm going to do you," Malcolm grunted. He was flushed and panting. But the look in his eyes melted me.

I fell back, tumbling to the floor. He rose and stood over me, a grin on his face. His cock was half-hard and drooling spunk. I lay on the floor and shivered. What was he going to do to me? Then I realized what my fantasy included. I wanted to be surprised by what he did. My thighs fell open. I waited.

Malcolm was still grinning as he dropped over me, turning me in his arms and forcing me onto my hands and knees. I felt lube squirting into my crack as he spread my legs and moved between them.

"Do you want my fingers up your ass? Do you?" Malcolm asked.

A finger dug into my hole. Thick and blunt, it spread my asslips apart and wormed deep into me. I moaned. "Yes! Finger my butt!"

Malcolm added a second and I arched my back and opened up for him. The ache pulsed in waves, into my guts and balls and cock. He added a third finger and I cried out. I dropped my head and became all asshole. Malcolm, my fantasy boy, crammed his fingers way up my quivering slot.

My cock exploded. As pleasure pulsed and beat through me, my body flailed around Malcolm's fingers. As I came and came, spurting on my carpet with reeking joy, one thought coursed through me with my fleeing jism.

There was too much to want. Too much for one night. Too much for a lifetime.

Albert Jesus Chavarria

Thursday, 3:00 a.m.

Okay, so it's three in the morning and I'm fucking this skinhead in a public restroom. The park is deserted and being the middle of the night, there's no real threat of surprise. Aside from us there are more than a few mosquitoes in here. I've given up trying to shoo the ones at my calves and ankles. Others I watch as they circle around and land on his back. I'm distracted by this and I think he notices. "Slap my ass," he says. I slap his ass. It's terrific. My red handprint rises up in the smooth whiteness after the first few times, shows me the blood underneath. I'm tempted to swat a couple of the mosquitoes. I leave them.

We met on an online chat. Not something I would normally do, but I'm trying to be adventurous, to try new things. He's read my profile, knows my last name, and knows I'm Hispanic. We're talking on the phone now. He's a skinhead – the real deal; goose-stepping, Hitler on the bookshelf kind of guy. I'm strangely intrigued. He's got this Puerto Rican/ public restroom rape fantasy. "Bareback," he keeps saying. "No condoms." Not that he asks, but I assure him I'm recently tested, negative. We both know I could be lying. I'm the one who knows for sure. It doesn't seem to matter. He already has these ideas about me and about how this whole scene is supposed to be played out. They're all pretty specific. He's given this some time; gotten it all figured out, knows exactly what he wants. "I wanna be fucked by a darkie." He actually says this. I mean, this could all be a huge set-up. There could be a whole gang of skinheads waiting in that restroom, but I don't think so. For some reason, I'm not really afraid of that. I'm not really Puerto Rican either, but feel like I'm up for playing the part. Besides, who says "darkie" anymore?

"Harder!" he says. I pump away harder. This is starting to feel like an act and I'm having a little trouble getting into character. All of these pieces add up to his fantasy not mine. "Say something." I do my best; "Oh yeah fucker, you like that big dick in your ass. . . ." Do people really talk like this, I wonder. Or is it just in the movies? I know this dialogue. There is a script to this, the Porn Talk, another part of the act. "Naw, man," he says, "in Spanish." Now, I am not a Spanish speaker so I rack my brains trying to remember my college lessons. The only thing I can think to tell him is to vacuum the floor. He responds favorably to this. Little by little it starts to come back to me and I ask him the prices of various articles of clothing. This line of questioning gets a nice rhythm going, making it suited for the action at hand. I think I inform him that the parrot is waiting in the living room. I also let him know that he should not walk in front of, or behind the bus when exiting. I've memorized this phrase from the plaques on the bus that warn of oncoming traffic. I feel confident now I could tell him how to push out the window in case of an accident, but I'm starting to doubt the conjugation of my verbs. Plus I wonder if I'm pushing it, he might also ride the bus and have some knowledge of public transit Spanish.

Of course I do all of this in the most menacing tone I can muster. I figure this scenario is much more about delivery and much less about actual content. So, coupled with the sounds of exertion in my voice, it's all pretty convincing. It also seems to do the trick. He gives a good, long "Uuuuh, uuuuh!" and comes into his own hand. I mean he catches it, every drop of his whole load. And I'm thinking this couldn't get much stranger when his excitement and orgasmic convulsions take me over the edge and I shoot inside of him, a lot, just like I agreed to do. It is a relief and release in more ways than one.

He pulls away from me and goes to the sink. He rinses his cum down the drain and washes his hands, not once, but twice. I'm watching this while I button myself up. He steps back to me and puts his head on my chest. He looks up, hurt. "Why would you do that? What would make you do that to me?" "Do what?" I ask. "Come inside of me. How could you do a thing like that? Don't you care about me at all?" I'm flabbergasted; pull away. I look him square in his dewy eyes, all that tough guy posturing gone and I see this wounded child in Doc Marten lace-ups. "Look buddy," I say, "this was your idea. You asked for every part of this. And if there's one thing I've learned, it's that you've got to give the people what they want."

Shaun Proulx

Porn Stars

"You're like a porn movie." Saying this to him, I feel old, desperate – I *am*, compared to this kid in the passenger seat. But I mean it; it's true. His lean stomach is silk. Touching it, I feel my own hand's roughness. My fingers pass through the down of his bush, beneath the beat of his pumping, his knuckles rap mine. He looks at me. Chin to chest, he studies himself, relaxing further down the seat.

> My jerking fist hits his hand. It's dark where we're parked, but I see his wedding band. I'm like a porn movie? I look down at myself to see how so. T-shirt pushed up under pits. Jeans shoved to ankles. No underwear. Jacking impressive meat. I slip down the seat; my spread knees press the glove compartment. My ass is sweaty wet. The leather sticks to me; I shift and it's like a fart. I wonder who usually rides in this seat. For three hours tonight I was just some tall pimply brainer alone in a bar overflowing with guys. Now I'm a porn movie.

I don't speak, I can't. The kid's eyes find mine – I'm transfixed. He's expressionless, just as he was minutes ago when I first spotted him from my parked van, stepping off the twenty-four-hour bus that links city to suburbs, dropping off Friday party boys all night. I'm across the street. Due home after working a double. Waiting, risking, hoping. The kid lights a cigarette, strolls. Nervous, I start the car.

> A minivan pulls alongside me as I walk home, passenger window down. Dude behind the wheel – Italian maybe, or Jewish – is almost bald. Gut poking from golf shirt. Heavy bags under the eyes. I bet there's a Lion's Club sticker on his bumper.

My heart jumps around my chest. It's all I can do to not step on the gas – still be home on time – but I summon my nerve. He steps from the sidewalk through shadows to the curb, tall, slender, beautiful. "Hi," I manage. Wonder if this is really happening.

I nod. He is old enough to be someone's father – mine, for example. He checks my crotch, looks away uneasy, ashamed. I pull the passenger door open. No explaining to anyone I know just climbing into some guy's minivan at two a.m. But I'm horny. A little bit drunk.

Incredibly, he slides in, and I am astounded at how hot he is: blond hair, intelligent eyes, very tall. I drive away. We stare ahead. Nothing is said. It's a dream; we pass darkened rows of cloned houses. Of its own will, my hand slowly reaches out to touch the kid's long leg. Slowly, like I might burn my self.

I take his hand. It's warm, clammy, little. I guide it. Fat fingers squish my prize pack. A sharp breath. He can't believe his luck.

I am hard, I'll burst, but we're finally here: a quiet dead-end I know. One hand driving, the other between his legs. I pull under the deep darkness of a group of maples and park, slide from my seatbelt; pull his T-shirt up.

I lift my ass; push my jeans down. His lips are on my semi, capturing it all into his mouth. He sucks my skin like a baby and then starts moaning like one.

I'm lost; this is ecstasy . . . until I rise for breath, gasping. "You're like a porn movie." The words barely come. The kid strokes.

I look down, then over at him. Lock eye contact, spanking away. My bag slowly tightens until suddenly I grunt and a hot white ribbon spills out. Keep staring at him. Both breathless. His eyes widen.

Breeze rushes into the van – it's so hot out – I'm alive, marinating; my mouth opens, all I do is look at him in the shadows while everything about me falls away. An instant later, my bliss is over. *Searing beams of a flashlight are illuminating us.* I fail to comprehend, eyes wide, body frozen, mind numb. There's an order to get out and as I do there's the uniform and there's the badge and there's the flash/flash in my mind: my life is over/how could I do this? The boy is out, wiping his stomach, and then I see something in the glare I hadn't before: Is this kid even of age? My knees buckle.

> I shield my eyes with one arm. Fucking light! The cop doesn't ask what we're doing. It's obvious. But he keeps his flashlight on me. Asks how old I am. I see the old guy. Terrified, gonna keel over. The cop asks me again. The old man's shaking. "Twenty-one," I lie. I drop my arm, standing into my full height. The cop studies me. Our eyes meet. I don't blink.

Mercifully we're told to just go and the officer calls us faggots and the boy mutters "Fuck you" but that's fine because now we're driving away and I'm thanking the kid profusely. He lights a cigarette – I'll have to explain the smell – and says an address, staring ahead. After five silent minutes we arrive at a non-descript low-rise. He gets out; I go to thank him again –

> I slam the door. "Peace," I say, smiling. "Go straight home." The old man nods. I watch, under the streetlight. As he pulls away something catches my eye and I laugh out loud: a Lion's Club bumper sticker. I'm still smiling after I get upstairs, into bed, jack, and fall asleep.

I'm home but don't turn into the driveway. The house is dark. My mind replays exquisite, edited flashes, I still smell cigarette, and if anyone sees me just sitting in my van staring at my home *at three a.m.* I no longer care, I don't. The blinds in the bedroom window upstairs are shut. My front door is beige. My foot presses the gas; I go. Minutes later I am parked across from the bus stop again, and just in time.

R.E. Neu

Greek to Me

It wasn't easy convincing my landlord that my air conditioner was really broken. He kept saying that the noise and smoke were nothing out of the ordinary, and he stood in the blast of superheated air oohing and aahing like it was a tropical waterfall. When his face took on the color of a medium-rare steak, though, he gave up pretending, and in exchange for a glass of ice water he called a repairman. The next thing I knew somebody was pounding on my door at 7:30 in the morning.

"Open up!" a voice growled as I glared at my clock in disbelief. "I'm here to fix your air conditioner!" I threw on a towel and opened the door and if I wasn't fully awake before I certainly was now: the sight of this guy was as bracing as a double espresso. I don't mind old or out of shape folks provided they wear something to hide it – like baggy clothes or the Houston Astrodome – but he had on less than Britney Spears. I tried to avert my eyes as he lumbered in but I couldn't help but notice the corduroy short-shorts, scuffed brown boots, and a tool belt, with lots of blotchy red nakedness in between. I trailed after him until he found the air conditioner, and after the removal of his tool belt sent his shorts plunging to new depths, I fled to the shower. When I returned, the air conditioner was still grinding like a cement mixer and he was on my bed, engrossed in an old copy of *Drummer*.

Oops. "I'm a musician," I lied. "I thought that was an instruction manual."

"No," he said thoughtfully, "I don't think it is. Though some of the guys look a little like Ringo." I hadn't picked up an accent before so I was surprised when he pronounced it "Reengo." He smiled and showed a jumble of teeth splayed like a mouthful of shredded wheat. "Don't be embarrassed. I am Greek. My people have been that way for thousands of years. A man has a wife to bear children, and a younger man to teach. It is his duty. Take Aristotle – he invented geometry and logic and the helicopter. He meets this kid Socrates and embraces him like a son. He teaches him philosophy and politics and initiates him into sex. Not just slam bam thank you ma'am sex – manly sex, like a big bear hug. Except they were, you know . . . naked."

I couldn't think of anything to say. I didn't know anything about gay sex in the past because I'd been trying to get some in the present. But long ago I'd visited a civilization where men bonded together and paired off and left the women to their own devices. It was called "San Francisco." And while Castro Street wasn't the Parthenon and a kaftan wasn't really a toga, it was fun while it lasted.

He pulled a screwdriver from his toolbelt and pried the front cover off my air conditioner. "Me, I'm sad to say I have not found a boy to tutor. I'm not as smart as Aristotle, but I've learned a few things and I want to pass them on."

Now, to say I wasn't attracted to this guy was an understatement. Though he was butch as Hoss Cartwright's left testicle, he also had a belly domed like a turtle, and his hair was a shade of black found only on newborn mink and Wayne Newton. He had a thick thatch of chest hair but it started halfway between his nipples and his navel, and his legs were lumpy and red. But his story made me nostalgic. I looked at the wrinkles around his eyes and started to yearn for a time when sex wasn't just a temporary bond between strangers, something to kill a couple minutes between laundry cycles. When it meant sharing, and forming a bond so tight it could only be expressed by physical affection.

To make a long story short, he showed me how to adjust my thermostat and then we did it. He undressed me slowly and yanked his shorts down, and with paint-splattered boots still tied to his feet he had his way with me. "We are like Socrates and Aristotle," he panted. "I share my years of knowledge and then take you from behind." He wasn't particularly instructive, as I'd been in that position once or twice before, but knowing it was a time-honored tradition made it special. Before I even straightened up, he was gone.

I woke up in a great mood the next morning, despite the fact this was the second day in a row somebody was pounding on my door at dawn. As I wrapped myself in another towel, I realized something had changed. No longer was I a shallow gym rat with no connection to the past: now I was a shallow gym rat tied to history. I flung the door open like I was greeting a fresh new life.

"Hey," my landlord said, grimacing at my pale pink flesh. "Did my guy fix your air conditioner?"

"He sure did," I said, blushing. "It's running great now. That Stavros is a terrific guy."

He looked like your dog would if you asked it to mix you a martini. "Stavros? You mean the husky old guy who needs more clothes? That's my wife's uncle Patsy. He ain't Greek – he's half-Irish and half-Italian. Funny you should say that, though, cuz once he told a guy he was Greek, and they actually –"

By the time he saw my mouth drop open, it was too late.

"Oh, jeez. You didn't fall for that 'mentor' crap, did you? The Socrates and Aristotle speech?"

I nodded as blotchy red flesh flashed before my eyes.

"I gotta have a talk with that guy. But you can't really blame him, I guess. That's the only way he can get laid." My mood was as limp as my towel now, and he was looking guilty. "Look, if you really want a mentor, I could give it a try. But I ain't doing any of that butt-pirate stuff."

I shook my head, smiling in gratitude despite slowly realizing that a seventy-year-old man had just turned me down for sex. "Thanks, Mr Carmelo. But it's really not the same without a Greek guy."

"I know what you mean," he said. "In the forties I sent away to Japan for a mail-order bride. They sent me a German Jew named Schotzi."

After he left I stood in the dark, listening to the air conditioner's calm hum and feeling the cold air swirl around me. Sure, he'd tricked me. He'd used me and thrown me away. But was it as bad as all that? Maybe "Stavros" wasn't going to be my mentor, but he'd taught me something very important.

If I was going to get anywhere in this world, I'd need to fake an accent.

Daniel Curzon

My Day by Eleanor Roosevelt

A cold, mean wind was blowing in from the ocean. I parked my car, trying to decide whether to have some Thai food first, with wine, and then go for the orgasm. Or should I be greedy – that is, have an orgasm first – hopefully, mind you, only hopefully – and then have dinner and the wine (a half carafe of house white), followed by a second orgasm. Hey, that's not greedy; it's just thrifty. Half a Viagra costs a pretty penny even on my medical plan.

I opted for the early-bird orgasm and circled the cruising area. Alas, the parks and grounds people are now starting to tear the wooden slats off the fence behind which a lot of us have tricked over the years. Can't stand the thought of someone having sex in a park. Fuck them.

I saw some old tricks of mine, including The Hood, who always wears the hood of his sweatshirt up, day or night, hot or cold, probably because his head is malformed on one side. (I've never seen his entire head.) Once upon a time I wouldn't have touched him because of what The Hood seemed to promise underneath, yet once we got together he was actually good sex, with lots of touching and holding, not just the hard stuff. But this night we were not interested in each other.

After some time – and the Thai restaurant near the ocean was going to close if I didn't hurry – some skinny young thing with less-than-perfect teeth and bad posture sauntered over, grinning and smoking. "You want to party?" he asked me. I guess he figured because I am heavy-set now and a man of a certain age I'd jump at his offer.

Sorry, not my type, never was. "No," I said.

The Youngun looked upset. "I just got here from Texas, and I don't know about this place yet. I was just trying to get a few dollars for something to eat."

Not from me, you're not! Jesus, that's the second time in a row someone has asked me for money. Well, I'm not there yet, honey. Is the word spreading among hustlers about this spot?

Skinny Tex grumbled his way off into the bushes. "Jeez, everybody's so cheap around here," he said.

Onward! I told myself.

A look here, a look there. I showed some underwear.

Bulging underwear.

A man, slight but not skinny, not young, not bad-looking actually, even with his grey hair, expressed some interest in my display, perhaps catapulted into desire by the two chunky guys making out nearby. He came closer. He reached out his hand toward my crotch. I allowed this to happen. I wanted this to happen. I'd rather go with someone who wants me than with someone I might want who doesn't want me but merely puts up with me.

He said, "Let's go somewhere, and I'll suck you."

Nice words to hear, but they always remind me of the vice cop who arrested me years ago. He too wanted to "go somewhere else." Fuck him too.

"How about there?" I said, pointing to a spot maybe five yards away.

"Okay."

I unzipped.

He pulled down his pants and turned the baseball cap backwards on his head. And knelt down.

My Viagra was working wonderfully. It swells everything, in case you haven't heard. Thank you, God.

In no time at all – as usual – I shot my load.

I think my gentleman caller was a little surprised at my rapidity. "Can you do it a second time?" he wondered from below as I patted my part dry with a handkerchief.

"Not right away," I demurred.

I hurried over to the Thai restaurant, but it was ten minutes to closing time. Damn.

I thought about ordering take-out and eating in my car. Instead, I drove to the Safeway a few blocks away, bought an Italian-style chicken breast sandwich and a bottle of peach-flavored ice tea. (Room temperature, but what the hell.) I also got a chocolate cake parfait. Yum, yum. I've really got to watch my weight, but when you've just been sucked off, you tend to forget.

In my car, with the news on the radio, I ate my sandwich and drank my healthy peach tea, choking from time to time. Of late my throat has been sticking (closing up) a bit, either from allergies (which I never had before) or maybe from age. I'm sixty-three goddamned years old! Thank god I look about forty-nine. All right, fifty.

Then I went back to the cruising area, and the same gentleman who had asked me if I could come a second time was still there. I made an offer he couldn't refuse and stuck my dick into his mouth for the second time in just over an hour. "Suck it," I said. "Suck that cock!"

He was agreeable.

It took me a little longer to shoot this time. I thanked him. Miss Manners says: "One should always thank someone after he or she has sucked your cock." (More straight men should learn this instead of insulting the very people who give them the greatest pleasure they will ever know in life.) Yeah . . . fuck them as well.

When I got home, I ate my chocolate parfait and tried to forget the fact that I am growing old and that yesterday my new female cat killed the lovely silver-green hummingbird who used to flit around the tree in my backyard. He lived there for several years. He won't be there now in the morning, flying around, curious, making clicking noises at the cat with his long little bill, darting near the window of my bedroom to check me out. It's not the cat's fault, though I scolded her. She's just doing what Nature tells her. And so am I. And so are we all.

Stephen Lukas

The Need for Touch

Urine, cafeteria-style cooking, and cleanser smells launch the dog's nose into a twitching spasm as the elevator doors open. Kevin follows Gracie past reception where one of two nurses breaks into an appreciative smile and scurries around the desk to pet her. *Thank you*, she wags with her tail. Somewhere close by a woman's voice bleats a demanding, hysterical crescendo: "Mrs Rose. *Mrs Rose. Mrs Rose!*"

Today's first visit is with Dr Jay, the door just beyond the nursing station. Kevin learned they are his only visitors, ever. Always alone and wheelchair-bound, this aged man responds to the sight of the runty, unimposing beagle. The most he's offered them which, on this floor, is a lot are a few blinks of recognition that Gracie manages to sniff out from behind the clotting smog of dementia. Her woebegone eyes and merry disposition work magic with most residents on D12, the advanced Alzheimer's floor. Patients' hands instinctively reach down to scratch her head, or caress her tri-color coat. All but a few still have a lingering need for touch. She is fed imaginary treats, and not so imaginary pills if Kevin isn't vigilant.

Dr Jay, this evening in beige-with-brown-trim pajamas, is looking out the large picture window when they arrive. Gracie rises on her hind legs. *Hello, I'm here.* Kevin watches as Dr Jay turns his gaze to the furry guest. He recalls being informed Dr Jay had been a medical officer in the Navy. Maybe he used to consign veterans here, when "the time" came. Kevin wonders. Other residents display pictures of once familiar loved ones. But only last year's milk calendar hangs on the severely whitewashed walls of this over-heated room. June, apparently, is carrot muffin month.

"Hello, my friend," croaks a phlegmy British accent. Kevin is startled. When they make eye contact, another first, Kevin realizes it is not the dog being addressed and sees that the doctor is clutching something in his lap.

"Hello there," Kevin says. "This is Gracie. I'm Kevin. How are you today?"

"Today . . . good," Dr Jay answers reflectively. "Sit, please," he adds, nodding towards the chair near the bed. Kevin obeys. Gracie, folding her tail beneath her backside, sits sidesaddle. Kevin sees that Dr Jay is studying him, and for a while they stare at one another in silence. Kevin grins awkwardly, feeling unsure of what next to say.

"I miss . . . my friend," the doctor splutters, glancing back out the window overlooking misty Halifax harbour. Dog-therapy volunteers are coached to avoid asking questions of residents with advanced dementia, as they are easily confused, often resulting in heightened agitation if they forget what they've only just been asked. Stalling for time, for a response, Kevin observes several ships in port, their lights veiled under the gathering fog. But not HMCS *Montréal*, Marc's ship. Kevin pictures Marc, in his uniform, his hair wind-blown, on her deck somewhere in the Arabian Sea and rubs at his suddenly dry, tired eyes. Dr Jay's right hand is gently kneading Gracie's velvet ears.

"I have friends I miss too," Kevin responds finally and softly, the handle of Gracie's leash resting in his hand. Dr Jay's blue eyes snag on the nametag clipped to the right front-pocket of Kevin's jeans.

"I have a friend . . . his name," he says, his voice falling away. "I've been here for six months . . . years maybe, a long time, I think?" He squints, his mind digging. Kevin waits. After three months of volunteering at the Veteran's Villa, the same three months Marc's been at sea, he knows to respect the silence, that not all voids require filling. Gracie sits patiently at Dr Jay's slippered feet. Both the dog and the volunteering were Marc's idea. So Kevin could *stay busy. Occupied. Feel useful.* This floor, however, was Kevin's choice.

"I miss . . . will they . . . he will come back to get me . . . take me home." It wasn't a question. Hands fumbling, Dr Jay wrestles with what Kevin now sees is an ancient, waxy-looking wallet in his lap. With a quivering hand, he offers Kevin a small picture. Gracie looks up, watching their fingertips touch as the photograph is exchanged. In cracked black and white, two young men in smart-looking naval suits beam at the camera, embracing, safely, at the shoulder. A frigate for background. Wartime.

"I can remember . . . his . . . we. . . ." The words hang in the air. "Please find out if he's coming . . . maybe we can . . . go home, I'm not sure why. . . ." Dr Jay looks around the room questioningly, but not confused.

This time the silence lasts more than a few moments. Eventually,

Kevin rises to excuse himself to "make the rounds." He tugs gently at Gracie's leash. Before turning to leave, Kevin leans over to return the photograph. Dr Jay's hand moves to accept it, but suddenly diverts its course, lurching at Kevin's waist. Gnarled fingers graze downward, once, on the fly of Kevin's jeans before retreating. Kevin glances at the door before bending down and kissing, lightly, the old man's forehead. Dr Jay reaches up and strokes Kevin's face with his knuckles, gently and clumsily, before taking back the photo in his hands.

"I'll bring Gracie back to see you again. Soon."

At the door, Kevin turns for a final glance and sees in the window's reflection Dr Jay watching him leave. The doctor waves not at Kevin, but at his departing silhouette, mirrored perfectly by the fog clawing against the window, as if it wants in. In the hall, Gracie turns not to the next room, but back to the elevator. On the ride down, Kevin chews absentmindedly on the tip of his left thumb, more aware than ever of the raspberry-colored lesion budding just under the nail.

Simon Sheppard

The Phenomenology of Cocksucking, Part 1

A book by Marguerite Duras is on the bedside table. Bryce picks it up, riffles through it, puts it down again. He's wearing green corduroys and what looks like a hesitant smile. Standing near the bed, he shifts from one foot to the other. Charles gestures for him to sit down, patting the bed several times with his left hand. Bryce sits beside him.

"I didn't think I'd see you again," Charles says.

"It's been a while since college," Bryce replies. He's no longer smiling. He sighs and flops back on the bed, the flurry of his blond hair shining against the dark purple Indian print spread. Seeing the bedspread has reminded him of the cloying incense he used to burn, back when he and Charles were friends.

"Anyway," says Charles. "I'm glad you're here." He lays his left hand, the patting one, on Bryce's right leg, gently, just above the knee. The ripples of corduroy feel warm to his touch.

Bryce tilts his head back slightly. There's a poster against the Vietnam War above him; to him, it's upside down. He could brush off Charles's hand but he doesn't.

Beneath the corduroy, Bryce's dick is, perceptibly, getting hard. Outside the window, beyond a tattered pull-down shade, a siren whirls past.

"I've wanted to do this," Charles says, "for quite a while."

"Yes," says Bryce.

"You had a girlfriend. Always."

"Yes," says Bryce. He reaches down for Charles's hand and draws it upward.

"Want to smoke a joint?" Charles asks, his hand pausing midway up Bryce's thigh.

"Later." Bryce arches his crotch upward and Charles's hand slides quickly upward, cupping the bulk beneath the fly. He looks up at Bryce's face. Bryce has closed his eyes.

Charles leans across Bryce's body and nuzzles his cheek against his onetime friend's hard cock. Bryce moans and shoves his crotch upward.

Charles moves his face so his mouth is against the hard-on, gnawing at it gently. The corduroy tastes fresh, like laundry detergent. The light coming in through the window is red with sunset. Charles lifts his head and moves his left hand to Bryce's crotch. His fingers tremble as they pull down the zipper, awkwardly undo the belt and unbutton the green pants. Another siren, mysterious.

He looks up at Bryce, lying there silent, eyes closed, lips just slightly parted. He wouldn't look any different if he were asleep. Bryce's underpants are grey cotton briefs. Charles just lies there for a long moment, his own dick pressing hard into the mattress. This is, he's thinking, something he's wanted for a very long time, almost too long to remember why.

The siren has passed and everything seems silent as Charles lays his hand against Bryce's hard cock. Heat radiates through the cotton.

He fumbles as he pulls the underwear down far enough for him to see most of Bryce's penis, pulled flat against pale belly by the underwear's elastic waistband. It's considerably smaller than he would have imagined, and uncircumcised, a ring of tender pink flesh revealed just beneath the pointed cockhead. He looks up at Bryce's face. A glass of water on the bedside table, next to the book, is glinting with the last rays of the sun.

Looking back down at the cock, he pulls the waistband down further, past Bryce's balls. The sac is a pretty pink, and the sparseness of the few golden hairs on its wrinkled terrain contrasts with the abundant cloud of blond pubic hair in which the shaft nestles.

"Suck me," Bryce says.

So Charles does. He places his nose against the unnaturally silky, warm shaft, inhaling just a hint of old piss. He sticks his tongue out, laps at the little jewel of wrinkled flesh just south of the cockhead, then licks further down the smallish shaft. When his lips reach the base of Bryce's shaft, he opens wide enough to take one of the balls in his mouth; in contrast to the undersized shaft, the ball is large and meaty. He sucks on it for a minute, then releases it and quickly maneuvers Bryce's dickhead into his mouth, flicking his tongue against it. One of Bryce's hands comes down on the back of his head, pressing down. Charles takes the whole cockshaft into his mouth. It doesn't even reach the back of his throat. He sucks vigorously at the hard flesh, then slides his lips up and down and up again.

"Mmm . . . you're good," Bryce murmurs, in that little-boy voice he used to use when he was stoned. Charles wonders how much of a basis for comparison Bryce actually has.

Bryce has unbuttoned his shirt, revealing a little thicket of fluffy golden hair mid-chest, and is stroking his flat, very pink nipple with his right index finger, making circles. He stares straight up at the ceiling, an awful white stucco with sparkly bits.

Charles almost shoots off in his pants but holds back just in time. He's completely into sucking cock now, nursing hard at the swollen flesh as though it will yield up some secret or another if he keeps at it long enough. He uses his tongue to stimulate the ridge on the underside of the shaft. The flesh is slippery with saliva; it would be shiny if the room weren't almost dark. Bryce has stopped paying any attention at all to him, but he doesn't mind. He doesn't mind.

There are moments in every homosexual man's life when the entire universe comes down to a dick in his mouth. This is, for Charles, one of those moments. He's gotten what he wanted, which has turned out to be, rather strangely, a few inches of spongy tissue engorged with blood. He gulps down all of Bryce's hard-on again, lips down around the base, his chin against soft balls, his nose buried in blond bush, and sucks and sucks and sucks.

"Marguerite Duras was *such* a pretentious twat," Bryce says. And then he comes, salty as somebody's tears.

James Chum

Fan Dancer

I must have seen you at least ten times rummaging through back alley dumpsters and panhandling on Davie Street before I recognized you. When it finally registered that the skeletal, sallow-skinned man with the haunted eyes and rags for clothing was actually someone I'd lusted after years ago at the Gandy Dancer, my heart caved in.

Fifteen years ago, you had been the hottest man in Vancouver – at least I thought so. What a crush I'd had on you! My friends all teased me about it. I'd go to the Gandy on Friday nights and hide behind a pillar or a small crowd of your braver admirers to watch you dance, shirtless, twirling a pair of silver fans. God, you could move! You'd dance non-stop for hours – every movement was fluid, sensual, self-assured, infused with some mysterious and compelling power. They said you did drugs, but I didn't care. I was totally enthralled.

Many a night I'd go to the Gandy and not even set foot on the dance floor if you were there. I'd just stand by my pillar and watch you dance in that whirling vortex of light, flashing fans and disco fog. Your sweat-slick body gyrating, bathed in the reds, blues, and golds of the strobe lights spinning and flashing above you as you twirled your fans, splashed perspiration like holy water on the surrounding crowd.

Though I longed to, I never was brave enough to ask if I could dance with you. My friend Joey used to threaten he'd ask you on my behalf but I told him to fuck off. No, we never even talked, though I bumped into you once coming out of the men's room. I remember how I flushed and how my eyes took a dive to the floor as I mumbled, "Excuse me," and shuffled aside to let you pass. I still remember the heat, the heady smell of sweat-wet denim and poppers. I spent the rest of that night, like all those other nights, just watching you, until the last song was played, the lights came on, and the last desperate cruisers paired off. You always took your time leaving. I'd always hurry home alone, ears ringing, clothes smoky, and my mind a happy blur of disco music and swirling images of you, fanning me with your fans, dancing for me. Well, in my dreams anyway.

When I got back to my apartment I'd peel off my clothes, climb onto my bed and beat off, playing back those images over and over in my mind, fantasizing what it would be like to touch you, feel the sweat on the hairs of your well-muscled chest, linger for a while on the hardness of your nipples then slowly run my hand down over your slick, taut belly, tracing the thin line of silk that went down past the sweat-soaked leather belt, down to the ample mound of worn blue denim, one silver button already open, teasing. The force of my ejaculation always knocked me on my back.

Then one day you just disappeared. Later, I heard from Joey that you'd moved to L.A. Rumor had it you were living in a mansion, kept by some high-powered Hollywood closet case. Years went by, but I never forgot you. Every now and then I'd hear a favorite dance tune by Lime or The Flirts or Yaz and all the charge-filled memories would come back.

How you used to turn heads back then. But the day I recognized you, begging on the sidewalk, people rushed to get by you or looked the other way. The man of my dreams of my coming out days was homeless: health gone, looks gone. The way you looked perhaps your mind was gone too. I hoped so – that somehow this was all one merciful, numb fog, like those nights on the dance floor – that none of this hurt.

If Joey were alive I'd tell him about you. But he died the year Gay Games were here. They're all dead – or have moved back to Toronto or Montreal. There's no one left in Vancouver I can talk with about you now.

From that day I recognized you my mind flipped all over the place. I thought about trying to talk to you, to find out if you had a place to stay. I thought about going through my closets and taking you clothes. I considered taking you food. I thought about phoning AIDS Vancouver, BCPWA, even an ambulance. But in the end I didn't do anything. I don't know why. It was just like fifteen years ago, back in the bar: me, hiding behind a pillar, too afraid to reach out, too afraid make a move – to connect.

Yesterday, I bundled up and ventured out into the cold to buy liquor for the holidays. It was dark out. The frosted streets were bustling with frantic, last-minute shoppers. Outside the liquor store, a man in a Santa cap bobbed in the cold trying his best to play Christmas songs on a five-stringed guitar. I tossed him a loonie and pushed my way inside. By the time I'd picked out some wine and a bottle of Bombay Sapphire I was drenched with sweat. As I eased my way towards the cashier I heard the wail of sirens. From the back of the long line I could see an ambulance and a VPD patrol car pull up across the road. By the time I got outside a crowd had gathered in the alleyway behind the Gay & Lesbian Centre. I wanted to see the cause of the commotion so I shifted my precious load, crossed the street, and joined the growing throng.

Lights from the ambulance danced amber red along the alley's walls. Men in rubber gloves lifted something wrapped in a blanket from out of a dumpster. I was about twenty feet away, but even in the dark I recognized you in the eerie strobe lights. Your face was ghostly grey and more skeletal now. In that instant my grip loosened and my bag of bottles fell with a crash. I watched dazed as they lay you on a stretcher, covered you up, put you in the ambulance, and drove away.

Tonight I stare out my apartment window at the Christmas lights, biting my fingernails, trying to remember you as you were fifteen years ago: alive, bathed in reds and blues and golds, in disco fog, potent, beautiful, self-assured, dancing with your silver fans, shirtless, splashing sweat like holy water. But I can't rid my mind of the images of you sick and homeless, your crazy, haunted eyes, your thin, stained, shaking hands held out, begging on the street. All I can think of is you cold and alone dying in that dumpster. The image of your strobe-lit, lifeless face haunts me, and all I feel is empty inside.

Shaun de Waal

To All the Boys I've Loved Before

I'm floating in a darkened space, on my back, suspended, though there doesn't seem to be anything beneath me. Lights flicker vaguely. Shadowy figures surround me. Some of them I recognize as they come before me; some of their names I know, others I don't. Keith is on my left. I'm sucking his big uncut cock, and running a hand over his flat belly. He kisses me, a deep kiss with a swirling tongue. Jacques is on my right; I turn my head and get his fat cock in my mouth. I suck it deep. Then back to Keith's. He moves his cock rhythmically in and out of my mouth and he moans with pleasure. Ivan is sucking my cock, swallowing it as far as it will go. Then his mouth moves over my balls, and takes each one in his mouth, one after the other, and rolls it around. I feel his tongue move down my perineum and touch my hole. He lifts my legs and sticks his tongue in my hole. Now Will is sucking my cock. At the same time, he pushes a finger past Ivan's mouth, wets his finger there, and slides it into my hole. My hole tightens around it; he wriggles it around, and my hole loosens. Brenn straddles my face and fucks my mouth. I grab his butt and finger his hole. Robert is lowering himself onto my cock; I feel it pushing up into his ass, his ass opening to receive it, and he groans. I thrust into him while he leans forward over me and I feel his tongue touching my fingers and rimming Brenn's ass. Brenn fucks my face harder. I reach up and grab his nipples in my fingertips; I twist and pull. Now Daniel is rimming me and sticking two fingers up my ass. Brenn and Robert vanish. Daniel comes and kisses me; our tongues entwine. Xavier appears and starts sucking my cock. He pulls the foreskin closed and tongues that rose. I can reach his lightly hairy ass with one hand; I caress it. I reach under his balls and grab his long uncut cock and play with it. Shanyi appears, his small cut cock very hard. He slides it up my ass and fucks me. Then he is gently pushed out of the way by Hugh, who fucks me while I rim Andy, his round white ass suspended above my face. Andy and Hugh lean toward each other over my body and kiss. I'm being turned over by invisible hands. I'm face down now, and Pete's ass is in front of me. He is holding it open with his hands. I stick my tongue in his hole, jam it as deep as it will go, fuck him with it. I stick a finger up his ass, then two, and rotate them. He goes Aaaahhh. My ass is in the air. Ed takes Hugh's place – the cocks are getting bigger. I can feel Ed shove his cock into me. And then I feel Gavin beneath me, and my cock is gliding into his ass. He wriggles, staked on it. I fuck him, pulling my cock almost entirely out and then pushing it all the way in again, feeling Ed's cock in my ass, mimicking those movements, and I grab for Gavin's slender, pointy cock, which is rock-hard and wet. I stick a fingertip under his foreskin and move it around. I feel his cock jerk. Pete's butt is on my right, and Brian's is on my left. I rim them both, in turn. They are playing with each other's cocks. I stick my thumb up Brian's ass while Ed fucks me. Then Ed and Pete and Brian and Gavin disappear and I'm floating on my back again. Many hands are caressing my body. I reach out and feel chests, bellies, butts, strong arms. Lee looms over me – his cock is huge. He whispers something in my ear, kisses me, then lifts my legs up and pushes his cock deep inside me. Carl is sucking me at the same time. I am delirious, dreaming. I throw my head back, and feel it cradled by several hands. I'm on my knees and there are cocks all around my face, pointing at me like spears. I go from cock to cock, sucking them. Hands holding my head guide me from one to the other, moving in a crazy circle. Then I'm on my back again, Pierre and Tinus sucking me simultaneously, their lips meeting in a kiss when they move up to the head. I have a hand on each of their heads; I can feel short hair, long hair. Nicholas is rimming me. I feel delicate lips on my cockhead, a wriggling tongue in my hole. Then they are gone and Ax is there with a big black dildo. He grins at me wolfishly and nudges my hole with the head of it. Slowly, still grinning at me, his teeth flashing in the half-light, he pushes the dildo up my ass. It feels like I might burst. My cock is throbbing, bursting. With one hand Ax plays with my cock, then caresses my chest; I reach up and grab his thickly muscled arm, feel the big veins traversing it just beneath the surface. He laughs. The dildo goes deeper. Everyone is standing around me. They are jerking their cocks in their fists, crying out with pleasure. One by one they come, shooting hot drops over my chest and belly. They seem to burn into my flesh. Then, one by one, they start to piss. I can feel the dildo in my ass as, one by one, they piss all over me, all pissing at once, the warm jets mingling with the cum, streaming over my torso, my thighs, my cock, my face. I erupt. I dissolve.

J.B. Droullard

Suspended in Space

I may have passed on by now, but I am alive through you. You prolong my life force by opening these pages and reading. You give me new life through the seemingly effortless saccadic movements of your eyes across this slick printed page. You cannot help yourself. You cannot stop. Like touching yourself where you are told not to, you read on.

In reading these words, we are sharing a thought. A similar pattern is evoked in the synaptic networks of your brain, as existed in mine when I wrote this. Now, I am kissing your lips with my pen. I am rubbing your nipples hard through your thin white T-shirt and I am unzipping your pants. Slowly. Innocently, you smile, feigning complete naiveté as I free your thick one loose from the folds of your underwear.

It springs out and is already hard, but you turn your back to me. What a nice inviting ass you have! Like two perfectly risen loaves of fresh dough against the already baked tan crust of your lower back. I roll on a neural prophylactic, and make it wet with the Elbo Grease lubricant I bought last year in Amsterdam.

There is only a tiny tug of resistance as I enter you with my fully erect words. You squirm slightly underneath me, but then you adjust and succumb. You grab yourself and start to rub hard. I can feel you deep inside to the very core of your being. Your thrusts are making me cum.

I pinch your nipples as we shoot our loads You, deliberately onto your white briefs spread out beneath you, and me somewhere very deep inside. We are one with all men since time immortal who have had hard sex with other men. One, together in this peculiar universe of manhood. One, in a huge shuddering cataclysmic orgasm. One in the mammoth primordial ejaculation – a huge ocean of phosphorescent white sperm drifting deep in outer space, where we were propelled by our own orgasm and are now suspended. Drifting, timeless, living forever, and absorbing nutrients by osmosis from the gleaming rich translucent opalescent suspension we are floating in. . . .

Notes on Contributors

RICHARD ANDREOLI writes for *The Advocate*, *Instinct Magazine*, *Los Angeles Confidential*, and *Playboy TV*. He's covered sex addicts, guys who sell their underwear online, and his favorite temp jobs of delivering Red Bull to Anna Nicole Smith and waiting tables at leather sex parties.

G. MERLIN BECK is a sadist/writer who lives in San Francisco and works in Silicon Valley. Beck's short fiction appears in several anthologies, including *Roughed Up: More Tales of Gay Men, Sex, and Power*; *Erotic Travel Tales II*; and *Love Under Foot: An Erotic Celebration of Feet*.

JOHN BRIGGS writes short fiction and poetry, sculpts wood, bakes bread, and takes long walks in Vancouver. In his spare time he holds down a full-time job in the graphic arts.

BLAISE BULOT divides his time between Boston and New Orleans. His published writings range from homoerotic short stories in anthologies, through novels, articles, and poems, to scholarly reviews of nonfiction books in *Lambda Book Report*, *Gay & Lesbian Review*, *White Crane Journal*, and *Journal of Homosexuality*.

RACHEL KRAMER BUSSEL's (*rachelkramerbussel.com*) books include *The Lesbian Sex Book (2nd edition)*, *The Erotic Writer's Market Guide*, and the erotic anthology *Up All Night*. Her writing is published in numerous publications and over twenty erotic anthologies including *Best American Erotica 2004* and *Hot & Bothered 3*. She has appeared on *Naked New York* and *Berman & Berman*.

ALBERT JESUS CHAVARRIA is a sheep in wolves' clothing. He currently lives in Galveston, Texas, where he writes about art and other trifles.

DAVID J. CHEATER has lived in Canada and Germany. This is his first professional sale although he has published research articles in Jewish interest magazines and gay publications. He is presently researching "Native Americans in Speculative Fiction" and hopes to have the bibliography accepted for publishing in the near future.

TK Chornyj lives and skates in Vancouver. TK's work has appeared in the queer punk zines *Faggo*, *Cruising*, and *The Make Out Club*. This story is for Richard.

James Chum wants desperately to escape his demi-monde of "if onlys" and "what ifs," and finds that writing, sometimes, is a good way to exorcise the ghosts that haunt him. "Fan Dancer" is dedicated to the memory of Lee Andrews and all the guys who danced at the Gandy.

Daniel Collins loves "having written," non-digital photography, artistic men, Buddhist study, and traveling.

Billy Cowan: Northern Irish, shaven head, blue eyes. Home: Manchester, U.K. with Jamie and Reb. Likes sex and Staffy Bull Terriers but not together. Hates writing and theatre. Recent winner of the Writing Out 2002 international competition for best new gay play, *Smiling Through*.

Jameson Currier is the author of a novel, *Where the Rainbow Ends*, and a collection of short stories, *Dancing on the Moon*. His short fiction has appeared in the anthologies *Men on Men*, *Best American Gay Fiction*, *Best Gay Erotica*, *Best American Erotica*, and *Making Literature Matter*.

Daniel Curzon is the author of several books, including the very first gay protest novel, *Something You Do in the Dark* (1971). His new book is a nonfiction narrative about the dark side of the Internet: *What a Tangled Web*.

J.R.G. De Marco lives in Philadelphia and Montréal. Look for his new book, *Mr. Dead Leather;* available at *Amazon.com* and elsewhere. His work appears in *Quickies 1 & 2*, *We Are Everywhere*, *Men Seeking Men*, *Hey Paesan!*, *GLReview*. He is currently writing a mystery and a non-fiction work. E-mail: joseph@josephdemarco.com

Shaun de Waal works for the *Mail & Guardian* newspaper in South Africa. He is the author of the short fiction collection *These Things Happen* (1996) and the graphic novelette *Jackmarks* (1998). His graphic stories can be seen at *gmax.co.za/play.html*.

Clayton Delery is a native of Louisiana, where he lives and teaches writing. He has published creative and scholarly works in such journals as *Text*, *The Xavier Review*, *The James White Review*, and *Garden, Deck and Landscape Magazine*.

Christopher DiRaddo is a Montreal-based publicist who is tired of promoting other people's work. He decided that it was about time he put pen to paper and write something of his very own. *Closet* and *When I See Him, Maybe I'll Know* are his first two published stories.

J.B. Droullard has published two other pieces under this nom de plume. The author is a professor at a major University in Florida. He's spent the past year on sabbatical from teaching, working on an autobiographical novel.

Stephen Emery is a born and bred British Columbian, though he has also lived across Canada, in the U.K., and in Japan. He has been a freelance writer for various small magazines, and is also a singer, songwriter guitarist. He now works as an adult educator and curriculum designer.

Kyle Faas is a writer and photographer based in Toronto. Well, physically anyway. "Sweater" is his first published story.

Douglas Ferguson was born and raised in Saskatchewan and currently resides in Calgary, Alberta. His work has appeared in the two previous *Quickies* anthologies. He is the author of a novel called *The Forgotten Ones*, and is currently working on his second novel.

R. W. Gray's short prose and poetry have appeared in ARC, *Absinthe, Grain, Event, The James White Review, Dandelion,* and *The Blithe House Quarterly* and the anthologies *Quickies 2* and *Carnal Nation*. He has also written two serialized novels, *Tide Pool Sketches* and the forthcoming *Waterboys*, both published in the newspaper *Xtra! West.*

David Greig is a Toronto artist, writer, psychotherapist, and co-founder/organizer/facilitator of the Gay Men Over 40 Project, a gay men's community health initiative. Selected writing and digital art are on his web site: *dawgwerk.com*

A lapsed Buddhist who admits to killing spiders, *Danny Gruber* lives in central Oregon. His work has appeared in *Beau, In Touch for Men, Indulge,* and other magazines. When not hanging out in men's locker rooms, he peruses the web for independently made films. He dreams in black and white.

Television host and drag artiste *Darrin Hagen* is the author of *The Edmonton Queen: Not a Riverboat Story*. He is the first Queen in Canada to host a national television series, Life Network's *Who's On Top?*, for which he received the AMPIA award for Best Male Host.

Wes Hartley is a longtime resident of Vancouver. His stories and poems have appeared in journals and anthologies such as *Prairie Fire, Queer View Mirror, Contra/Diction*, and *Quickies 1* and *2*. He's presently hard at work on a novel in the form of a journal: *Picturepostcards Found In The Attic.*

Trebor Healey is the author of the novel, *Through It Came Bright Colors* (Haworth Press, 2003). His short fiction has appeared in *Best Gay Erotica 2003, M2M, Blithe House Quarterly, Lodestar Quarterly, VelvetMafia.com, Queer Dharma*, and *Ashé!* For more info: *treborhealey.com*

George K. Ilsley is the author of *Random Acts of Hatred* (Arsenal Pulp, 2003), a collection of short fiction, the title story of which was first published in *Quickies 2*. "Clamp and Groove" is part of a work-in-progress exploring the relationship between Tom and Sebastian.

Scott Johnston resides in London, Canada. He is thirty years old.

Shane Keleher is a thirty-year-old, queer, Toronto-based writer working towards his MA in English Literature. "It's in the Shoes" marks his fiction debut.

Robert Labelle is a graduate of the MA program in creative writing at Concordia University. His work has appeared in other Arsenal compilations such as *Quickies* and *Queer View Mirror 2*, as well as in *Pottersfield Portfolio*. "Père Grâce" is an excerpt from a longer work.

Joe Lavelle lives in Liverpool, England. His short fiction has been published in Britain, U.S., and Canada. His feature articles have appeared in various British publications. Joe has been working on a novel for far too long and has recently completed a screenplay about gay men working in straight porn.

V.K. Lem grew up in a mixed-race family eating both rice and potatoes. He lives in Toronto and avidly follows the work of Asian-Canadian authors and artists.

Tom Lever's work has appeared in *Quickies 1* and *2*, *Bear Book I* and *II*, *American Bear*, and in various other anthologies. He lives and works in Germany with his huzbear Bob.

SHAUN LEVIN is a South African writer living in London. He lived for many years in Israel, where he worked as a journalist. He has published a novella with recipes, *Seven Sweet Things* (2003), and his stories appear *in Modern South African Stories* and in recent *Best Gay Erotica* anthologies, amongst other collections. See more: *shaunlevin.moonfruit.com*

LINDA LITTLE lives and writes in River John, Nova Scotia. Her award-winning first novel, *Strong Hollow*, was published by Goose Lane Editions in 2001. She is currently at work on her second novel, *Grist*, from which this piece is excerpted.

CHRISTOPHER LUCAS lives and writes in the sublime southwest with his partner of eleven years. He has written several short stories, appearing in *The Church-Wellesley Review*, and in the anthologies *Bar Stories and Latin Boys*. "Park & Ride" was originally an impromptu reading at a Five-Minute Erotic Reading competition which took first place. He can be reached at Jebalucas@yahoo.com.

RAYMOND LUCZAK, editor of *Eyes of Desire: A Deaf Gay & Lesbian Reader*, has written four other books. He has also directed the films *Ghosted* and *Guy Wonder: Stories & Artwork*. Nine of his stage plays have been performed throughout the U.S. His website is *raymondluczak.com*

STEPHEN LUKAS called Toronto home until moving to Nova Scotia in 1995. His writing has appeared in *Atlantic Books Today*, *Runner's World*, and *Atlantic Progress*. He is a sales director for a client relationship management firm. He and his partner Peter live with their real-life beagle, Gracie, just outside Halifax.

HARRY MATTHEWS, a native of Cincinnati and a graduate of Williams College, has lived in New York City for the past few decades, exploring its sexual by-ways and working in publishing, international education, and tourism. This is his third appearance in *Quickies*.

MATTILDA, AKA Matt Bernstein Sycamore, is the author of *Pulling Taffy* (Suspect Thoughts Press), from which "All Faggots Are Fuckers" is excerpted. He is the editor of *Tricks and Treats: Sex Workers Write About Their Clients* (Haworth) and *Dangerous Families: Queer Writing on Surviving* (Haworth, 2004). He is currently at work on a new anthology, *Resisting Assimilation: Alternatives to the Gay Mainstream*. Visit *mattbernsteinsycamore.com*

Sean Meriwether's work has been published in *Lodestar Quarterly*, *Love Under Foot*, and *Best Gay Erotica 2002*. He is the editor of *Outsider Ink* and *Velvet Mafia: Dangerous Queer Fiction*. Sean lives in New York with his partner, photographer Jack Slomovits. Visit him online at *seanmeriwether.com*. "The Bathroom Rebellion" is for Greg Wharton and Ian Philips.

Marshall Moore is the author of the novel *The Concrete Sky* (Haworth, 2003) and the collection *Black Shapes in a Darkened Room* (Suspect Thoughts Press, 2004). He lives in Seattle. For more information about Marshall and his writing, visit his website: *marshallmoore.com*

Jordan Mullens hangs out in pretentious cafés where he writes love poetry and says hello to whoever looks his way. He's subject to spasms of unrequited lust and often falls for men seen in the windows of passing trains or on elevators just before the doors close. He lives in Montreal.

R. E. Neu has written humor for publications like the *New York Times Book Review*, the *Los Angeles Times*, and *Los Angeles Magazine*. His short stories have appeared in a few anthologies, and for many years he was a contributing writer to *Spy* magazine. His column "Sucks in the City" appears irregularly in *Frontiers* newsmagazine.

Toronto writer/actor *Shaun Proulx* contributes to *Xtra!*, *Instinct* (L.A.) and is co-founder/editor of the e-zine *GayGuideToronto.com*. He's appeared in Toronto productions of *The Most Fabulous Story Ever Told* and *Unidentified Human Remains and the True Nature of Love* plus indie films including *Die Mutter* (Toronto International Film Festival, 2002). *shaunproulx.com*

Canadian-born *Andy Quan* has lived in Sydney, Australia since 1999. His smut has been published widely and he's the author of a short fiction collection, *Calendar Boy*, and a book of poetry, *Slant*. Pay him a visit at *andyquan.com*

Andrew Ramer lives in San Francisco. He is the author of *Two Flutes Playing*. His stories can be found in *Best Gay Erotica 1998* and *2002*, *After Words*, *Kosher Meat*, *Found Tribe*, and online at *Doorknobs and BodyPaint*, *Riverbabble*, and *Tattoo Highways*. An interview with him appears in *Gay Soul*.

Sandip Roy is a lapsed software engineer who now works as an editor and writer and radio host in San Francisco. His work has appeared in *Quickies*, *Men on Men 6*, *Chick for A Day*, as well as *Salon.com*, *San Francisco Chronicle*, *San Jose Mercury News*, and others. His commentaries can be heard on National Public Radio. "Mourning Becomes Electric" is for Dibs.

Antonio Ruffini lives for most of the year in Johannesburg, South Africa. There he has won a couple of prizes for science fiction short story writing, and, once upon a time, to everybody's surprise, including his own, actually won a silver medal at a provincial Karate competition.

Simon Sheppard is the author of *Kinkorama: Dispatches From the Front Lines of Perversion* and the award-winning *Hotter Than Hell and Other Stories*, and his work appears in nearly 100 anthologies, including *The Best American Erotica 2004*, *Friction 7*, and *Best Gay Erotica 2004*. He loiters shamelessly at *simonsheppard.com.*

Donn Short's first play *The Winter Garden* won the du Maurier Arts National One-Act Play Competition. His most recent play, *Full Frontal Diva*, received the 2003 London Borough of Newham Writing Out Award, an international playwriting prize, and was the winner of the PTC Award at the Jessies in Vancouver.

An MFA grad from UBC, *Michael V. Smith* is a writer, videographer, and occasional drag queen. He has a monthly sex column, *Blush*, in Vancouver's *Xtra! West* and freelances for the *Globe & Mail*. His novel, *Cumberland*, was nominated for the *Amazon.ca*/ Books in Canada First Novel Award. You can find out more at *michaelvsmith.com*

Sam Sommer is a writer, director and scenic designer living in NYC. In recent years his plays, *'Til Death Us Do Part* and *Attic* were produced off-Broadway. A number of his short stories have appeared in gay anthologies including *Queer View Mirror 2, Quickies 1* and *2, Boy Meets Boy* and *Skinflicks*. He is the recipient of two OOBR (Off-Off Broadway Review) awards (for scenic design) for his work on *Cowboys* and *Tango Masculino.*

O. Spleen was diagnosed HIV positive in 1999. Having survived tuberculosis and a heart operation, he documented his experiences in his first novel *Depravikazi*, already widely acclaimed for its brutal honesty. As a performer he has, among other things, extolled the virtues of Arthur Rimbaud and laid an egg from his rectum.

Jay Starre lives in Vancouver, where he pumps out gay erotica for such magazines as *Men*, *Torso*, *Indulge*, and *American Bear*. Gay anthologies he has written for include the *Friction* and *Buttmen* series.

Matt Stedmann's erotic fiction has appeared previously in the Alyson Publications anthologies *Men for All Seasons* and *My Biggest O*. His non-fiction work was included in the Canadian anthology *ReCreations*, which was nominated for a Lambda Literary Award.

HOREHOUND STILLPOINT's short stories and poetry can be found in *Thrills, Pills, Chills, and Heartache*; *Tough Guys*; *Out in the Castro*; *Law of Desire*; *Poetry Nation*; *Of the Flesh*; *Poetry Slam*; *Quickies*; *Quickies 2*; *Queer View Mirror 2*; *Roughed Up* and his little Kapowbook, *Reincarnation Woes.*

RON SURESHA is author of *Bears on Bears: Interviews & Dicussions,* and a self-published recipe book, *Mugs o' Joy.* He is editor of *Bearotica, vols. 1 & 2.* A story of his also appeared in *Quickies 2.* Other writing of his may be found at his website: *suresha.com.* He lives in Providence, Rhode Island.

ROYSTON TESTER is originally from England. His work has appeared in *Quickies 2, Blithe House Quarterly, Descant,* and *New Quarterly*; forthcoming in *Everything I Have Is Blue* (Suspect Thoughts Press). Most recently he wrote on "monogamy" for *The Love That Dare Not Speak Its Name* (Boheme). He lives in Toronto.

COLIN THOMAS is the theatre critic for the *Georgia Straight* newspaper in Vancouver and has won the Chalmers Children's Playwriting Award three times. *Sex Is My Religion*, his first play for adults, is published in *Plague of the Gorgeous* and he's just finished *Fairy Christmas*, a television script about a boy who wants to fly.

ROBERT THOMSON is a Canadian-born writer, singer/songwriter, and producer. He is the author of two volumes of short fiction *Secret Things* and *Need.* He works as a disc-jockey in Toronto.

GERKE VAN LEIDEN is the nom de plume of Germany's best-selling gay author Stephan Niederwieser. Niederwieser has published five novels, short stories in various gay and heterosexual anthologies (such as *Boy meets Boy*), and the textbook *Sextips für Schwule Männer*. For more information visit his website: *stephan-niederwieser.de*

BOB VICKERY is a regular contributor to various websites and magazines, particularly *Men* and *Inches.* He has four anthologies of stories published: *Skin Deep, Cock Tales, Cocksure,* and most recently *Buddies* (Cole Valley Press), and he also has stories in numerous other anthologies. Check out his website: *bobvickery.com*

JOHN SHANDY WATSON is a freelance travel writer and editor based in London. He studied English Literature and Creative Writing at Concordia University in Montreal, the fabbest city on the continent, and one that he still misses terribly. He can't stand belly-buttons.

Barry Webster has published in many venues including the *Washington Post*, the *Globe and Mail*, *Prairie Fire*, *Event*, *Fiddlehead*, and *Harrington Gay Men's Fiction Quarterly*. He has just completed his first collection of short stories, one of which was shortlisted for a National Magazine Award.

Michael Wilde is a filmmaker and freelance writer. In his spare time he enjoys making zines, culture jamming, and being in passionate but doomed relationships with the wrong men. When he grows up he'd like to become a cyborg super spy just like on television. Cute guys totally dig spies.

Born and raised an Okie and now living in New Mexico, the setting of many of his plots, *Mark Wildyr* has a keen interest in personal and sexual development and the interaction between diverse cultures. His erotic gay stories have appeared in works published by Companion Press, Alyson Publications, and STARbooks Press.

About the Editor

James C. Johnstone's writing has been published in the Lambda Literary Award-winning anthology *Sister & Brother: Lesbians & Gay Men Write About Their Lives Together*, *Flashpoints: Gay Male Sexual Writing*, *Prairie Fire*, *Icon Magazine*, *The Buzz*, and *Homefronts: Controversies in the Queer Parenting Community*.

He is co-editor, with Karen X. Tulchinsky, of *Queer View Mirror: Lesbian and Gay Short Short Fiction*, and *Queer View Mirror 2*. He is also editor of *Quickies: Short Short Fiction on Gay Male Desire*, *Quickies 2*, and the upcoming *Donors & Dads: True Stories of Gay Men & Fatherhood* (The Haworth Press).

Up to 9/11, James worked as a Japanese language interpreter, translator, and tour escort, but while the world changes, and recovers, and when he's not straining his eyes at the city archives working on contracts as a house genealogist (see *homehistoryresearch.com*), he's happily ~~stalking~~ stocking shelves at the Gourmet Warehouse.

photo: Daniel Collins